Hoops
AND
Hearts

ALEXA ASTON

OLIVERHEBERBOOKS

Prologue

DALLAS

Sawyer Montgomery listened as his opposing counsel addressed the jury in her final summation. Like him, Elizabeth Pope sought to make a personal connection with each juror, looking them directly in the eyes. She was a formidable attorney. Polished. Prepared. Someone who fought passionately for her clients.

And she was the love of his life.

They had begun dating during their final year at Baylor Law School, though they had known each other since they were first years. Elizabeth drew others to her with her winning personality and compassion for all. She had been a part of Sawyer's study group during 1L and 2L, but things had turned romantic just before the start of their last year. They had dated that year and the two following graduation and were now engaged to be married in two months' time. This was the first time, however, that they had gone up against one another in a courtroom.

Usually, they tested their opening and closing arguments on one another, giving the other critical feedback. They

1

hadn't been able to during this case since they were opposing counsels. He had to admire his fiancée, though. She was convincing as she implored the jury to find the defendant not guilty.

Dispassionately, he took notes as she spoke, thinking of ways he could counter the points she was making in his own final argument. Though Sawyer believed he had proven his case beyond a reasonable doubt, Elizabeth now chipped away at small pieces he had presented throughout the trial. It wouldn't surprise him if he didn't receive the usual, unanimous verdict he was known for achieving.

Elizabeth thanked the jurors for their time and returned to sit next to her client, causing Sawyer to rise and move closer to the jury box, where twelve citizens were seated. They would begin their deliberations soon and determine the fate of Anthony Simpson.

He walked the jury through the state's case, detailing each portion of evidence against the defendant and doing his best to negate the points Elizabeth had made. Still, his gut told him that his fiancée had done enough to place reasonable doubt in the minds of at least a few jurors.

Ending his summation, Sawyer told the jury, "I hope that you will carefully weigh the evidence the State of Texas has presented to you and find the defendant, Anthony Simpson, guilty in the murder of Jane Rockwell. Thank you for your time and your service. The citizens of Dallas County appreciate how much you have invested of yourselves in this case, and they are depending upon you to render a unanimous, guilty verdict and send Anthony Simpson to prison."

Sawyer returned to the prosecution table without glancing at Elizabeth. He listened as Judge Johnson gave final instructions to the jury, who would first break for lunch before beginning their deliberations, and then they were led from the courtroom.

Now, the waiting game began.

He rose, as did Elizabeth, and they moved closer to one another. All he wanted to do was run his fingers through her strawberry blond hair and kiss her beautiful, rosebud mouth. Instead, he kept things professional, not revealing an inkling of their relationship. To anyone watching them, they would merely see two attorneys chatting briefly about the case they had just tried.

"Nice job with your closing, Counselor."

She gave him a half-smile. "Same to you, ADA Montgomery. I won't say it was a pleasure going up against you. You are a very tough opponent. You articulated your case perfectly, and your witnesses gave good testimony without seeming rehearsed." Her smile widening, she added, "Then again, I believe my arguments were solid and that my client will walk out of here a free man."

"Want to grab some lunch?" he asked.

"I wish I had time to, but I have a new trial starting in two days. I need to finish interviewing a couple of witnesses before working on my opening statement. Maybe you can help me work on that later tonight," she added huskily.

"Maybe I'll hear it—and then help you out of whatever you're wearing," he replied, causing her to laugh.

"If I don't see you back in court for the verdict later today, I'll see you at home," she told him.

He smiled at her. "Ditto."

They had stolen *ditto* from the movie *Ghost*, a film where Patrick Swayze's character Sam had trouble voicing words of commitment to Demi Moore's character, Molly. When Molly would tell Sam that she loved him, he would merely reply *ditto*, never speaking of love. Then Sam was killed by a mugger—and it was too late to speak what was in his heart.

Sawyer and Elizabeth had begun using the word to convey their feelings without alerting others around them to their involvement. No one at work knew they were dating, much less engaged. If his boss had known about their relationship, he never would have allowed Sawyer to try the Simpson case against Elizabeth, citing it would be a conflict of interest. They both were passionate about their jobs, however, and had actually looked forward to finally having the chance to face off against one another in court. After having attended law school with Elizabeth and coming in as salutatorian to her valedictorian, he knew what a powerhouse lawyer she was, one with a keen mind and attention to details that others often overlooked. Occasionally, he sneaked into a courtroom to listen to her for a few minutes, but it had been eye-opening watching her as he tried an entire case against her. It made Sawyer proud of her.

He left the courtroom, opening the bottom drawer of his desk once he was back in his office and removing a package of peanut butter crackers from his stash. He ate them while drinking a Diet Coke and began working his next case, reading witness interviews from the police department.

Hugh James, the Dallas District Attorney, appeared in his doorway. "How did it go?"

"I think we had a solid case against Anthony Simpson. The evidence should speak for itself." Sawyer paused. "However, you know that juries can often ignore facts and vote based upon emotion. Elizabeth Pope is very skilled at manipulating a jury's emotions. Did she raise enough questions for there to be reasonable doubt?" He shrugged. "We'll soon see."

"I wish we had Pope in this office," the DA said. "She's

got a great track record. You know her, don't you? Didn't you both attend Baylor Law at the same time?"

He nodded. "She was the top of our graduating class and had multiple job offers from all kinds of big-name law firms. The fact that she went to work in the public defender's office for peanuts speaks to her character."

"Win or lose this case, Sawyer, see if you can draw her back from the dark side. This office could use a smart, thoughtful attorney like Pope."

"I'll see what I can do, Hugh," he said solemnly, biting back a smile.

As passionate as Elizabeth was about defending the downtrodden, he was just as passionate about prosecuting criminals and bringing them to justice. He doubted he could ever convince his fiancée to join him in the DA's office.

They had talked, however, about starting their own firm after they married. Montgomery & Montgomery. They had brainstormed about the kind of law they might practice and the type of clients they wished to represent. While nothing had been settled, Sawyer thought it would be amazing to go to work every day with his beautiful, intelligent wife and then be able to come home and spend his nights with her.

He received a text at four-thirty to return to the courtroom. The verdict was in after about four hours of deliberation, and he looked upon that as a good omen. The longer juries were out—especially on murder cases—the more likely they were to render a not guilty verdict.

He slipped back into his suit's jacket, straightening his tie as he headed toward the elevators. He and Elizabeth had talked about whoever won this case, they would go out for a celebratory dinner, with the loser paying.

Entering the courtroom, he saw she was already at the defense table. He nodded to her as he took a seat. The judge came in and called the courtroom to order, and the jury was led in by the bailiff and seated. The judge asked if they had reached a verdict, and a Black man in his mid-forties who had been elected foreman rose.

"We have, Your Honor."

He handed the results of the vote to the bailiff, who took it to Judge Johnson. He glanced at the paper handed to him, his face set in stone, not betraying anything.

Sawyer's heart began thumping harder. He wanted this win. He truly believed that Anthony Simpson had murdered Jane Rockwell and should be locked away for his crime. Then again, Elizabeth had made a few excellent points in Simpson's defense, so the door had been left open.

When he heard the not guilty verdict announced, he maintained his composure as the courtroom erupted. Simpson's family, seated on the first row behind the defense table, leapt to their feet, cheering. Judge Johnson called for order, and everyone calmed down. The judge then thanked the jury for their service, and the courtroom was dismissed. Sawyer watched from the corner of his eye as Elizabeth hugged Anthony Simpson and then hugged his wife and two teenaged children.

He hung around until she turned to him, offering her hand.

"Counselor, it was a well-fought battle."

As he shook her hand, he said, "Hugh James gave me the mission to try and lure you from the dark side into the light of the DA's office."

She chuckled throatily, causing desire to flare within him. He released her hand.

"Hugh James—and the DA's office—is the last place I would ever want to work. You know that."

"I do. I told him I would try, though. I'll report back that I failed miserably. That the Angel of Justice has vowed never to leave the public defender's office."

Sawyer referred to the nickname a journalist had given Elizabeth after a particularly long and grueling murder trial. He loved to tease her about it every and now and then.

She leaned in. "Anthony Simpson really is innocent," she insisted and then grinned. "I guess that means you'll be buying dinner tonight since you lost."

"Name the place. I'll make a reservation."

"You know I love a good steak dinner at the end of a long trial."

He laughed. "Al Biernat's, it is. Meet you there? Seven?"

"Sounds good. See you then."

Sawyer went to report back to Hugh James, who scowled as Sawyer entered the DA's office.

"You lost, Montgomery," the district attorney growled.

"I did. I'll be calling the jury members over the next day or two, polling them as to why they voted the way they did."

It was one of the quirks of the Texas legal system that allowed prosecutors to contact jurors. Naturally, the juror did not have to reveal anything about their particular service on a case, but a handful always chose to speak to him about what had occurred during deliberations. Sawyer found their words insightful, and he had learned quite a bit from those conversations, things that had helped him in future cases which he had tried.

"Did you approach Pope about switching sides?" Hugh asked, sounding surly.

"I did. The Angel of Justice wasn't biting, sir."

His boss frowned. "I didn't think she would, but I'm not going to let up. That woman would be an incredible asset to this office. I'm going to see that she moves over here by hook or crook."

"Good luck with that, Hugh," Sawyer said breezily, knowing that Elizabeth would never change her mind. She would either continue in the PD's office, or the two of them would begin their own law firm. He could see that happening in the near future. Right now, their careers consumed a majority of their waking hours, and it was hard to share a meal together, much less a night out on a date. Once they had kids, though, they would both need to dial things back. If they had started their own law firm by then, hopefully it would give them more time together, as well as time to be good parents. He and his sister Darby had grown up with two wonderful, supportive parents, and he wanted to emulate his mom and dad's parenting style as much as possible.

Sawyer returned to his office and made their dinner reservation before working another hour. He asked his assistant to compile a list of the jurors' phone numbers so he could begin calling them tomorrow.

Because tonight was strictly for him and Elizabeth.

They met at the famous steakhouse, him ordering a New York strip, while she requested her usual filet mignon. Both liked their steaks medium rare. They shared sides of whipped sweet potatoes and roasted mushrooms but passed on dessert when the server asked.

As Sawyer paid the bill, he leaned over and whispered in Elizabeth's ear, "*You're* the dessert tonight," causing another of those low chuckles which had him hot for her.

They returned to their apartment in Oak Lawn, and he made love to her. In the afterglow, they lay entangled in one another's arms. He had never been more content than in this moment.

"I can't wait to be Elizabeth Montgomery," she told him. "You know, of course, that I'll continue to go by Elizabeth Pope at work. We'll have to report our marriage to both our bosses, though. I already feel bad that we've kept quiet about it for so long."

"I know. I can just see Hugh's face when he finds out that I've been sleeping with the enemy. He will not be a happy camper. I'll be raked over the coals and have to listen to a long lecture about fraternizing with the enemy."

"You don't think he would believe you threw the Simpson case?" she asked indignantly. "If he does, I'll show up at the DA's office and give him a piece of my mind."

He kissed the top of her head. "Hugh will get over it. Don't worry about me. I can take care of myself. But now that we've argued opposite sides of a case? As far as I'm concerned, it's a one-and-done."

"Everything always comes back to basketball with you," she teased, referring to how college athletes would play their freshman year and then leave a university for the NBA.

Sawyer hadn't had that opportunity. While he was a talented enough player to earn an athletic scholarship to the University of North Texas, he had suffered a horrific knee injury his senior year, curtailing any idea of a career in the pros. Instead, he had turned his passion for basketball toward the law and was happy in the work he did.

And with the woman he loved.

They fell asleep, waking at four-thirty in order to go their separate ways. Elizabeth would drink a cup of coffee and scroll through her emails before going for her usual run, while Sawyer hit the Y for his own workout. He showered at the Y and left for his office. His first order of business was to call yesterday's jurors. Surprisingly, he reached half of the twelve. Three agreed to speak to him about the trial and the jury's decision. All three said the same thing. The verdict was influenced by the small holes Elizabeth had poked in the state's case.

He had lost to the better attorney, and he wasn't saddened by that.

Mid-morning, Sawyer went to the break room to get a Diet Coke and see if any Danish might be left. Three other attorneys were huddled, looking as if they were gossiping.

"What's up, guys?" he asked, pulling a can from the fridge and popping the top.

"We were just talking about the hit and run this morning. Did you hear about it?" Jack Schneider asked.

Sawyer shook his head. "No. Why?"

Schneider laughed. "For a moment, I'd almost think you were behind it. Except you're such a Boy Scout, Montgomery."

He frowned. "I don't get it. What are you talking about?"

The other ADA shrugged. "The hit and run involved Elizabeth Pope. Apparently, she was out jogging and was struck by a car. The driver left the scene without rendering aid."

Panic raced through him. "Where is she?"

"In the morgue," Schneider replied. "DOA."

Reeling, Sawyer, stumbled from the break room without a word, returning to his office, closing and locking the door. Anguish filled him. It felt as if his soul had been ripped from him.

Elizabeth was gone.

And nothing would ever be the same again.

CHAPTER

One

Paisley Roberts felt energy brimming inside her. She glanced around the dressing room of the Las Vegas Aces, seeing both determination and eagerness on the faces of her fellow teammates. Today's final game of the regular season with the New Jersey Hurricanes would decide which of the two teams moved on to the playoffs.

She was determined to lead her team to victory.

These women meant everything to Paisley. They were the only family she had, just as previous teammates had been over the two decades she'd been playing basketball. She had never known who her father was. Her drug-addicted mother's parental rights had been terminated by a jury when Paisley was only four years old. She had immediately gone into the foster care system, bouncing from house to house, never finding a home as she sprouted taller than any kid at school.

By the time she reached seventh grade, Paisley had reached her full height, an inch over six feet, towering over everyone in her middle school, including her teachers. But she found a home on the basketball court that year. Her first coach had seen Paisley's potential, and while she had three children of her own, Coach Callahan still went through the prep of becoming a foster parent and fostered Paisley from the time she was twelve.

Coach Callahan was a tough woman, and Paisley had soon realized she was never going to be loved by the coach. Their relationship was transactional. Paisley's job was to make Coach Callahan look good. In return, the coach gave her room and board. She didn't care. Having a permanent foster home with Callahan allowed her to stay in one place, honing her athletic skills. She moved into AAU competitive basketball, and the rest was history.

Paisley had won two state titles in high school, with Coach Callahan being moved up to serve as the girls' varsity basketball coach, riding her foster child's coattails. Paisley had been offered numerous athletic scholarships and chose to play at Baylor University in Waco. The school already had several NCAA national championships under its belt. Paisley led the school to another national championship her sophomore year and the NCAA championship game her senior year.

Then when she was barely twenty, she played in her first Olympics in Madrid, taking home a gold medal. She had been named to Team USA again for the next two Olympics, as well, and it was assumed that she would also be on next year's roster and compete for the gold in Rome. She would be thirty-two by then and figured it would be her last Olympics.

She focused on the game at hand now. As a former number one draft pick in the WNBA, she'd had a lot riding on her shoulders from the moment she entered professional sports. Paisley had lived up to her hype and even exceeded all expectations, bringing new fans to the sport in droves.

You were only as good as your last game, however, and the Las Vegas Aces needed a win tonight to move to the first round of the playoffs. They'd been plagued with injuries this year, but everyone was back for tonight's showdown, healthy and ready for a victory.

The team took to the floor for warmups, and her shot rang true. As it happened with any basketball player, there were nights Paisley was more on than off.

Tonight, she was definitely on—and with every three-pointer she made, the growing crowd settling into their seats cheered.

They returned to the locker room, and she downed a Gatorade to stay hydrated. Coach Armstrong gave a pep talk, and the team went out to their home court, their enthusiastic fans cheering wildly during the player introductions. As usual, Paisley received the biggest hand from the crowd. Fortunately, her teammates never showed any signs of jealousy because they knew her to be the heart and soul of the Aces. She had already taken them to the playoffs seven times since she'd joined the team, two of those resulting in championships. The hope was that they would repeat that this year since the team's starters were the same as last year's.

They tipped off, and her pregame nerves dissipated as always, a calm descending over her. She liked to think of it as her Zen zone.

By halftime, the Aces were up by four. The locker room was quiet, but she could still feel the energetic buzz surrounding the players present. She went over to Lisa Fowler, their center, and gave her a couple of notes. No one minded that Paisley did this. It was something she'd started doing since she'd played her first game in seventh grade. Her situational awareness was honed better than any other existing player's, and she often saw things other players—and even coaches—didn't.

The center took the advice in stride, and the team returned to the court.

By mid-fourth quarter, the game was tied, the Aces having lost the lead they'd held up until that point. Paisley took the ball down the court, running the offense like clockwork, and the Aces moved ahead of the Hurricanes again. With three minutes to go, they now led by three points.

Nikki Jones fouled her soon after the next time Paisley dribbled down the court, something which had gone on all game, though the refs had seemed to turn a blind eye to it. Jones was the new golden child of the WNBA, and it seemed she could do no wrong. Paisley had learned not to complain to refs. Instead, she kept her head down and played to the best of her ability.

She moved to the foul line and made both her free throws. Paisley was the most consistent free throw shooter in the league, and it surprised her that Jones had fouled her when she did. Then again, the refs hadn't been calling anything against the rookie, and Jones probably thought she could get away with the foul.

The Hurricanes came back quickly, Jones hitting a three-pointer. The Aces only held the lead by a single basket. It wasn't enough, especially with what time was left on the clock.

Coach Armstrong called a time-out, and the team huddled around her as she diagrammed the play to be run, looking to Paisley, who nodded in agreement. Paisley knew it was up to her to execute the play flawlessly. If she did, their shooting guard would be in a perfect position to attempt a three—and the Aces needed those three points desperately.

As she brought the ball down the court again, Nikki

Jones was all over her. Fortunately, Paisley handled the ball with ease, running the play exactly as Armstrong had outlined. When Rashida Roundhouse sank the basket, the arena erupted. Paisley couldn't help it. She shot a smug grin at Jones, who looked ready to explode.

And then all hell broke out.

Jones rushed her, something Paisley was unprepared for. She knew just how physical a basketball game could be. Most sports fans believed football, with all its hard hits and tackling, was the roughest American sport. She would love for those casual, armchair fans to play in one professional basketball game and suffer the elbows to ribs and temples alike. She knew some players played dirtier than others, but this rookie caught her off-guard, especially because Paisley didn't even have the ball and the play was already over.

Just as Nikki Jones reached her, Paisley threw up an arm to protect herself, but Jones shoved her. Hard. Somehow, Paisley managed to keep her balance, stumbling back several steps. As the Aces fans jeered, she turned to see if the closest ref had witnessed the attack the entire arena had seen.

That's when it went from bad to brutal.

Suddenly, Paisley was hit in her back, completely caught off-guard by the hands that slammed into her. The unexpected blow caused her to pitch forward. She fell to the court, both knees slamming the hard surface. Immediately, she knew something terrible had happened by the pain reverberating through her. Then someone was on her back, as if they were in a wrestling match, and a free-for-all brawl broke out on the court. She found herself buried, a pile of players atop her. By the time the weight of the others had been lifted from her, Paisley knew she was in serious trouble.

Lisa and Rashida lifted her to her feet, ready to help her back to the bench. The refs were ordering teams to opposite ends of the court as fans howled in displeasure. But Paisley couldn't even manage a single step. She cried out, a loud gasp escaping her lips. Sagging, her teammates threw her arms around their shoulders and carried her off the court. While she finally was able to put weight on her left foot, her right knee screamed in agony.

The trio reached the Aces bench, and as tears filled her eyes, she shook her head at Armstrong.

"I'm in trouble," she got out, biting back a scream because the pain was now magnified, radiating through her.

Her knee throbbed viciously. A wheelchair was brought, and Paisley was settled into it. She found she couldn't even bend her knee and had to flex her foot, keeping the leg stiff as she was rolled away and taken immediately to the medical facility within the arena.

Everything after that became a blur.

An hour later, she had been taken by ambulance to the nearest hospital. The Aces team doctor had accompanied her, and she now listened to the head of the emergency room and a surgeon as they gave her the bad news. Through her haze of pain, Paisley understood that she had a fractured patella.

Dr. Patel, the ER guy, said, "This is an uncommon injury, Paisley. Only one percent of athletes' knee injuries involves a fractured patella. Basically, this is a break in your kneecap, which is a small, flat bone which covers your knee joint and protects it, like a shield. Any fracture impacts your ability to bend your knee."

He whipped out a pad and pen and began sketching to help her understand. All the while, the gnawing pain made it hard to concentrate on what he said.

"You have quadriceps and a patellar tendon that attach to your patella," he told her. "This is how you can flex and extend your knee. The knee is covered with cartilage, and that acts as a cushion for your knee joint. The X-rays showed your excess swelling is from the hemarthrosis. Blood from the broken bone pieces which have collected in the knee joint."

Dr. Patel smiled sympathetically at her. "I'm going to hand it over to Dr. Sinclair now. He's in charge of your case now. I wish you a speedy recovery, Paisley."

She couldn't even muster the strength to say goodbye and turned to the surgeon. "What now?"

"We also had a CT scan done to help define the type of fracture you suffered," Dr. Sinclair told her. "Your injury is called a comminuted patella fracture. Unlike a transverse one, where the patella breaks into two pieces, a comminuted is where your kneecap has shattered into three or more pieces. I won't know if it's stable or unstable until I open you up and take a look. If it's unstable, some of the bone pieces might be too small to reconnect. If that's the case, then I'll remove them and work with what I have."

Dully, she said, "So, I'm having surgery."

"Right away. I'll also clean up any cartilage damage that I find, but I need to warn you that there's a strong possibility of post-traumatic arthritis."

He shook his head, empathy in his eyes. "Your recovery will be long. Slow. Painful. But I've followed your career. You're a dedicated, disciplined athlete. My gut tells me that you'll do whatever it takes so that you're able to walk again."

His words were like a knife to her heart. If walking again was the goal, then she was really up a creek.

"I'll have the surgery then."

Papers were brought for her to sign. In the midst of it, she asked if the Aces had won the game.

The team doctor, who had remained with her, said, "Yes. But the game was called after the brawl. Since we were ahead, we'll move on to the playoffs."

"And Nikki Jones?" Paisley asked, not bothering to contain the bitterness in her voice.

"She's been suspended indefinitely for her actions against you. The league's brass plan to conduct an in-depth investigation into the incident."

Jones may have been suspended, and she would most likely have to pay a hefty fine, but she would go on to play.

Paisley never would again.

She had been lucky her entire playing career. She'd suffered a few ankle sprains. A stress fracture in her left foot, which had healed during an off-season. A nagging case of plantar fasciitis had occurred in her right heel, but she had done PT for it. Even three years later, she continued doing the set of exercises the therapist had given her to perform each morning after she got out of bed to keep it at bay.

But she had never experienced serious injuries. No ACL tears. No hip, thigh, or wrist ailments. The fact that she could not bend her knee now let her know how bad her injury was, especially with Dr. Sinclair saying the end goal was for her to be able to walk again.

A nurse came by and notified Paisley that she would be taken to the operating room in the next ten minutes.

Dr. Sinclair appeared again. "I know you have a few minutes to process things. Do you have any questions for me?

"What is the recovery time for a patella fracture?" she asked neutrally.

The surgeon's face gave away more than she wanted to know, and he said, "Usually three to six months. Of course, it depends upon the severity of the injury. As I mentioned, I'll know more once I get inside and clean things up and do the necessary repairs."

He smiled. "Don't worry, Paisley. Once you're out of

recovery and have a good night's sleep under your belt, we'll talk again."

It was already September. Six months from now, TEAM USA women's basketball roster would be announced. Paisley knew she wouldn't be named as a player—and that thought sapped her spirits.

Even though she had already determined the answer, she asked, "Will I be able to come back from this injury, Dr. Sinclair? Play with the Aces again?'

"I don't like to make predictions before surgery," he told her. "I'll be blunt, though, Paisley. At your age—and with the wear and tear on your knees after playing basketball for two decades—I would say the possibility of playing at the professional level again won't occur. I know you're a competitor and want to come back from this injury. Even in the best of circumstances, your mobility is going to be limited. You won't be able to play world-class basketball anymore."

She nodded, desperation seeping through her every pore. "Thanks for your honesty, Dr. Sinclair. Do you really think I'll be able to walk normally again?"

"Absolutely. I guarantee it. It's going to take a helluva lot of PT—and dedication on your part—but you'll be able to live a normal life. It won't be one running up and down a court because your knee will not be able to take that severe pounding, but you'll be able to walk. Work out. Live a fairly active life."

A shadow crossed his face. "It just won't unfold on the basketball court. For that, I'm truly sorry."

"I understand," she said, despondency washing through her. "Let's go get this done."

Paisley saved her tears. She could hold a pity party when she was alone.

Hours later, she woke up in a hospital room, feeling a

little sluggish. She vaguely remembered being in a post-op recovery room, coming in and out of consciousness, but she had charge of her faculties now. She noted the sunlight streaming through the window and knew it had to be the next day.

A nurse greeted her. "Good morning, Paisley. How are you feeling?" she asked brightly.

"Like a truck ran over me. Multiple times," she admitted.

"I'll go get Dr. Sinclair. He wanted to know the minute you were awake."

The nurse returned with the surgeon a few minutes later.

"Everything was successful. I was able to make the repairs needed and only had to remove two bone fragments which were too small to be reattached."

He told her how long she would be in the hospital and that he had already contacted a physical therapist who specialized in sports injuries, especially those to the knee.

"Rodney is going to take excellent care of you, Paisley. You're going to come through this."

He looked at her with kind eyes. "I also hope that you'll be willing to see a mental health specialist. It's going to be a lot, the physical exertion of rehab. What may be even tougher for you, though, is adjusting mentally and emotionally to your situation. I know how passionate you've been your entire life about basketball. It's going to be a difficult adjustment to living a life off the court. I hope you will let me recommend someone specializing in talk therapy."

Paisley knew he was right. The life she had led up until this point would be very different from the one which followed.

Nodding, she said, "Give me the name. I realize I'm going to need all the help I can get, Dr. Sinclair."

The nurse returned. "Paisley has a waiting room full of

coaches and teammates, Dr. Sinclair. What should I tell them?"

He looked to her. "You don't have to see anyone now. You're barely awake after major surgery."

She knew this would most likely be the last time all these people would be gathered to see her. They would be practicing and then playing in playoff games around the country. Once the season ended, her teammates would scatter to various places, some heading to their homes in other states, while others would be going to play in Europe's women's basketball league, where the pay was much better than in the US. It was her last chance to say a proper goodbye to the family she loved and the sport which was in her blood.

"No, have them come in. All of them. But only let them stay a few minutes before you chase them out."

Dr. Sinclair said, "I'll go tell them they can stay ten minutes."

The nurse helped place more pillows behind her and then raised the bed so that Paisley was sitting up.

"I'm Peggy. I'll be taking care of you this shift. And I'm a pit bull when it comes to sending visitors on their way. I've followed your career since you were in college. I played basketball myself back in the day. AAU and high school, but I still love the game. You've been a great role model for girls. I won't lie to you, Paisley. You're in for a rough rehab, but if anyone can do it, it's you. You're physically and mentally tough."

Peggy touched her hand to Paisley's shoulder and squeezed. "And I'm Team Paisley all the way."

The door opened, a flood of people entering the room. She saw the looks on the faces of her teammates. Hopeful. Worried. She glanced to the head coach and shook her head. Armstrong nodded to her in return.

Everyone crowded about the bed, wanting to hold her hand and wish her well, saying they were dedicating the remainder of their season to her.

She told them, "It took a lot of guts to claim yesterday's victory over the Hurricanes. If you can do that, you can do anything," she said. "And I'm going to be cheering you on all the way to the WNBA Finals. Bring home that championship for me."

The room erupted in cheers, and then Peggy shepherded everyone out.

When the last person had left, the nurse returned to Paisley's side. "I know you're probably still a bit groggy. You need to get some sleep now. Rest is restorative."

The nurse left the room, leaving Paisley all alone. With all her teammates and coaches now gone, she finally gave in, hot tears spilling down her cheeks.

Paisley hoped she had the strength for what lay ahead as she moved toward the next chapter in her life.

CHAPTER
Two

WACO, TEXAS—TEN MONTHS LATER ...

P aisley rose at four in the morning for her usual workout. She used to be a runner. Then a jogger. Finally, at the ripe old age of thirty-two—and post-surgery and rehab—she was a walker.

She did a series of stretches for half an hour which focused on strengthening, stretching, and range-of-motion. Her fractured patella, while now officially healed, had caused lingering stiffness and muscle weakness, and she continued months after surgery to retrain her knee so that it moved as it did prior to her injury.

At least Nikki Jones had been banned for life from playing in the WNBA. Still, the rookie had simply moved to Europe and now played for a Russian team, making five times what she had earned playing in the US for the Hurricanes. Paisley pushed aside thoughts of Jones. She'd learned through her talk therapy sessions that no good came from dwelling on Jones or the incident between them.

Instead, she now set out on her daily walk, trying to keep her swirling thoughts at bay. She limited the first part of the walk to twenty minutes, entering the building where the Baylor's women's basketball team held their workouts. As a former team member, the head coach had granted her privileges to the facility, and Paisley spent another half-hour on strength training.

After her workout, she walked back to the apartment she was renting and showered, blow-drying her long, chocolate brown hair, and then brushing it until it fell into soft waves. Usually, she pulled it back in a high ponytail, but she wanted a more polished look for today's job interview with the Hawthorne High School principal and athletic director.

Once she drank a protein shake, Paisley brushed her teeth and applied a coat of lipstick, the only makeup she ever wore. She went to her car and headed north on I-35. She would go through Ft. Worth and then angle toward Hawthorne.

As she drove up the interstate in light traffic, Paisley couldn't help but think where she was supposed to be in ten days.

In Osaka, getting ready to play in the Olympics.

She cursed aloud and then began utilizing one of the breathing techniques which she had learned from Dr. Langston to calm herself. The therapist had shared several of these exercises, as well as teaching Paisley about meditation, which she practiced regularly.

It didn't matter that she had three gold medals to her name. National championships in college and in the pros. What was important was the here and now, the new life she hoped to build for herself.

Possibly in Hawthorne, Texas.

Though she'd never held an official title, she'd been coaching others her entire life. She was good at critiquing other players and had shared her insights with her teammates from the first day she'd stepped onto the basketball court. She had taken countless younger players under her wing, mentoring them at various levels. Paisley believed she was a born coach. Perhaps Hawthorne High School would be the first stop of many in this second chapter in her life coaching players for pay.

The head women's basketball coach at Baylor had been the one to approach her about this job opening. Paisley had held many conversations with Maggie as she had rehabbed at her former alma mater these past few months. Maggie was from Hawthorne and still in touch with many friends in her hometown. The high school's basketball coach had recently taken a job in Austin, leaving the position Paisley was interviewing for today vacant. Maggie's personal recommendation had helped Paisley land this interview.

Admittedly, she was a little scared to start a new career, but it was time to move on from being a player and officially join the coaching ranks. Paisley had majored in secondary education at Baylor and had been encouraged to keep her teaching certificate current, even while she played in the WNBA. Now, she was glad that she had listened to that advice. If she did land this job, it would mean fewer hoops she would need to jump through before she started her new job.

When she reached Ft. Worth around eight, the morning traffic was heavier than she had expected, making her slightly anxious. Once she passed through the city, the way to Hawthorne was smooth sailing. Since she arrived well before her interview time, she drove around the small town for a few minutes, familiarizing herself with its layout.

She finally made her way to the high school and turned into the parking lot. Though it was only the third week of July and school wouldn't start for another month, the parking lot had several cars in it. What she assumed was the student parking lot on the side of the school also had numerous cars in it.

Getting out of her vehicle, Paisley heard the strains of a band playing in the distance and figured that summer band practice was going on at the football stadium, which sat next to the high school. She knew band members worked just as hard in their own way as did basketball players, spending hours in the summer before marching season even started, perfecting their moves on the field. The same was true of drill team members and the cheerleading squads, as well as the football team participating in their preseason workouts.

Excitement began to fill her as she entered the building. If she could be a part of something again, she believed it would help her mentally. It had been hard for her to leave her Aces teammates behind since they were all the family she had, even though she had never really allowed any of them to become too close to her.

Maybe she would find a new family in the halls of Hawthorne High School.

She went to the office and gave her name to a clerk, who asked her to take a seat, offering Paisley coffee or water. She said yes to the water and asked where the closest restroom was since it had been almost four hours from Waco to Hawthorne. The clerk directed her to a faculty restroom within the office area.

When she came out, the woman handed her a bottle of water and said, "Follow me, Ms. Roberts. Mrs. Biggerstaff and Coach Sutherland are ready for you."

Paisley had always been one to do her homework, and she had thoroughly scoured the Hawthorne High School website, as well as conducting internet searches of Blanche Biggerstaff and West Sutherland. The principal was entering her twenty-fifth year of education, having taught in two other districts before joining Hawthorne ISD as an administrator.

West Sutherland, on the other hand, was even more famous than Paisley herself. He was a homegrown product of Hawthorne, having won a wide receiver scholarship to Texas A&M. West had been drafted by the Dallas Cowboys and played with the NFL team for a decade before retiring and returning to his hometown to coach the Hawks football team. He was also the district's athletic director, the reason he would be sitting in on her interview today. It would come down more to whether West wanted to hire her. At least that's what Maggie had said.

Paisley tried to tamp down the sudden flutter of nerves, telling herself if she didn't land the job in Hawthorne, she was bound to find another coaching position.

She entered the conference room, and both its occupants rose to greet her.

"Paisley, it is a real pleasure to meet you," Blanche Biggerstaff said, offering her hand. "I'm a big fan of yours. I played volleyball and basketball myself in high school. I've followed your career over the years. It was a pleasure to watch you compete, especially for Team USA."

"Thank you," she said graciously, having heard the same thing hundreds of times before.

West gave her a lopsided grin and held out his hand. "Same here, Paisley. I'm another fan. You really made your mark on the Olympic landscape, not to mention helping Baylor to bring home another national championship. And it's thanks to athletes such as yourself that the WNBA is finally getting the recognition it deserves."

"I appreciate that, West," she said, feeling more at home. "And I'll admit I'm a little sad not to be playing on this year's Olympic team."

Dr. Langston had taught Paisley that it was all right to experience sorrow in being left off the team and not being about to compete for her country. This was the first time she had vocalized it, though.

He looked her in the eyes. "There's always a time to step away from playing the sport you love. I did it. You've done it, as well. I can tell you from my own personal experience that coaching has turned out to be even more rewarding than being on the playing field myself. I hope that will prove true for you, as well."

"Why don't we take a seat and get to know each other?" Blanche suggested.

For the next half-hour, Blanche and West told Paisley about the town of Hawthorne and the high school itself. They spoke of the district's educational philosophy, emphasizing how each student can learn, and that they wanted to open opportunities for students to participate in learning experiences beyond the classroom, mentioning everything from mentoring programs to intramural sports.

"We have an excellent academic reputation, as well as a terrific sports program in the district," West told her. "We coordinate closely with our middle school coaches so that they're teaching a watered-down version of our offenses and defenses in various sports. By the time athletes arrive at the high school as freshmen, they've already been exposed to and have played in our various systems, from football to basketball and beyond."

Paisley had said very little so far, finding it odd that they had talked so much about the town and the school district. Then again, she believed they were trying to entice her to come to Hawthorne. After all, she was a big name in the world of sports.

Or at least she had been.

"Do you have any questions so far?" Blanche asked.

"No. You and West have answered them, outlining the school's pedagogy and mission statement, from students to student athletes. It sounds as if Hawthorne High School has a lot going on and would be a great place to work."

West said, "That was the easy part." He grinned. "Now, we're ready to grill you."

He wasn't kidding. They asked her at least three dozen questions, getting her perspective on everything from curriculum to handling discipline to working with her colleagues. Then West drilled down, asking very specific questions about the type of program she would run and how she would handle her student athletes. Paisley felt good about her answers, however, and comfortable with the pair.

At the end of an hour, Blanche and West exchanged a glance, and she knew the job was hers if she wanted it.

A deep yearning suddenly filled her. She wanted to be part of this school. This town. To truly belong to a community for the first time ever.

Although she had always considered her basketball teammates her family, Paisley had held them at arms' length. She had never formed close friendships with any of them. She had discussed this with Dr. Langston at length during their therapy sessions, and the therapist said a lot of Paisley's feelings were rooted in the fact that she had been abandoned by her mother at the tender age of four, causing her to mistrust everyone around her, keeping her from forming serious attachments, be they friendships or love interests.

While it appeared to outsiders that she was close to all her teammates, it was more a transactional relationship, the same as it had been with Coach Callahan when she had fostered Paisley. Callahan had used Paisley's talents to springboard to a better job with the school district. Once

Paisley had graduated and could no longer offer anything to the woman, Coach Callahan had never contacted her again, letting her know that their time together was done. That meant she had nowhere to go during breaks from college, and Paisley had crawled inside the loneliness and embraced it. It had been a bitter pill to swallow, but she had learned to close herself off from any close relationship from that point on, knowing that others only valued her for her basketball skills and not for who she was.

She decided she would take this job in Hawthorne. Became a Hawthorne Hawk and work with her players, bringing out the best in them, just as she had done with her fellow teammates over the years. Then she would move on. A new school. A new town. She was fooling herself to think that this situation might be different. They merely wanted her to coach here because of her fame and basketball knowledge. She would do the best job she could in this position, and when a new opportunity came along, she would take it without a backward glance.

Paisley looked at West Sutherland now, his gaze warm and friendly. Welcoming. She turned her eyes to Blanche Biggerstaff, who gave Paisley a big smile.

"We would like to offer you the girls basketball head coach position," the principal said. "I don't know if you've interviewed with other schools or not, but if we could have your decision by—"

"I'll take it," she interrupted. "I know with school starting around the corner, I need to get settled. So do you. I know you're going out on a limb for me, Mrs. Biggerstaff."

"Blanche," the principal insisted.

Nodding, Paisley added, "I haven't officially coached. It's not on my resumé. It may cause some in the community and the school board concern. I *have* been coaching all my life, though. Mentoring other players. Giving them feedback during and after games. Helping coaches draw up new plays."

She grinned. "I guess I'll finally have an official title. I like the sound of Coach Roberts."

The pair rose, and Paisley followed suit, shaking hands with both of them again.

Blanche said, "Welcome to Hawthorne, Paisley. It's a wonderfully supportive community. Our high school sports teams have many rabid fans." She laughed. "And that's just the students. You should see their parents and the rest of the town."

"I know oftentimes that girls sports aren't the same draw as boys."

West shook his head. "That's not the case in Hawthorne. Blanche is right. You'll be amazed at the turnout for home games. And the fact that we're getting such a well-known face is going to be icing on the cake."

"I don't want to trade on my Olympic or WNBA fame," she insisted. "If that's the only reason I'm being hired for this position, then maybe I shouldn't accept it."

West met her gaze. "We want you because you're the best candidate, Paisley. You've got the best basketball knowledge, plus you have a passion for the game, coupled with a nurturing spirit. You're going to be a fantastic coach." He paused. "And you've got a challenge ahead of you. I think that's why Coach Finnerty left us."

"You must be referring to the Lady Hawks' record the past two years."

Part of her deep dive into Hawthorne High School had included researching the basketball team over the last five years Coach Finnerty had been head of the girls basketball program. While Finnerty had brought home two district titles early during her tenure, she had a losing record her final two seasons. But it surprised Paisley that Finnerty hadn't made a lateral move when she left. Instead, she'd jumped two classifications within the UIL system, landing a job at a large high school in an Austin suburb. Then she had discovered that Finnerty's brother-in-law was the athletic director in the district she had gone to, and it made more sense.

"I know the girls have had a couple of losing seasons." Determination filled her. "That's going to change on my watch."

Blanche smiled. "We like a positive attitude. You're going to fit right in, Paisley." Turning to West, the principal said, "Give her the grand tour, Coach. I'll call admin so they can have the contract drawn up. You can head over there after Paisley has seen the school and facilities."

"Thank you, Blanche. I'm grateful for this opportunity."

"We're happy to have you on our faculty, Paisley. Stop by my office after you've seen everything. I'll have a packet pulled together for you. It's one we give all our new teachers. It'll give you dates of teacher trainings and keys to your rooms. You can have your picture taken for your employee badge when you go to admin, and that will allow you access into the building and field house."

The principal offered her hand again. "Thank you for wanting to be a Hawthorne Hawk."

West took her around the high school, showing her the cafeteria, auditorium, faculty lounge, and the copy room. They went to the gyms, and she was pleased to see there were two, one a normal size and another quite large. She could envision pep rallies in this gym.

"There's a schedule as to when each team gets to use which gym," he told her. "Sometimes, you'll be running practice on half the court, and another team will be using the other side. It might be volleyball. Gymnastics. We're lucky a bond package passed several years ago which allowed us to build a second gym and stands. Because of that—and the size of the new gym—we host a lot of tournaments and playoff games."

West led her to the locker rooms, and she saw the facilities were more than adequate. They left the main building and headed over to the field house, where the coaches' offices were located.

"As the district's athletic director, I've chosen to house here instead of over at admin. It's more convenient as the head football coach to have my home base be here, plus it helps me keep an eye on all the other sports at HHS. I've got an open-door policy. You can come to me anytime about any issue. I'll be sure to get you Hope Sewell's contact info. She's your assistant coach."

"Why wasn't she considered for this position?" Paisley asked, curious.

"Hope is a great teacher and has the potential to be a great coach. Last year was her first year to teach and coach, however. She chose not to interview for the position, saying that she wanted more seasoning before becoming a head coach."

"Do you think she'll resent me? I've never coached a day in the public schools. She's got more experience than I do."

"Your situation is pretty unique, Paisley. You've competed successfully at every level of your sport. Plus, as you yourself said, you've been coaching informally during your entire career. This is merely a formality, giving you a title and paying you for what you've done on the side for years. No, I think Hope is going to enjoy working with you. She'll learn a lot from you. On the other hand, I hope you'll be open to whatever she brings to the table."

She noted that West did not say Hope would be working under Paisley. He had chosen the phrase working *with* instead. That spoke volumes to her about the kind of program West ran here.

"I'll also make sure you get the names and numbers of the coaches at the middle school. As I mentioned, we try to closely coordinate our programs, so the players have an easier transition from middle school to high school athletics. I know bringing in a new coach means new offensive and defensive schemes. The sooner you can introduce your plays to the coaches, the better they can pass them along to their athletes."

"I'd like to at least see Coach Finnerty's playbooks first. Talk to Hope. See what was working and what wasn't." Then she paused. "You haven't shown me my classroom yet. I forgot to ask what I would be teaching."

"Sorry we forgot to mention that. Coach Finnerty was also our PE instructor. The students have a separate teacher for health, so you won't need to worry about that component. Let's stop by the gym again. There's a separate coaching office there for whoever is the PE teacher."

She saw that office and was pleased that she would be teaching physical education. She was also certified in math and knew that came with a lot of tutoring for some students. She wouldn't have to worry about how to work out a tutoring schedule, much less how to even begin to teach math in a classroom. Her student teaching days had been well over a decade ago, and she knew much had changed in the class-room since then. Teaching PE would be easier and a lot more fun than teaching algebra or geometry.

They returned to the main office, where Blanche met them, carrying a canvas bag with a Hawk on the side. She handed the bag to Paisley.

"Inside is the handbook for faculty members. There's also a folder with the specifics for this coming year. The academic calendar, as well as the basketball schedule—preseason and district—and the new hire teacher training dates. Also, a set of keys. Everything is labeled and color coordinated. Once you sign your contract, you'll be free to come and go as you like and make whatever preparations you want before staff development starts. West can help familiarize you with all the state UIL rules regarding your basketball program. I've already talked to Dr. Sutherland, our superintendent, and he can't wait to meet you and have you sign your contract."

"I thought Paisley and I could grab a late lunch before we head to the ad building since it's already after one," West said. "I'll call Dad and tell him we'll be there around three."

He glanced to her. "Yes, my dad is the superintendent of Hawthorne ISD. He allowed Blanche and the previous AD to hire me. It's a small town, though, so you're going to run into my relatives. My cousin Darby is the cheer coach and sponsors student publications at HHS. She'll be a great reference for you because she also came to the classroom late. Darby worked for a decade before moving back to Hawthorne and stepping into her role as an educator last year. I'll make sure to give you her number, as well."

Paisley thanked Blanche again and told her that she would be seeing her soon. West told her they could go to lunch in his truck. On their way to the parking lot, he dialed a number and smiled down at his screen.

"Hey, babe."

"Did you hire her?"

"Yup. Paisley's right here with me. We're gonna grab some lunch."

"Jen and I got caught up in work and had just taken a break. I put in an order at Pizza Palace, and Jen was about to leave and pick it up. Why don't you two come here and have lunch with us? I ordered extra so we'd have some for dinner tonight or lunch tomorrow. That way, I can help tell Paisley about Hawthorne."

They had reached his truck, and West looked to her. Paisley nodded.

"Okay, we'll save Jen a trip and bring the pizzas home. Love you."

"Love you, too."

West hung up, and they climbed into his truck. "I hope you don't mind stopping by my house. I'm a new dad, and I need my Kate fix. Badly."

As he started the truck, he added, "Kate is our daughter. Born six weeks ago and named after Kelby's mom. It's incredible how one little newborn can bring a grown man to his knees and have him talking gibberish."

She couldn't help but laugh, hearing this big, athletic guy talking about his baby.

"Do you have family, Paisley?"

She felt herself tense and tried to relax. "No. I grew up in foster care."

"I didn't know that. My brother-in-law also went through the system. His name is Dr. Eli Carson. He's the medical director at Triple H."

"Oh, I passed by it on my way into Hawthorne. It's a really nice facility for a town this size."

"Hogan Health is the parent corporation. They're putting in hospitals and medical offices in towns about Hawthorne's size throughout a five-state area. Eli's wife, Autumn, is my younger sister. She's in charge of all the nurses at the hospital. I also have another sister, Autumn's twin. Summer is a novelist." He beamed. "And she just married my best friend, Chance."

"You mentioned Darby was your cousin," Paisley said, fascinated by how West was connected to people in the town.

"Yes. Darby married Eli's brother, if you can believe that. Jace wound up being adopted when he was young and didn't even meet Eli until last year. Jace is my sports agent. He goes into Dallas a couple of days a week. The rest of the time, he works from his home office here in Hawthorne."

She laughed. "Anymore family members I need to know about?"

"I've got one more cousin in town. Darby's brother, Sawyer. He's a lawyer here in town. He used to be an assistant district attorney in Dallas, but he missed small-town life. We all get together pretty frequently. You'll have to come sometime. It'll be a good group of people for you to meet and hang out with."

"You've been very welcoming, West, but I'm going to have a lot on my plate, being a first-time coach and teacher. I doubt I'll be socializing much," she told him, wanting to shut the door on getting to know others so she could focus on her new responsibilities.

He turned onto the town square and pulled up in front of Pizza Palace. "I'll be back in a few. This'll be the best pizza you've ever tasted. Mario and Mischa moved here from New York, and they know how to make a damn fine pizza."

She watched him enter the restaurant and felt bad for a moment. He had been extending the branch of friendship, but she had thrown up a big, red flag, planting it in front of herself and telling him to halt. Paisley hoped it wouldn't influence their working relationship. As the district's athletic director, she would report to West Sutherland. She would also work closely with him on budgetary matters. He was a decent guy, though. Hopefully, he wouldn't hold anything against her. Paisley simply wanted to do her job. Coach her players. Get the best out of them.

And then move on.

She wasn't in Hawthorne to make friends. As much as she yearned for community, the life of a coach was transient. They moved around, going from school to school, district to district. She had never let her guard down before, and she wasn't going to do so in Hawthorne, especially since she only planned to stay a couple of years before trying to make her way up the ladder. Even Maggie had hinted to her that if she coached for a couple of years, she would find a place for her on Baylor's coaching staff. Paisley would do her best and keep to herself. It had worked fine for her up until now.

Even if Dr. Langston had encouraged her to form friendships during this new phase of her life.

West returned to the truck with a couple of large pizza boxes in hand. He opened one of the rear doors and set them on the floorboard.

As he got behind the wheel again, he said, "I didn't even think to ask what kind of pizza you liked. I'm sorry about that, Paisley. Hope you'll find something you like in what Kelby ordered."

"Not a problem," she assured him. "If it's pizza, I'll eat it. The toppings don't matter. I'm all about the crust. And having played in New York and eaten pizza there, I'm really looking forward to tasting this."

He told her a little more about growing up in Hawthorne during the ten minutes it took to reach his house. And boy, was it a house.

"This is the only thing I've ever splurged on," he shared. "I made great money playing for the Cowboys. I still make decent money through endorsement deals. Kelby and I designed this house with a growing family in mind. It's our forever home, so we went all out. It's got everything we want. I'm not embarrassed by it because I earned every penny that went into paying for it."

As they climbed from the truck, she said, "Good for you, West. Although WNBA players are paid a pittance compared to our NBA counterparts, I understand how hard I've worked for the money I've earned over the years. You don't have to apologize to me about your house."

He retrieved the pizza boxes, and they went to the front door.

"I know this all has to be pretty overwhelming for you, Paisley. Moving from Las Vegas. Starting a second career. A new state and a new life. If you ever need to talk about anything, feel free to bend my ear. I've been where you are— and not that long ago. Both of us are former pro athletes. Both of us had knee injuries and went through painful rehabs. We've both started a new chapter in our lives, taking up the challenge of coaching teenagers. There may be a point when you miss being out on the court and just need someone to talk to about it."

"Do you miss being on the playing field?" she asked quietly.

He grew thoughtful. "I thought I might, but that hasn't happened. I feel as if I were born to coach. The satisfaction I get from working with my staff and players is way more than when I was scoring touchdowns on Sunday afternoons. It also helps that I Zoom with my therapist once a week. She's a great sounding board and keeps me grounded. Being married to Kelby and having Kate also helps. A lot."

West opened the door and indicated for Paisley to enter. She was glad to hear that he had easily made the transition from pro athlete to civilian life. If a Super Bowl player could be happy coaching in a small town, maybe she would be, too.

CHAPTER
Three

Sawyer was looking forward to seeing his sister. Darby had been away from Hawthorne for five weeks now. The first week had been spent at a cheer camp in San Antonio, where she'd taken the JV and varsity squads to learn new cheers and dances. The month which followed had been spent in Europe with Jace. The couple had returned to Hawthorne as of last night, however, and he'd invited them to have dinner with him. Darby had asked Sawyer if he would grill burgers, and he'd readily agreed, figuring she was tired of rich European foods and in the mood for a juicy American cheeseburger.

He left his law office on the town square and drove to the two-bedroom house he'd been renting ever since he'd moved home to Hawthorne. At the time, he'd been lucky to lease it since Triple H's staff had brought a few hundred employees to the small, sleepy town. Since then, a few apartment buildings had been erected, and some new home construction had begun, as well. He knew he was throwing money down the drain by continuing to rent, but purchasing a home was a big move.

Especially because he'd be the only one living in it.

He'd recently turned thirty-six and never would have dreamed he would still be single. Then again, no woman had caught his eye since Elizabeth. Her death seven years ago had sent him into a downward spiral, and Sawyer had buried himself in work. He'd kept quiet about their relationship, and no one in the DA's office had known how deeply he had mourned the only woman he'd loved.

Then he'd finally hit a wall. Total burnout. He'd burned the proverbial candle at both ends for years after his fiancée's death, and Sawyer had realized overnight he had nothing to give anymore. He was wrung completely dry. The thought of entering a courtroom and fighting to put away another criminal left a sour taste in his belly. He'd resigned his position immediately and moved back to his hometown, taking over Isaiah Smith's practice. The feisty retired lawyer still owned the building in which Sawyer had his office, and he paid Isaiah a nominal rent each month for the office since being on the town's square was an ideal location.

Sawyer had been fortunate that his undergrad degree had been paid for with his basketball scholarship, but he had gone seriously into debt for law school. On his district attorney salary, he'd barely made a dent in the money he had owed. Upon his return to Hawthorne, West had paid off the balance of the loan and its interest. Though he'd protested, not wanting West to spend so much money, his cousin had said it was an investment in Sawyer and the town of Hawthorne. Truth be told, West had more money than Midas and hadn't missed what he'd given to Sawyer to pay off the loans. West had a generous nature and fat bank account, thanks to his days in the NFL. He accepted the salary the school district paid him, but he'd told Sawyer he would coach for free if they ever asked him to do so.

Once Sawyer arrived home, he changed into a T-shirt and shorts. The summer heat was stifling, hovering around one hundred and two. Thank goodness his grill was shaded by an old oak tree. They would definitely eat inside tonight and relish the air conditioning.

He'd already made up the hamburger patties the night before. While he waited for Darby and Jace to arrive, he cut up a watermelon and placed the slices in the fridge to cool. He also fried up some bacon and crumbled it in canned pork and beans, adding diced onion and green peppers, ketchup, and brown sugar to the mix. The beans went into the oven to bake. They were Darby's favorite, next to the chili he made. Chili was a weekend dish, though, so he was home to nurse it for several hours. Besides, it was too dang hot to eat chili in July.

The doorbell rang, and he went to answer it. His sister and brother-in-law stood on the porch, and he ushered them inside, out of the heat, before wrapping his arms around Darby, giving her a bear hug. Something was very different, though, and Sawyer pulled away, his eyes falling to the loose top she wore.

Beaming at him, Darby said, "Yes. I'm pregnant. We wanted you to be the first to know."

He enfolded her in his arms again, happiness spilling from him. If he didn't have any kids, being an uncle to Darby's children would be the next best thing.

Sawyer released her and offered Jace a hand, shaking it and then hugging him, as well.

"Congratulations, you two. I'd grab beers to celebrate, but I guess that's off-limits now."

"Give Jace one. He can drink for two," his sister teased, following him into the kitchen. She sniffed. "Baked beans?"

"Yes. When you asked for burgers, I figured out you were really asking for baked beans."

She sighed. "As much as I enjoyed visiting Europe and trying some new foods, all I could think of at times was a cheeseburger and your baked beans, Sawyer."

He laughed. "I also made potato salad last night so the flavors could settle. Just like you like it."

"You're the best big brother," she declared.

"Let me go light the grill, and then we can talk for a few minutes."

"I'll do it for you," Jace offered. "You two get started. But I will take that beer when I come back inside."

Sawyer poured a large glass of iced tea for Darby and grabbed a Shiner Bock for himself. They sat at the kitchen table.

"Tell me everything. The baby. The trip. Cheer camp."

She took a sip of her tea. "Camp was great. It was a weird feeling, being at a cheer workshop as a sponsor instead of one of the instructors, but the squads had a wonderful time. They learned a lot. The rising seniors stepped up, showing the leadership I was hoping for. The dances lacked a little creativity, though."

"That's because you weren't choreographing them," he said, mentioning one of the jobs Darby had held with Cheer USA during her tenure.

"My co-captains said they were going to rework the dances and implement original steps of their own. In fact, they've sent me a few videos, and I really like what they've done." She sighed. "I'll start working with them come Monday. Same for the newspaper and yearbook staffs. They come back early and start planning the year. Yearbook comes up with the theme and how to cover it before school even starts. They block out the sections and assign who'll be responsible for what pages. Newspaper always likes to have an edition waiting for students on the first day, so they've been covering events in Hawthorne and working on stories about different students all summer."

"How is the baby going to factor into all this?" he asked.

Her hands came to her belly, and a satisfied smile touched her lips. "The baby was made during spring break when Jace took me to Maui for our delayed honeymoon. He or she will be due mid-December or so. Yes, it will complicate our lives a little. If the baby's on time, my maternity leave would be up a few days before the cheerleaders compete at nationals in February. Since they'll be defending last year's title, they have a lot at stake."

"They'll have to do a lot of practicing on their own," he noted.

"Actually, they do that already. But I'll need to be very selective in finding a sub who is willing to put in the extra hours after school—even on weekends—to get them ready for the competition. Legally, I can't go near them. I can't even go up to school while I'm on maternity leave. We'll work it out somehow."

"When will we know if you've got a he or she?"

Darby grinned. "Tomorrow. I already have an appointment at Triple H with my OB/GYN first thing in the morning. I'm seeing Dr. Bennett, same as Kelby did with Kate. Since I'm almost five months along, she's scheduled a sonogram after my appointment with her. By this time tomorrow, we'll know the gender."

Jace appeared. "The grill's hot enough. Ready for the burgers."

"Put all talk on hold," Sawyer said to his sister, retrieving a beer and handing it to Jace.

"I'll grill the burgers," Jace said. "You can bring out the onions and mushrooms."

Sawyer's grill had a side panel. Any time he cooked burgers, he also brought a pan of mushrooms and onions mixed with a little olive oil outside to grill.

"They're already chopped. I'll get everything now."

He pulled out the burgers. "I've already seasoned them. I did that when I made the patties." He glanced to Darby. "Hope there's not too much garlic in them for you."

"I'm fine," she assured him. "I'm eating everything in sight. Haven't had but a few whiffs of nausea, and that was a few weeks ago."

He handed over the platter of patties to Jace and poured the olive oil in a pan, bringing it and two zip locks of veggies with him. Jace took everything from him.

"I've got this covered," his brother-in-law said. "Go talk with Darby. She's been dying to see you."

Sawyer returned inside. As he puttered about, pulling out potato salad and toasting buns, his sister told him about London, Paris, Rome, and Florence. Neither Darby nor he had ever been to Europe, and so he gobbled up everything she told him.

"In each city, we tried to do some day trips. From London, we took a tour to the Cotswolds. Saw Stonehenge and Bath. Another day we took the train down to Canterbury and saw the town and cathedral. Versailles was just a short train ride from Paris. The palace is phenomenal, but we enjoyed the gardens and the Queen's House quite a bit. And Italy is for eaters, Sawyer. My gosh, every meal was better than the one before it. The pasta. The pizza. I only hated that I had to forgo the wine.

Jace said it was terrific, both the whites and reds. We'll have to go back someday." She grinned. "Maybe even take the kids with us, unless we leave them with their uncle Sawyer."

"That would be fine with me. I'm glad you got to see some of the places you've always wanted to go," he said wistfully.

He and Elizabeth had planned to spend their honeymoon in Florence and Rome. He had a deep love of history and architecture, and she was a fan of Renaissance art. A lump formed in his throat, and he swallowed hard, forcing it down. Even after all this time, it hurt to think of her.

Darby stood and came to him, wrapping her arms around him.

"I'm sorry. I forgot that you and Elizabeth had planned to go to Italy."

"It's all right," he assured her, kissing the top of her head. "If I ever do go someday, she'll be with me in spirit."

She pulled away, her gaze connecting with his. "I didn't know it still hurt so much. Sawyer, you need to move on. I'm not saying forget Elizabeth. I know you'll never want to do that. But I think it's time for you to date a little. Have some fun. You're everyone's go-to guy. You solve all our problems. Give great advice. Listen when we need a friendly ear. But you don't do anything for yourself."

He removed the buns from the toaster, setting them on the table. "Well, the dating pool isn't huge in Hawthorne. I've actually gone out a couple of times since I came back."

"Obviously, no one interested you enough for you to pursue a second date."

"You're right about that."

"There are some single teachers at HHS. Say the word, and I'll set you up with a few of them." She brightened. "In fact, I met someone today who's just been hired. She would be perfect for you."

Before he could balk at going on a blind date, Jace appeared with a platter of burgers and a skillet of veggies.

"Set everything here," Sawyer said. "I'll take the beans out of the oven. And we've got watermelon for dessert."

It took a few minutes to fix their plates, and then they sat at the kitchen table. He asked Jace a few questions about their trip, and his brother-in-law was all too happy to tell Sawyer about visiting everywhere from Churchill's War Rooms to the Vatican Museum to Notre Dame Cathedral.

"And the gelato is to die for," Darby told him. "We would eat it twice a day. My favorite was a stracciatella, a smooth vanilla gelato with crunchy chocolate shards. Jace was wild about gianduia, which was a blend of chocolate and hazelnut."

"I would like to go to Italy and eat my way through the various regions," he said. "I watched a show on CNN where Stanley Tucci visited different areas. It blended travel and architecture, plus he focused on the foods each region in Italy is known for. He'd make the recipes with locals. It was definitely food porn for the eyes."

They ended the meal with the slices of watermelon, and Darby mentioned how much sweeter fruit tasted to her now that she was pregnant.

Jace offered to clean up, allowing brother and sister to sit a bit longer and talk. As he had anticipated, Darby turned the conversation back to him dating. His sister could be like a dog with a bone, relentless.

"Seriously, I met a new hire at Kelby's today. And no, I didn't tell Kel I was pregnant, but I think she guessed. She was sweet enough not to say anything, though. Kel is smart enough to know I would officially want you to be the first to know." She paused. "But I'm calling her in the car on the way home once we leave so she'll know for sure."

Darby stopped speaking, looking scattered for a moment. "Sorry. My thoughts go haywire a little bit every now and then. I guess it's pregnancy brain. Anyway, she called me to come over because West had just hired a new girls basketball coach and thought it would be a good idea for her to meet a fellow teacher."

"Yeah, he told me Coach Finnerty had left."

Sawyer had not been a fan of the basketball coach and was glad someone had finally replaced her.

"West brought her home to meet Kelby and Kate. Of course, Jen was there since she's working out of their house these days. Kelby's starting to ease back into work, but she still hasn't arranged childcare for Kate. I think they want to find someone who can come to the house and watch Kate. That way, Kel could keep nursing without much fuss."

She paused. "What was I saying? Oh, yeah. West brought the new coach home. He and Blanche had interviewed her this morning, and he'd shown her around HHS. They ate a few slices with us, and then he was going to take her to admin to meet Uncle Joe so she could sign her contract and get her badge. Anyway, she's really nice. And very tall. Confident. Very striking. I didn't know who she was, but Kel and Jen certainly did. It seems she played for the US in the Olympics. Chocolate brown hair and very expressive eyes but a little closed off. Then again, she was just meeting everyone for the first time."

Sawyer had an inkling who the new coach might be and asked, "Was her name Paisley Roberts?"

Darby brightened. "That's her! I think it would be great if you'd ask her out. Just show her around Hawthorne. See if anything sparks between you."

"We'll see," he said.

She shook her head. "You look and sound exactly like Dad. I'd ask to do something, and I'd get a 'We'll see' from him." Darby frowned. "And that was usually a big, fat no. Come on, Sawyer. What have you got to lose? Paisley's single. She obviously plays basketball, so you have that in common. She's a new face in town."

"We'll see," he repeated, causing his sister to laugh.

Jace appeared, a container in his hand. "The kitchen is sparkling. I took the liberty of putting a few watermelon slices in here since Darby is wild about fruit these days."

"Good. Even though I bought just half a watermelon, there is a lot of it. In fact, give me that container. You can take the other one. There has to be more in it than this one."

Jace made the switch, and Sawyer walked the couple out to their car, congratulating them again on the baby.

"You better call me the minute you know the gender," he told them.

"We will," his sister promised. "And you call West and get Paisley's number."

Jace looked at his wife quizzically. "What do you have up your sleeve?"

"I'm trying to set Sawyer up with the new basketball coach. I think they'd be perfect together."

"Baby, let's let Sawyer make his own decisions where his love life is concerned."

"Thank you, Jace," he said. "Take her home and get her out of my hair."

Darby rolled down her window after Jace started the car. "Call West. Get the number. That way, when I talk with you tomorrow, you can tell me where you're taking Paisley on your first date."

Sawyer waved as Jace's sports car pulled away, thinking

his brother-in-law would need to get a more family-friendly car so that a car seat would fit. Those two would have a lot of changes coming their way, but they would be terrific parents.

Something tugged at his heart, and he decided that Darby might be right. It was time for him to put himself out there. See what the world had to offer a guy in his mid-thirties.

He pulled his cell from his pocket and touched the screen.

West answered. "Hey, Sawyer. What's up? Darby just called Kelby, and from what my wife says, your sister is pregnant."

"She is. She's officially telling Kelby now. But I'm calling about something else. I have a favor to ask."

Sawyer took a deep breath. "Would you be willing to pass along Paisley Robert's phone number to me?"

On her last morning in Waco, Paisley did her usual morning workout. Stretches, followed by her walk, and then she entered the facilities at Baylor. It didn't surprise her to find Maggie already working out there herself. The coach nodded to Paisley, who went to the weights and began some light lifting.

They completed their workouts in companionable silence, for which Paisley was grateful. Maggie was the closest thing Paisley had to both a mother and friend. Her college coach had taken a young player under her wing and had continued supporting Paisley even after she left the university for the pros.

When they both finished, they grabbed bottled waters and sat a moment.

"Are you packed? Leaving soon?"

Paisley nodded. "I'll leave after I get home and shower. Packing didn't take long."

Even all these years later, the little Paisley owned easily fit into her sedan. She supposed it was left over from her foster care days, where everything she owned needed to fit into one brown grocery sack. It really hadn't changed once she landed with Coach Callahan's family. She never had a bedroom of her own there. Instead, she slept on a couch in the office, her clothes neatly folded and placed in a corner of the room on the floor. Paisley had dreaded her feet growing because Coach Callahan bitterly complained about having to keep her in new shoes.

As an adult, she now realized how little Callahan had given to her foster child, merely using Paisley to climb the athletic ladder and further her own career. Only after Paisley had graduated did Maggie share that Callahan had angled for a job at Baylor once Paisley had accepted a full ride to the school. Maggie had told the coach that her staff was set and that she had no openings. It was then that Callahan cut all ties with Paisley, seeing that her foster child had no more use to her.

Because of that, she'd had nowhere to go during holidays from school. Maggie had stepped in and become Paisley's go-to. She ate Thanksgiving and Easter dinners with Maggie's family and even stayed at their house over long breaks, such as Christmas, since the dorms closed. Fortunately, her athletic scholarship allowed her to remain on campus year-round, allowing her to take classes during both summer sessions while having access to the workout facilities and gym.

It was during her years at Baylor that Paisley truly honed her basketball skills. She'd spent hours working on her free throws. Three-point shots from different spots on the court. Dribbling solely with her left hand so that it was just as comfortable doing so as her dominant right hand, a required skill for a good point guard.

Looking gratefully at Maggie now, she said, "I'm not

going to go all mushy on you. You know I never do sentimental, but you saved me in every way, Maggie. You taught me so much about basketball, but you taught me even more about how to be a gracious person. I can't thank you enough for how you've influenced my life in a positive way. I've been a better player, teammate, and person, thanks to your influence."

"You're family to me, Paisley. You always will be. And remember, coaching is in your blood. You've got this."

"You're the only person I would admit this to. I'm terrified of being a coach and in charge of a team of my own."

"You've been around enough coaches and players over the years. Think back and draw the best from the best and then make it your own. You'll be in charge of your own program, able to run it as you see fit. Not only to teach your athletes about basketball but teach them about life. Once you have a few years of experience under your belt, you know you're welcome here in Waco. I can always make room for another assistant of your caliber as soon as you have a little seasoning."

"I appreciate that more than you know, Maggie. For now, I'm going to be laser-focused on this job in Hawthorne. The team is in a bad place. Two losing years in a row and a coach who abandoned them. I've got to win their trust first. Then I'll work on the basketball end of things."

Maggie hugged her. "If you ever need any advice—or even a sounding board—I'm here for you, Paisley."

"I know that. Thank you."

She returned to the small, furnished apartment she had been renting since March, when she had completed the rehab which had been provided by the league. Her gut had told her that she needed to be away from everything in Vegas. No coaches or players were calling her by the end of those six months since they had been gearing up for their new season.

It had been the right move to return to Waco and be in familiar surroundings once again. Maggie's support had also helped tremendously.

Paisley showered and dressed. She placed her things in the car and then returned her key to the office, where the manager thanked her for being such a good tenant.

Once she was in her car, she texted Jen Adelstein.

> Leaving Waco now. Should be in Hawthorne between 11:30 and noon.

Almost immediately, Jen texted a thumbs up. As Paisley started her car and left Waco behind, she hoped she was doing the right thing by renting a room in Jen's house. She had met Jen at West and Kelby Sutherland's house the other day. Jen was from the Midwest and had worked with Summer, West's sister, at a publishing house in New York. Jen had recently left that job and come to Hawthorne, trying to figure out what to do next as she visited Summer. The timing had been perfect, with Kelby's baby due soon. The entrepreneur had been looking for someone to bring aboard her social media and branding business, and Jen's skills fit the bill perfectly.

Since Paisley needed a place to live, Jen had mentioned over the pizza lunch that she was renting a three-bedroom house a few blocks off the town square and that she was more than happy to rent out one of the rooms to Paisley for as long as she wanted it. Jen worked at West and Kelby's house and would be gone during the day. She told Paisley they could see as much or as little of each other as Paisley wanted. Jen had said she was open to becoming friends but if Paisley wanted just to be a roommate, that would be fine, too.

She figured she would be spending a majority of her waking hours at the high school. Renting a room from Jen meant she wouldn't have to look for an apartment. Since Jen's rental had come furnished, she also wouldn't have to worry about buying any furniture, much less kitchenware and towels. She could come and go as she pleased, so the arrangement suited her. Jen seemed to be really nice, with that Midwestern, open friendliness Paisley had seen in a couple of her teammates on the Aces. Maybe they would become friends, after all.

Darby Tanner had also been at that lunch. She was the cousin West had mentioned who taught at the high school. Darby and Kelby had been best friends for many years, and it was obvious they had a shorthand between them. Darby had looked pregnant to Paisley, but she hadn't mentioned anything, so Paisley kept quiet. Darby had given Paisley her number, telling her to text any time if she had questions about the high school.

She had also told Paisley that she'd be at the school frequently between now and the start of school in August. Her cheerleaders would be putting in practice time there, and the newspaper and yearbook staffs she sponsored would also be working. Darby said she hoped Paisley would text so they could have lunch a few times and get to know one another better.

Paisley had liked Darby and Jen. West's wife, too. Kelby Sutherland was a true beauty, and it was obvious that she was very bright. Kelby also appeared to have taken to motherhood and their six-week-old daughter Kate. Paisley had never once thought about having children. She had never even been around a baby before, but little Kate Sutherland had stolen her heart, with her large, inquisitive eyes studying Paisley.

It made her wonder if somewhere down the road she might think about adopting a child. Saving someone from the foster care system and giving that child all the love and attention she herself had never received.

Then again, the life of a coach was nomadic in nature, with frequent job changes. The hours, too, were long and unpredictable. Nights and weekends taken up with games and tournaments. Maybe she would simply learn to mother her players a little bit and give them a safe harbor to speak their minds.

She passed through Ft. Worth easily, the Saturday morning traffic light compared to what she had experienced just a few days ago. As she reached the other side of Ft. Worth and turned to head toward Hawthorne, her phone rang. That was unusual. No one ever called her. These days, few people even texted her.

Glancing down at her phone, she saw it was an unknown number. Still, she'd better answer it. It might be someone connected with Hawthorne ISD or the high school itself.

She tapped a button on her steering wheel. "Hello?"

"Is this Paisley Roberts?" a deep voice asked, causing goose bumps to dance up her arms.

Cautiously, she replied. "This is Paisley. What is this about?"

"You're going to think this is pretty odd, Paisley. My name is Sawyer Montgomery."

The name sounded familiar to her. She associated it with Hawthorne and then realized where she'd heard it before.

"You're West's cousin, right?"

"I am. West told me that he had hired you. I thought I would give you a call and welcome you to Hawthorne. I hear you're arriving today."

"How do you know that?" she asked sharply. Paisley had learned long ago to guard every detail about her private life, which is why she posted so rarely on social media.

The voice on the other end of the line chuckled. "You aren't from a small town, are you?"

"No. I grew up in San Antonio. Why?"

"You're moving to a small town. Hawthorne is full of good people, but news flies fast here. Everybody will be in your business. Know your business. That's the good and bad of living in a small town."

"Like you know I'm arriving today?"

"Exactly. I heard it from West, from my sister Darby—whom you met the other day—then from Jen. And my aunt Meg also mentioned it."

He paused, and neither of them said anything for a moment.

Finally, Sawyer spoke again. "I grew up in Hawthorne and then took a job in Dallas. And you know what? I missed that small town vibe more than I ever imagined. I missed walking down the street and most people knowing my name. I came back a year and a half ago, and I haven't regretted that decision. My sister and her husband are here. My three cousins live here, too, with their spouses. My aunt and uncle. I'm doing good work, helping others."

Curious, she asked, "What do you do for a living?"

"I'm an attorney. I have an office on the town square. I rent it from Isaiah Smith, who retired when I came to town. I took over his law practice and have added a few of my own clients to it."

She didn't quite know what to make of this call, so she remained quiet.

"I know you have to think this is the weirdest conversation with someone you've never met. I'm a basketball player. A former basketball player. I played college ball at UNT in Denton. I guess hearing you were coming to town, I simply wanted to welcome you. Let you know that another basketball player was around. Of course, I don't have the claim to fame you do. An injury ended my career in my senior year. I wasn't talented enough to make it to pros anyway, but I loved the game with a fierce passion."

"I'm sorry to hear about your injury, Sawyer. That it ended your playing days. It's rough when that happens because you are stuck with the fact that you didn't know that would be your last game. A lot of 'what ifs' linger."

"I made my peace with it a long time ago. I never miss going to any of the games at the high school. Guys or girls. There's a purity about high school basketball that isn't present in college or the pros. The innocence of the players. Watching them blossom before your eyes. Seeing what they're capable of unfolding over a season. Watching them when they can find their sweet spot on the court. It really is a thing of beauty. I look forward to seeing you make your mark with the Lady Hawks. They are in sore need of good coaching. They need to come together as a team and play like one, without individuals trying to grab their own glory. But you'll find all that out once you meet your players."

"I appreciate you touching base with me, Sawyer," Paisley said, not wanting their conversation to end but feeling it was wrapping up. He seemed like a nice guy. Friendly. And with him being West's cousin, she instinctively trusted him, which was something foreign to her. Paisley wasn't one to trust anyone, much less a stranger, but something in his voice calmed her. It definitely made her want to meet him.

"Well, I'll let you go," he said. "You've got my number in your phone now. I hope you'll use it sometime. I'd be happy to show you around Hawthorne. Answer any questions you might have. Maybe we can even grab a bite to eat sometime."

Paisley heard herself say, "I'd like that, Sawyer."

That surprised the hell out of her.

She never wanted to be around others once she left the basketball court. Being a loner was in her nature. She'd never even had a single date. Her life had been focused completely on basketball.

"If that's the case, would you care to grab a bite tonight? We could have dinner, and then I could drive you around town. Show you the sights."

Bluntly, she asked, "Are you asking me on a date?"

A low chuckle came from him. "Actually, I think I am. I don't really date, Paisley. Haven't for years. But I figured you were new in town. That we at least have basketball in common. No pressure, though. I'm not really looking for romantic involvement, but maybe you could use a friend once you get here."

"Then I'll say yes to dinner with a new friend," she responded, again surprising herself because this was so out of character for her. She didn't socialize. Period.

"Great. I know you've already had food from Pizza Palace, so we need to introduce you to somewhere else. Normally, I'd suggest Dizzy's Diner. It's the best food in town, but Dizzy only opens for breakfast and lunch. There's a good sports bar, though. Burgers. Wings. Nachos. And lots of TVs to watch in case we run out of things to talk about."

Her gut told her that wouldn't be the case.

"Okay, Sawyer. What time are we going to have this friendly dinner?"

"How about I pick you up at six? That's probably too early for someone like you, but people in Hawthorne have a tendency to eat early and hit the sack early."

"No, six is fine. I'm usually up between four and four-thirty to work out, so I go to bed pretty early myself."

Again, that low, intriguing chuckle sounded, and goose bumps sprang up along her arms again.

"Then you're going to fit right into Hawthorne, Paisley Roberts. Okay, then. I'll see you at six. Sonny's Sports Bar is super casual—everyone will be in shorts and T-shirts. You'll look out of place if you wear anything else."

Relief swept through her. Her wardrobe was severely limited. Knowing she could dress casually tonight was a huge plus.

"I'm renting a room from Jen Adelstein," she volunteered. "I can text you the address."

For some reason, her words caused him to laugh aloud.

"I already know that, Paisley. I'm certain at least half of Hawthorne knows that, as well. I'll see you at six. Bye."

"Bye," she said, tapping the button on her steering wheel again.

Paisley wasn't quite certain what to make of the call from Sawyer Montgomery, much less his invitation to have dinner together this evening. She decided not to question it, though. It seemed things were done a little differently in a small town, and she would have to become accustomed to that. She had known that she would be scrutinized by the community from what Blanche and West had indicated. The town's residents were heavily invested in the high school's sports programs, so she understood she would be under a microscope with her play calling and the record of her team.

It seemed, though, that she herself would be a hot topic of discussion, which caused her to wonder about being seen tonight in Sawyer's company.

Would people think they were dating?

Paisley had never lived her life worried about what others thought of her, though. She wasn't about to start now. She would go to dinner and hopefully make a new friend. The fact that Sawyer was a guy shouldn't make any difference.

And yet something told Paisley that this might be the start of something very new.

CHAPTER
Five

As Paisley entered the Hawthorne city limits, she wondered what it would be like, living in a permanent place. Almost a decade of her foster care years had been spent going from one household to another, and she had never truly fit in anywhere. As an adult, she had traveled to many cities in the US and Europe, playing in two different professional women's leagues, but she really had never seen those places. The flight would land, and she and her teammates would be whisked to a hotel or practice facility. Even during the decade she had played for the Las Vegas Aces, she only went to the same few places. The practice facility and game arena, with trips to the grocery store or Target in-between. She had never gambled a single time in Vegas, much less attended any entertainment shows. Her life had consisted of nothing but basketball.

Maybe she could find more of a work/life balance here in Hawthorne. She cautioned herself not to become too attached to the town or anyone living in it, however. As much as she might like to sink roots into this community, she had to remember she was only as good as the last game she'd coached. If she didn't put up winning numbers, West Sutherland would not renew her contract, and she would head to the next coaching position, which might be hundreds of miles from Hawthorne.

Knowing that, Paisley resolved not to try to make any friends. She would be cordial to Jen but merely treat her as a roommate, someone she shared a sleeping space with. At school, she would keep to herself, pouring everything into her players instead of buddying up to faculty members.

She reached the town square and turned off on one of the streets which dead-ended into it, driving a few blocks before turning right. The quiet, residential street would offer her solace. She would get to know more of the town's layout as she walked it every morning.

When she reached Jen's rental, Paisley was displeased to see several cars parked on the street in front of it. At least she was able to pull into the empty driveway. She would need to make sure she got a key from Jen and wondered if there might be room for her to park her car in the garage, especially since so many residents parked on the street.

Paisley knocked on the door, and it was quickly opened by her new roommate.

Jen gave her a wide smile. "Hey, Paisley. A few people stopped by to welcome you to Hawthorne."

At least that explained all the cars. While she wasn't up for company, she would play nice. If this welcome wagon included residents of the community, she didn't want them to leave with a poor impression of her.

As they stepped into the den, she spied four other women present. She recognized Kelby, West's wife and Jen's boss, along with Darby, her fellow faculty member at HHS and West's cousin. Hesitantly, she moved closer to them, wondering about the other two women. Their facial features were very similar, and then she noticed they both had the same turquoise eyes West possessed. One was tall, blond, and willowy, while the other had auburn hair and was much shorter. And very pregnant.

Jen said, "This is Summer Blackstone, my best friend from our days in New York at Liberty House, and Summer's twin, Autumn Carson."

Summer gave her a big smile. "We're so happy to have you come to Hawthorne, Paisley. The girls basketball team really needs a jumpstart."

"Let's hope I can provide that for them," she said.

"I'm Autumn," the other twin said. "It's a pleasure to meet you, Paisley. You're the talk of Hawthorne over the last few days."

She winced, recalling what Sawyer had said about how everyone knew everyone's business in a small town.

Kelby and Darby greeted her then, and Kelby said, "I picked up a few pizzas on the way over. It was the easiest to do instead of throwing together a lunch to welcome you. Let's go into the kitchen and grab some slices."

Everyone started toward the kitchen. Except Paisley. She stood a moment, trying to center herself. Then she noticed Autumn had hung back from the others.

"You must be feeling a bit overwhelmed from the others, Paisley," the woman said astutely. "I can understand that. Kelby and Darby have been friends since kindergarten. Both cheerleaders, with that effervescent personality. My twin was always the more outgoing of the two of us. I was the quiet one, so I know how overwhelming it can be to be around the three of them. They're all wonderful gals, though. They just want to open their hearts to you and help you become a part of Hawthorne."

"I appreciate their openness. It's just a lot for me. I'm pretty much a loner," she admitted.

"I get that," Autumn said. "I turned into a real loner during my first marriage. I put my husband through med school, working double shifts. I kept doing that during his residency because I thought I should try and make some money since he was never home. Little did I know he was making time for several women at the hospital we both worked at and ignoring his wife. His cheating just about destroyed any self-esteem I had. Overnight, I was broken."

Paisley was surprised by Autumn's candor.

"You exude calm. A quiet confidence. I can't imagine anyone cheating on you."

Autumn smiled. "That's thanks to my new job and a husband who truly loves me. Who believes I can do anything. I divorced Flint and left Houston and all the ugly memories behind. It took returning to Hawthorne to realize how isolated I had become. Fortunately, I had family here to help pick me up. I took a position which involves supervising the entire nursing staff at Triple H."

Autumn's face softened. "That's where I met Eli. His faith in me has helped me to become a stronger, more capable person. The person I was, all along, deep down inside. He believed in me—and now I truly believe in myself. I feel I can do anything now, thanks to Eli."

Autumn's hands went to her belly. "And I plan to raise this little girl to be someone who can stand on her two feet."

Still a little startled by how much of her personal life Autumn had revealed, Paisley asked, "When are you due? It looks soon."

"I've got about six more weeks to go. Sarah Elizabeth is named after her two grandmothers, and she's going to kick butt."

Paisley laughed. "I hope you're going to have her play basketball then."

Autumn placed her hand on Paisley's and squeezed gently. "You don't have to be alone in Hawthorne, Paisley. Plenty of people are already rooting for you. I hope you'll let down your walls a little bit and let others in. Mine surrounded me, and that's why I recognize that in others."

Kelby stuck her head around the corner. "Are you two coming?"

"We are," Paisley said, giving a nod to Autumn and feeling a little closer to her. Quietly, she said, "Thanks for sharing some of your story with me. I can be a little closed off."

The table in the kitchen only seated four, so they carried their plates of pizza back to the den. She answered a few general questions, but she mostly listened. Kelby and Jen told her about Social Synergy Creations, the business Kelby had started after returning to her hometown.

"I worked in several areas of business around the country," Kelby shared. "My ex-husband moved us around a lot. I came back to Hawthorne because my dad had a stroke. He passed away a year ago this past spring."

"I'm sorry to hear that," Paisley said, realizing that Kelby, too, had been married previously since she knew West had played for the Cowboys for many years.

"You would have liked him. Everyone liked Big Jim Blackthorne. He was one of those larger-than-life people who entered a roomful of strangers and instantly made friends. Once he was gone, I decided to stay in Hawthorne and start my own business. It began growing faster than I ever anticipated and I knew I needed help."

Kelby glanced to Jen. "That's when Jen came to town. She's been a godsend."

"I had no idea when I left New York to visit Summer that I'd be staying here," Jen said. "But SSC gives me the chance to do something new every day. We create websites. Mission statements. We work with individuals, corporations, and organizations with their branding. We handle social media."

Paisley shook her head. "I am not someone who's ever been bitten by the social media bug. My only account is on Instagram. I never even look at it. I think I've only posted half a dozen times on it. After I've won a championship. That kind of thing."

"That surprises me," Kelby says. "You're a big name in the sports world."

"Was," she said neutrally, not wanting any bitterness to bubble up.

"Why didn't your agent press for you to post more?" Kelby asked. "Or hire someone to handle your social media accounts for you?"

"My agent only helped me in negotiating my contracts. He never mentioned social media to me. I wasn't the Olympic gymnastics all-around gold medal winner or the men's decathlon star. Those are the kinds of athletes who get their pictures on cereal boxes. I was just a member of the basketball team."

"You never had any endorsement deals?" Darby asked, clearly surprised.

When Paisley shook her head no, Darby added, "That's plain wrong. You are definitely a role model others can look up to, especially young women."

She shrugged. "That boat has already sailed. I'm nobody now. It's far too late to try and get an endorsement deal. Not that I want any. I'm committed to this job at the high school."

"You might be surprised," Darby said. "My husband is a

sports agent. He reps West. If you ever change your mind, let me know. I can put you and Jace together."

"Thanks," Paisley said, touched at how strongly Darby seemed to feel about this.

The conversation switched to the upcoming football season and the team West would field. As she listened, Paisley thought how nice it would be if she could be a part of this group of women. They had shown up to welcome her today and had been open and friendly. They didn't possess any agenda. She was used to anyone trying to befriend her actually wanting something from her. That's why she had kept to herself for so many years. To be honest, Paisley didn't even know if she knew how to make a friend, much less be a friend to a group such as this.

"Okay, announcement time," Darby said. "Not that everyone here hasn't guessed, but I'm pregnant. I didn't just come back from Europe with extra pasta and gelato weight."

Everyone offered congratulations, and again, Paisley thought about how Kelby had just given birth and now Autumn and Darby were also pregnant. She thought of how she would love to have a child. Boy or girl. It didn't matter. She would go to their games. No, coach them. Read to them. Color with them. Build a fort and teach them to ride a bike. To have gone from never even thinking about having a family to suddenly desiring one was a pretty wild turn. She would really need to get hold of her emotions and think this through.

With the pizza consumed, Kelby said, "I need to get back and nurse Kate. I'm sure West has been reading the sports section to her." She looked to Paisley. "We're so happy you took the job at HHS. I know you'll make friends with others at the high school, but we'd love to have you as part of our group. No pressure. You'll be busy with your team, but I hope you know we're here for you, Paisley."

Kelby looked to the others. "Let's make sure to give Paisley our cell numbers."

She already had Jen and Darby's, but she added Kelby, Summer, and Autumn to her very short list of contacts.

Autumn said, "You'll need to get a new lineup of people. Doctors. Dentists. I can help steer you toward the right ones since I work at Triple H."

"You'll want to get your hair cut at The Style Shack. Betty Jo is terrific and reasonably priced," added Summer.

"Thanks," she said, feeling good about her start in Hawthorne. "I appreciate the kindness you've all shown me by turning out today."

"I know Mom and Dad will have you over soon," Autumn said. "Dad always invites new teachers for a home-cooked meal before school starts. Mom is the city's librarian. If you're any kind of reader, she'll be able to point you in the right direction."

"Actually, I read quite a bit," Paisley said. "I spent a lot of time on buses and airplanes, traveling with my teams. My Kindle is probably my best friend."

"What do you like to read?" Summer asked eagerly.

"Just about anything. I've been on a crime kick lately. Drawn to crime novels and true-life accounts about crimes."

"I never edited any crime novels," Summer said. "A few mysteries, but mostly women's fiction and romances."

Autumn wrapped an arm around her sister's shoulder. "Summer is writing a romance series set in a small town in the Texas Panhandle. It's wonderful."

"Is that why you came home to Hawthorne?" she asked. "To be a writer?"

"It is. They say write what you know. Being immersed in

a small town again has helped me to remember a lot of the little things which make small towns so special."

"I've never read a romance," Paisley admitted. "Maybe I'll start with one of yours once you're published. Well, I better bring my stuff in now."

"You want some help?" Darby asked.

"No. I don't have much. Thanks for the offer, though. And thanks to everyone who stopped by and fed me delicious pizza."

Jen laughed. "I know you must think that's all Hawthorne has to offer, but there are other food places. Dizzy's Diner is my favorite, but if you're a barbeque fan, you simply have to eat at Barbeque Bliss. There's also a burger joint. A sports bar. A nice steakhouse."

"I guess I'll need to try all of them since I don't cook."

As they all went out the door, Autumn said, "I've been learning how to cook with Eli."

Summer added, "I'm also learning how. Chance is great at making breakfast foods. You won't find a better omelet or French toast than what he makes. We're both working our way through his family's cookbook, though."

Kelby said, "We're getting together next weekend. We try to do so a couple of times a month. We'd love to have you join us."

Though she was reluctant to commit, a deep yearning suddenly filled Paisley. These women were offering her friendship. They didn't have to do so. They didn't want anything from her. They were just nice people in a small town, welcoming a newcomer.

"I'd like that. Text me the details, Kelby. And what I can buy at the store to bring."

"Will do."

Everyone went to their cars, and Paisley made two trips,

bringing her things inside. Jen had given her the choice of two different bedrooms, both equal in size.

Jen gave her a key and said, "The bathroom across from your bedroom will be yours. It's also the one guests use."

"You want me to keep things out of sight because of that?"

"Not really," her roommate replied easily. "I don't have guests over often. Make it your own."

Paisley gave her roommate a warm smile. "I want to thank you for taking me in. If I would've gone to an apartment, I think I might have been a little lonely. I don't need to be your best friend. You already have that in Summer, but it'll be nice to have someone to chat with when we're home."

"Warning. Do not say anything to me in the morning. Not until I've had at least one cup of coffee."

She laughed. "Oh, you're one of those people, Jen."

"The way you say that, I'm guessing you're a Sally Sunshine in the mornings, Paisley."

"I usually wake up pretty happy. I am an extremely early riser, however. I'll be very quiet, though. I won't disturb you."

"I get up about six-thirty. Have a couple of cups of coffee and scroll through my phone. Do half an hour of yoga. Then shower and dress and head to the Sutherlands' place. I don't have to be at work until nine. I usually leave there around five-thirty, so that puts me home a little before six. You can let me know if you want to cook together any night. Maybe we could even come up with a schedule if we want to eat together a couple of nights a week. Or you can just do your own thing. I'm happy either way."

"It's hard for me to say what my schedule will be once school starts. Even then, it'll change once the season starts. I'll have games a couple of nights a week. Some weekend tournaments. In these few weeks before school starts, I'm wide open to do whatever."

She hesitated. "Except for tonight. I'm going to have dinner with Sawyer Montgomery."

Jen eyed her with curiosity but didn't press her about any details. "That's great. Sawyer's a nice guy. He's the person everyone seems to depend upon, and yet I can't help but think he's a bit of a loner."

That was an interesting tidbit.

"I'm glad he reached out to you, Paisley."

"I think it's the basketball connection," she said. "Both of us having played in college. Okay, I'm going to go and unpack. I just wanted you to know how grateful I am to be renting a room here."

"I know you're a long way from Vegas, Paisley. I hope you'll find a home in Hawthorne."

She excused herself and went to her bedroom. Closing the door, she unpacked the little she had, putting things in drawers and hanging a few items in the closet. She definitely would need to do some shopping. While she didn't think she would need to dress in anything but athleisure wear at school since she was the PE teacher and coach, Paisley figured if she did socialize a little bit, she'd need more than her T-shirts and jeans.

Reaching for her phone, she ordered a few things online since it was next to impossible for a woman her height to find anything in a brick-and-mortar store. She changed the shipping address on her accounts at three different places, two clothing stores and one which sold shoes.

After she took her toiletries to the bathroom and filled the medicine cabinet and a drawer, she returned to her bedroom, needing downtime after all the socializing she had done. Paisley had talked more today than she usually did in a week.

And she still had dinner with Sawyer Montgomery to go.

CHAPTER
Six

Sawyer finished mowing and edging the lawn and came inside, downing a quart of ice water before jumping in the shower. He had turned to physical activities to keep him busy ever since he'd spoken with Paisley Roberts this morning, feeling embarrassed to have actually called the former basketball player out of the blue.

When he'd asked West for Paisley's phone number, it had been spur of the moment. Yes, Darby's pushing him had factored into the decision. So had his sister's announcement that she was pregnant. Sawyer had wanted to be a dad for the longest time. He'd pushed that dream aside when he'd lost Elizabeth.

But would his beloved have wanted him to give up on that dream?

He'd put a lot on hold since his fiancée's death. Sawyer hadn't done any traveling, something they had planned to do extensively before having kids. He hadn't dated, except for two blind dates after he'd moved to Hawthorne which had ended with a dull thud. He hadn't bought a house because he couldn't imagine being in it by himself. As his sister and cousins began to marry, though, it had put him in an awkward position, being around happy couples all the time. It had also left him feeling a bit envious because he wanted what they had. Desperately. And yet he felt it would be a betrayal of Elizabeth if he pursued another woman.

When he'd seen Darby and her small bump, though, it was as if a light switch had been turned on. Life was short. Damn short. Elizabeth had been cut down when hers was just beginning. His own parents had been killed on their way back to Hawthorne from Darby's college graduation ceremonies at UT. They were both were forty-eight and in the prime of their lives. They'd had a six-week cruise booked. They looked forward to both their children marrying so they could become grandparents. Then they were gone in an instant, killed by a drunk driver.

Sawyer was tired of his life being on an even keel. He'd stopped making any forward progress and had been treading water ever since his fiancée died. At first, he'd buried himself in work for years, not wanting a second of free time to remember how empty his life now was. When he'd been dangerously close to a mental and physical breakdown from the strain of all the cases he'd taken on, he'd chucked life in Dallas and left the DA's office to return to Hawthorne. While the slower pace of life had helped considerably, a restlessness now filled him.

No more treading water. He was going to start swimming again, all the way to the deep end. Do things that frightened him. Excited him. Made him glad to be alive. He was going to stop observing and start participating. Live as if he had nothing to lose.

And that included dipping his toe back into the world of dating. He only knew what he'd seen on TV about Paisley

Roberts. She might or might not be the answer to his final questions.

But he was ready to begin living again.

He dried off and then wrapped the towel around his waist as he shaved. He'd suggested dinner at Sonny's Sports Bar and told her to dress casually because his gut told him that was the only way she would accept a dinner invitation from a stranger. Their tenuous connection was West, and for a moment, Sawyer kicked himself. He should've asked West and Kelby to join them. That would have been a good way to break the ice.

Yet in a way, he was glad he was going to have Paisley all to himself. It would keep things real. He had always been good at reading juries, and he hoped that would now extend to Paisley. His gut would tell him if this was a one-time thing.

Or if something more might come of it.

Sawyer rinsed his face and cleaned his razor, then dressed in khaki shorts and a Dallas Mavericks T-shirt. It was one of his newer T-shirts. Most of the rest were faded and ratty looking. He was trying to score points tonight, and that meant making a good first impression without seeming to try too hard.

As he went out to his car, he texted Paisley.

> On my way. Hope you're hungry.

He didn't expect a reply, but he did receive a thumbs up from her and considered that a good omen.

As he turned onto Jen Adelstein's street, he took a few deep breaths, trying to calm the nerves which had grabbed hold of him. He'd been to Jen's a few times to pick her up since they only lived a couple of blocks from one another. While he thought Darby had hoped her brother and Jen would spark, from the beginning, Jen had seemed just like another little sister to him. Jen herself had even talked with Sawyer about it privately, telling him that she thought he was a great guy but that she merely wanted to be friends with him. He didn't know much about her background. Whether or not she'd left behind some guy in New York. He was just happy to add a new friend to his ever-growing circle here in Hawthorne.

Maybe that's what Paisley Roberts would be. A good friend. Someone he could watch a basketball game with. Grab a bite to eat. He would go into tonight with no expectations.

That way, he wouldn't be disappointed if they didn't click.

He pulled up at the curb, seeing a new vehicle sitting in Jen's driveway. It was a Hyundai Elantra and looked to be a couple of years old. It did bear a Las Vegas Aces sticker in the rear window, though, so it had to belong to Paisley. He also noticed a Baylor Bears license plate frame and recalled that she had gone to school there.

Should he text her again? Or should he go to the door? It had been so long since he'd done this kind of thing, he didn't know what proper etiquette dictated. Then again, his dad would've had his hide if he sat in a car and expected a girl to come out. Sam Montgomery had been a gentleman, through and through, and Sawyer wasn't about to disappoint himself or his dad, in case he was watching in amusement, perched up on some cloud.

He made it halfway up the porch stairs when the door opened, and Paisley stepped out.

She took his breath away.

Paisley wasn't a conventional beauty by any means. Her mouth was a little too wide and generous, but her rich, chocolate brown hair was long and full, hanging well below her shoulders. Something that had never struck him on TV, because shots of her were too far away, were her eyes. They were an espresso brown, rimmed with amber, drawing him in. It was also nice to look a woman in the eyes. He was six-four, but Paisley was only a couple of inches shorter than he was. Her build was tall and thin, but he knew from her playing days that she was deceptively strong.

"I'm Sawyer," he announced.

"Paisley," she responded, her voice low and rich. It made him want to hear her laugh, and he wondered if her laughter would sound as rich as her voice.

She offered her hand, and they shook.

Suddenly, electricity shot through him, taking Sawyer by surprise. The only time that had ever happened was with Elizabeth.

His gaze met Paisley's, and he could see she was shaken. Sawyer pumped her hand once and then reluctantly released it.

"Glad you listened to me and wore shorts," he told her. "Most women would have ignored what I recommended."

"I'm not most women," she replied confidently.

He was struck by her assertive air. This was a woman who had achieved what very few others had. She'd been a member of college and professional championship teams, as well as multiple Olympic teams. If she hadn't been attacked and injured her knee so severely last year, she would be flying to Osaka next week to participate in the opening ceremonies for the Olympics, decked out in red, white, and blue as a member of Team USA.

"I can see that," he said, eager to get to know her. "Ready to hit Sonny's Sports Bar?"

"Sure."

She accompanied Sawyer to his sensible sedan, which he'd owned for five years and planned to keep at least another five. Sawyer opened the passenger door for her, and Paisley climbed in.

She glanced up. "Mind if I adjust the seat?"

"Be my guest."

He came around and climbed into the driver's seat, and they both fastened their seat belts. As he pulled away from the curb, he asked, "How was the rest of your drive?"

"Not bad. Then again, it was Saturday morning, so I didn't expect traffic to be very heavy."

"I'm sorry I didn't warn you about the ambush." He glanced at her, seeing understanding fill her eyes.

"You mean the pizza brigade."

"Is that what they brought?"

"Yes. I'd eaten lunch from Pizza Palace earlier this week, when I was in town for my interview, but I didn't mind a repeat of something that tasty."

"It's a good, New York-style crust. I have it a couple of times myself each week," he admitted. "Although I like to cook, I usually eat lunch out. It's a good way to see others in town and lets me keep a finger on the pulse of what's going on in Hawthorne. But when I do that, I don't need a heavier evening meal. So, most of my cooking happens on the weekends. You've heard of weekend warriors when it comes to exercise? Well, I'm a weekend cook."

"I can make a sandwich," she said, laughing. "That's considered cooking to me. Slapping meat and cheese on bread or making a PBJ."

"No grilled cheese?" he teased.

Paisley shook her head. "That's real cooking. I wouldn't know the first thing about how to put a grilled cheese sandwich together."

"It's all in the mayo," he explained. "Not the butter."

Her nose crinkled, and Sawyer thought her pretty adorable at that moment. "No butter? Mayo? Ick!"

He laughed easily. "I'll bet every great grilled cheese you've eaten was prepared with mayo. It's actually pretty scientific. Yes, you do butter the inside of the bread, where your cheese goes, but you spread a thin layer of mayo on the outside that touches the pan. The mayo has nothing to do with the flavor. Actually, it doesn't even provide any. You don't taste it, which is why you've had it and didn't even know."

"Are you pulling my leg?"

For a moment, he pictured her naked in his bed, pulling on those long legs, licking his way up them to her core. Heat rippled through his body.

"Sawyer?"

He came back to earth. "Just trying to think how to explain it to someone who doesn't cook," he lied. "Basically, mayonnaise has a higher smoke point than butter. When fat reaches its smoke point? That's when you get a bit of a bitter, burnt flavor. Mayo is less likely to burn on your griddle, and that allows the cheese more time to melt into an ooey, gooey mess."

"Huh. I'm actually intrigued."

"I'll demo one, and you can eat and rate."

"You're on."

By now, they'd reached the square, and he pulled into a parking slot. Before he could make it to her door, she'd already opened it and got out. So much for being a gentleman. He wondered about her dating history. He'd googled her and couldn't find her name linked to anyone.

He placed his hand on the small of her back, guiding her

to the door of Sonny's. They entered, and he caught the smell of onion rings, causing his mouth to water.

Sonny himself greeted them. "I heard you were coming to Hawthorne, Paisley. It's an honor to have you eat at my place. I'm Sonny Smith. Used to quarterback the Hawks back in the day." He slapped his beer belly. "That was before a wife and four kids."

"Nice to meet you, Sonny," Paisley said. "Sawyer said this is a great place to eat."

"And watch games. Football. Basketball. Soccer. With the Olympics starting next weekend, most of the TVs will be tuned to the games." He winced. "I'm sorry. That must be a hard pill to swallow."

"It is," she said, not mincing words. "But I plan on catching every basketball game Team USA plays, both the men's and women's teams. And other sports, too. I may not be dribbling down the court in Osaka, but I'm there in spirit."

"Let me take you to a table," Sonny said.

The owner led them to a booth, and Paisley slid into one side, with Sawyer sitting across from her.

"Beers? Cokes? Sweet tea?" Sonny asked.

"I'll have iced tea," Paisley said. "Unsweetened."

"Make it two," he added.

"Coming right up."

After Sonny left them, Sawyer said, "You handled that very graciously. Hawthorne has always been mad for sports. The ones played here and beyond. This place is packed for Monday and Thursday Night Football. College games. Basketball and baseball. Wimbledon. The Open. And yes, even the Olympics. I'm sorry Sonny brought it up."

She shrugged. "It's a part of my life, one I'm very proud of. I have high hopes for this team. Do I wish I were there, running the offense as I brought the ball down the court? Of course. But there's a time to step away. Mine just came sooner than I'd hoped it would."

Paisley paused. "Osaka would've been my last Olympics. I'd already decided on that. And I'm happy with the roster they put together. My absence gave another athlete her chance at living her dream."

"That's a great attitude to have."

She sighed. "I do believe that, but it's really hard, knowing I won't be on that plane next Tuesday to Japan."

"Then we'll have to do something on Tuesday to take your mind off that. Something fun and maybe a little bit crazy."

The smile Paisley gave him caused Sawyer's heart to beat in double time.

"You're on, Montgomery. I like the way you think."

Now, all Sawyer had to do was come up with something wild and crazy.

That didn't involve sex.

And that was going to be pretty hard because suddenly, having sex with Paisley Roberts had shot to the top of his Things I'm Going To Do Someday list.

CHAPTER
Seven

Paisley walked the few blocks to the town square. She had contacted her assistant yesterday, and Hope Sewell had agreed to meet her for breakfast at Dizzy's Diner. She was looking forward to learning more about the basketball program from Hope, knowing the assistant would be critical in helping her to establish a winning tradition with the Lady Hawks.

She entered the diner. At seven o'clock on a Monday morning, it was over three-quarters full. A white-haired man in his mid-seventies with bright, blue eyes greeted her.

"You wouldn't happen to be Paisley Roberts, would you?"

"That's me," she confirmed.

"Boy, you're a tall drink of water," he observed. "I'm Dizzy Baker, by the way. Christened Delbert, but my daddy was a baseball fan and thought Dizzy Dean hung the moon. He's the one who started calling me Dizzy, and it stuck. This is my place. I'm glad you've come to Hawthorne, Paisley. I don't miss any home games at the high school. Ever," he said emphatically. "Grew up watching and playing the basics. Football. Basketball. Baseball, of course. Living in Hawthorne, though, I've become a huge fan of all the sports played by the Hawks. I've learned a lot about soccer. Tennis."

He grinned, leaning in to share a confidence. "And I think girls know how to play basketball better than boys. When I'm not here working the breakfast and lunch shifts, you can find me at whatever sporting event is happening after school that day or that night."

"It's good to know you're such a steadfast supporter of the Hawks, Dizzy," she said, thinking him quite a character. "It's nice to meet a true fan."

"Come with me. Hope's already grabbed a booth for you two."

He led her to a booth, where a woman slid from it and offered Paisley a hand.

"It's great to meet you, Coach," Hope said, causing a thrill to rush through Paisley since it was the first time anyone had addressed her that way.

She shook hands with Hope, who was about five-six, with brown hair and a light dusting of freckles across her nose and cheeks.

They took their seats, and Dizzy asked, "What would you like to drink?"

"Water, please," Paisley said. "And a glass of skim milk with my meal."

She noticed that Hope already had a cup of coffee and a tall glass of ice water on her side of the table.

"Be right back," Dizzy said.

She glanced at the menu already sitting on the table and then asked Hope, "What's good here?"

"What's not good?" Hope replied, laughing. "Seriously, you never get a bad meal at Dizzy's. Whatever you order will taste great. You'll have to come back at lunchtime and try his grilled cheese and tomato basil soup. Or even the tuna melt. They're my favorite things on the menu."

She perused the menu a moment, and then Dizzy returned with her water.

"Know what you want, ladies?"

Hope ordered the eggs Benedict, along with sides of hash browns and fruit.

Paisley said, "I'm going with Dizzy's Delight. Make the eggs over easy. Ham for my meat. Hash browns." She paused. "I'm in a quandary. I don't know if I should order the pancake, sourdough toast, or biscuit with gravy."

"The pancakes are light and fluffy," Dizzy told her, "but the sausage gravy we make here makes the biscuits to die for."

She handed him her menu. "Then I'll go with the biscuit and gravy."

As they waited for their breakfasts to arrive, Paisley said, "I'm sure you already know about me. I'd like to hear about you."

"I'm from a small town in the Panhandle," the assistant shared. "Youngest and only girl out of four siblings. I played every sport I could in elementary school. First base in softball. Setter in volleyball. Several different positions in soccer. But I fell in love with basketball when I turned ten and concentrated on it in middle school and high school."

"What positions have you played?"

"In middle school I started as a small forward. Switched to point guard and shooting guard. Freshman year, my coach put me at shooting guard, and I stuck with that all through high school. At my height, I was too short for center or forward. My ball handling skills weren't good enough to be a point guard and run an offense the way you've done during your career."

"Any college ball on your resumé?"

Hope shook her head. "I was a good but not great player in high school. Didn't receive any offers. Didn't expect any. I graduated from Texas Tech. Played intramurals, coed basketball while I was there."

"I know last year was your first year in coaching," Paisley said, "How did you choose Hawthorne?"

"You go where the job is," Hope said. "My coach in high school had played in college with Coach Finnerty. Half of getting a job in basketball in Texas is who you know. The other half is being in the right place at the right time. My coach recommended me, and that was good enough for Coach Finnerty."

Dizzy arrived bearing plates with their breakfasts. Paisley put ketchup atop her golden hash browns and dug into her meal. The biscuit and gravy was everything the diner owner had promised. The eggs were cooked to perfection, and the ham was smoky and slightly sweet. It was the hash browns that won her over, though. Without a doubt, she knew she would become a regular at the diner.

"I need to know everything about our team," she said after they'd eaten in silence for a few minutes. "Why the team hit the skids. Who the returning players are and what skills they have. I especially want to learn about the offense Coach Finnerty ran and what holes were in it. Same with the defense."

Hope looked at her reluctantly. "I don't really feel right saying anything bad about Coach Finnerty's playbook."

Looking steadily at the assistant, Paisley said, "While I hope we become friends, Hope, our relationship is, first and foremost, a professional one. Just as a doctor wouldn't reveal sensitive medical information about a patient and a lawyer wouldn't share confidences his client had voiced, nothing goes further than me when we talk. About anything. I want to make our basketball team into a winning one. I want to create a culture of learning and respect. I don't need to know every little thing that went on before I arrived, but you've got to help me out here. I swear whatever you tell me stays with me.

She grinned. "After all, I did spend a lot of time in Vegas."

Her quip caused Hope to laugh, and Paisley crossed her fingers, hoping that broke the ice between them for good. Trust among coaching staffs was vitally important if any success were to take place.

Hope swallowed. "I was in a tough position last year," she began. "Being a first year, I knew to keep my mouth shut from the beginning and just try to learn. Also, Coach Finnerty was the type who wouldn't have listened even if I did voice an opinion. She was pretty much one of those *my way or the highway*-type coaches. While I believe in discipline, she went overboard with it. A girl might miss a critical free throw during a game, and the whole team would be required to stay after that game, running dozens of laps."

Hope took a sip of her coffee. "First of all, I don't believe in physical punishment when someone misses a shot. It would've been a better use of time if that one player maybe had been required to practice extra free throws. That would've been beneficial. Not running on tired legs after a demanding game. I also thought it was wrong to make the entire team stay to run laps. It got to where the girls were paranoid about making a mistake, which just made them prone to doing so. You could tell they began to dread games instead of enjoying playing their competition."

Paisley was horrified at hearing this.

"From what I gathered, the first few years Finnerty coached in Hawthorne, she inherited a great team and didn't have to do much coaching. Once those players graduated, though, she was under a lot of pressure to produce the same kind of results. She cracked the whip hard, thinking harsh discipline would force the players to be better. Instead, talented athletes left the program. Sometimes, for other sports. Sometimes, just to get away from Finnerty."

Hope shook her head. "Part of me feels like I'm betraying her by saying all this, but it needs to be said. You're not inheriting much of a team, Coach. We barely have enough girls to have five starters on the court."

It was more serious than she could have imagined. Paisley had been in worse situations before, though.

"Let's talk offense first."

Hope elaborated on the offense run last year, and Paisley asked for the assistant's honest feedback. Hope opened up, throwing out ideas she had and would have liked to try.

"A lot of what you're saying makes sense. We're definitely going to incorporate your ideas into our offense this year."

Surprise filled the younger woman's face. "Are you serious? You mean you'll consider using some of my plays?"

"I'll do more than consider. We *will* use some of them. The same will be true for plays our players suggest. They're the ones out on the court. They see more than we can, sometimes. My coaching style is collaborative, Hope. I may hold the head coach title, but I want you to feel on equal footing as far as contributing play material."

After that, Hope visibly relaxed, ideas gushing from her. Paisley began taking notes on her phone, excitement filling her.

They talked about the defense next and how Finnerty had only played one-on-one. While that worked in the right situation, if there were a mismatch in height among players, it could prove to be a real disaster.

She said, "I'll mix up one-on-one with zone coverage."

Tears sprang to Hope's eyes. "You don't know how happy I am to hear this, Coach. I've looked up to you for so many years. You're proving to be even better than I ever expected."

"I'll admit that I don't have your coaching experience. I always did help out my teammates, however. I would give them tips during a game when I saw something going on that they could take advantage of. I also mentored younger players who joined teams I played for. But I'm not the be-all, end-all, Hope. As I said before, this is a collaboration."

Pausing, Paisley then asked, "Would you have time to go up to the high school now? Maybe look through the playbook with me?"

"I'd love to, Paisley," her assistant said enthusiastically, calling Paisley by her name for the first time.

Dizzy wouldn't let her pay for her breakfast, telling Paisley that the first meal for a newcomer to his diner was always free. She thanked him, certain she would be back in the future.

Since she had walked to the diner, Paisley rode with Hope to HHS, swiping her employee badge for the first time to gain entrance into the field house.

Hope said, "I shared an office with Coach Finnerty last year. Actually, sharing is not the word I should use. I had a desk here, but she liked the space to herself."

"I won't be like that, Hope. We'll need to be together. Bounce ideas off one another. We're going to draw up plays together. Look at game film. You and I will be joined at the hip."

Her new assistant beamed. "I'm going to learn so much from you, Coach. I can't wait to get started."

They opened up various notebooks, going through countless numbers of plays the Lady Hawks had used last year.

Paisley said, "I'm not going to ditch this playbook. I'm seeing some good things here. I have lots more I want to add, though. I'm sure you're feeling the same."

Hope went over to the desk which was hers. She pulled out a manilla folder and handed it to Paisley.

"These are plays I drew up last year. Coach Finnerty only looked at a few of them before she told me that she was the coach and the only one who would be running the offense and defense without interference." Hope paused. "I believe there are some good plays in here."

"I know there are," Paisley agreed. "I can tell you've got basketball knowledge, and it's ready to flood from you. If you don't mind, I'd like to take this home with me and study it. Familiarize myself with it and the rest of the previous schemes. I won't know what we can use and what needs to be discarded until I meet the players, though. I've got to evaluate the skills they possess and tailor things to them."

She sighed. "We're going to have to recruit like mad, Hope. Injuries are hard to predict. I don't want one of them to cause us to forfeit even a single game. Since we barely have enough players to field a team now, we're going to have to go out and find girls willing to give the program a chance."

"The good thing is, you have a name, Paisley. You've won championships at every level. There'll be girls who have watched you on TV. Girls who want to *be* you. That will definitely attract a few more players to the team."

Paisley glanced at her watch, seeing it was almost one o'clock. "We've been at this for several hours now. I know this is your summer break, and I didn't mean to take up so much time."

"Not a problem, Coach. I was eager to see who West would hire. Worried a little about how I would get along with the new coach, but I can tell this is going to be a fantastic relationship. While I'm working alongside you, I'm going to be picking your brain like crazy." Hope smiled. "After all, it's not many coaches who get the opportunity to be mentored by a three-time Olympian."

Pushing talk of her past aside, Paisley said, "I need you to draw up the list of who has already committed to play this year. Put together a profile of each individual, telling me their talents and weaknesses. Then compile a list of anyone who did play in the program and left. Those still here at HHS. I'll be contacting the middle school coach next to see which players are incoming freshmen and what they're like."

"I'll have it for you by tomorrow. I'm sure Marsha Zelman at the middle school would love to meet with you."

"No rush. Take a couple of days. I've still got a few things to clean up on my end. What about meeting with Marsha on Thursday here if she's available?"

"Definitely," her assistant said enthusiastically.

"I'll reach out to Marsha and see if that's good for her. If not, at least you and I can meet together. Thanks for spending time with me today, Hope. You're going to be a real asset to this program."

"It'll be nice not to be shoved to the side. I appreciate you valuing my input."

They returned to Hope's car, and she dropped Paisley at Jen's house. Going inside, she realized she was still full from her large breakfast at the diner and decided to simply open a can of soup for a light lunch. She would need to buy some groceries to stock the pantry and fridge and might as well do that after she ate.

She had put off meeting with Hope tomorrow because Tuesday was the day she was spending with Sawyer Montgomery. He'd told her to block out the entire day for them to do something out of the ordinary. She couldn't image what that might entail, especially in a small town such as Hawthorne, but she was looking forward to being in his company again.

Paisley was definitely attracted to the former college basketball player. He was three inches taller than she was, with a lean yet muscular frame. His hazel eyes had drawn her in during dinner last night, making her feel as if she could confide in him. She could imagine running her fingers through his thick, caramel hair, something she had never done with any guy.

She'd never had a single date. Not one. In high school, she was so much taller than most of the guys and totally focused on basketball, knowing it and earning good grades would be her ticket to a free college education. Once at Baylor, she spent a majority of her day around women. In the dorm. At practice. Most of her education classes were filled with women. Any time a guy was enrolled in one, he would sit with the handful of other guys.

Sometimes, she would informally scrimmage with guys who were in the gym, be they players on the men's basketball team or others hanging around the gym. But just as she'd thrown up walls around her to keep other girls from getting too close to her, she'd done the same with guys. Because of that vibe, she'd never been asked on a date.

Once she'd turned pro, Paisley felt enormous pressure on her. As a number one draft pick, the Aces had invested heavily in her, and she dedicated herself to being successful in the WNBA. Once again, she was around mostly women, her teammates or other athletes. Every single one of her coaches during her tenure with the Aces had been female.

That made this attraction to Sawyer unique. Where she had said very little to other guys throughout her entire life, Paisley had an actual conversation with Sawyer—and he had seemed interested in what she had to say. She wondered if anything might come of their budding friendship. If things might go beyond friendship.

Hopefully, she'd get a better read on him as they spent an entire day together.

Eight

Sawyer had suggested doing something wild and crazy to keep Paisley's mind off not being on the Team USA plane to Osaka. He couldn't think of a thing that fit that description within the city limits of Hawthorne, so he had looked further afield. He had a good idea and ran with it, booking reservations. He would need to sound her out now, however, to see if she was up for something of that magnitude. If not, he had a Plan B and even a Plan C waiting in the wings.

He couldn't imagine what was going through her head on today of all days, the day she would have left to compete in her fourth Olympics, a rare feat for any athlete. He knew how squirrely he'd been early on in college, and thought, too, how she'd had so much maturity by her first Olympic experience. Paisley had been a cornerstone of the women's basketball team for three Olympiads. But teams moved on. Players were injured or simply aged out and could no longer perform at their previous levels. He wondered if anyone had bothered to reach out to her from Team USA since her career-ending injury or if she would even want to watch her former team-mates play any of their games on TV. If she did, he would be more than happy to watch with her.

He didn't want to make comparisons between her and Elizabeth, but some were occurring naturally. Of course, they didn't physically resemble one another in the slightest, which was probably better. What they did have in common, though, was that they made him feel at ease around both of them. Talking to both Paisley and Elizabeth was incredibly easy.

Sawyer thought back to his first day of law school. It was in Constitutional Law class that he'd first laid eyes on Eliza-beth. He'd noticed her right away. She was beautiful. And obviously bright. Their law professor had asked a question, which appeared to stump the entire class. Elizabeth was the only one to raise her hand. Though Sawyer had waited for her to be skewered, having already heard about the profes-sor's reputation, the answer she provided was insightful and inspiring. It set the bar for the class. It definitely made Sawyer want to be a better student and a better lawyer.

Within a few days, they had joined the same study group and remained in it all three years of law school. From the beginning, they had an easy camaraderie between them, as well as a healthy competition over grades. She had teased him, calling him Sawyer the Future Lawyer.

Then things changed. When they weren't looking, friendship blossomed into love.

He was offering Paisley friendship now—and a part of him hoped that he could finally put the past behind him and that he could find romance again.

And love.

Paisley was her own woman, however. Sawyer deter-mined not to constantly compare the two women. If friend-ship was all that ever occurred between them, he would take that as a blessing. Sawyer had enjoyed their dinner together last week. Paisley had seemed a bit guarded at first. Then again, he was a total stranger to her, while he knew something about her.

Since then, he had done his usual lawyerly thing, a deep dive into the internet, scouring for information about her. She'd had a storied career. One of the best in women's sports. Paisley had been on good teams and great ones, contributing so that they became better. She had great basketball smarts, and that kind of thing couldn't be taught. It was innate. Her ball handling skills were incredible. He watched a few videos of her bringing the ball down the court, and Sawyer could almost see the wheels turning in her head, mapping out the offensive options available to her, deciding which play to call. She had the skills necessary to be a good coach.

And heaven knew the Hawthorne Lady Hawks needed her badly.

He hadn't asked Paisley any particulars about the players she would be coaching, not knowing how much West had divulged about the team. Knowing his cousin, West would've kept quiet, not wanting to influence his new coach's perspective. By now, though, Paisley would have contacted Hope Sewell. If she were smart, the assistant would have placed all her cards on the table and held nothing back from her new boss. Sawyer would ask a few general questions today of Paisley and see what she had learned about her team. He would even offer himself up as someone she could bounce ideas off. While a lot of people had opinions about the Lady Hawks, Sawyer at least had a ton of basketball experience under his belt. Either Paisley would be interested in doing so —or she wouldn't. It would be up to her.

As a courtesy, he texted that he would be at her house in ten minutes. Sawyer had come into his law office early this morning to finish a few things. Working for himself, he had come to enjoy setting his own schedule. Nothing pressing was on his calendar, which was why he had been able to take off all of today.

He took a last glance at his email and then flipped the sign on the door from open to closed. Locking up, he went out the back door. He always parked in the alley in order to give potential clients more parking options in front of his office. He drove the few short blocks to Jen's rental. Before he could get out of his car, Paisley came bounding down the porch stairs, her long legs going on endlessly in the biker shorts she wore. He had suggested she wear them, as well as a form-fitting shirt.

She came toward the car, and he noticed the swing of her ponytail. Sawyer got out of the car and came around to open the passenger door for her.

"Service with a smile," he quipped as she climbed inside his car.

He returned to the driver's seat and asked, "Did you hydrate as I told you to?"

"I'm always good about doing that, but I did down an extra bottle of water after I showered this morning. So, what are we actually going to do today, Sawyer?"

As he pulled away from the curb, he asked, "Are you afraid of anything? Spiders? Heights?"

She hesitated a moment and then said, "Snakes. I don't do snakes. I got in trouble on a school field trip to the zoo in third grade. The teacher tried to get me to go into the reptile house, and I wasn't having any of that. She took my hand and yanked me into the darkened building, and I howled like a banshee. Broke away from her and ran as fast as I could. A parent chaperone chased after me and stayed with me while the rest of the class toured the place."

"Any particular reason why you don't like snakes? Or do they just creep you out in general?" he asked lightly.

He glanced over and saw Paisley swallow hard. "It goes back to my first foster home," she said quietly. "I was barely four and had just been taken away from my mom. Didn't have a dad named on my birth certificate. Mom was a drug addict. I'd already been in and out of foster care for weeks at a time before that, but this was different. My mom's parental rights were terminated, and so the state was looking for a more permanent placement. Or at least as permanent a placement as you can get."

Sawyer focused on the road ahead of him as he said, "Something bad happened there. You don't have to tell me. It can stay in the past."

"No. I think I want to talk about it." Paisley shifted in her seat. "The foster dad had a snake in a long glass case in his bedroom. The couple had a son. I think he was maybe eleven or twelve. Then three foster kids. Two boys older than I was and me. At the time, I didn't understand much of anything, but looking back? I realize they were the kind of people who liked to draw the extra income the system pays to people who become foster parents. Some of those people actually do spend that money on the kid they're fostering. Buy them new clothes. A toy. Pick up extra groceries."

"And this couple wasn't like that?"

"Not by a long shot. They didn't pay a whole lot of attention to me. I think they were mad that a girl had been placed with them. I got the impression they wanted another boy. That I was an inconvenience."

For a four-year-old to pick up on something like that, Sawyer figured the foster parents were sending a pretty strong message. He tamped down the anger that rose in him, thinking how helpless Paisley had been. How alone she must have felt.

"Their boy was cruel to me. Said nasty things. Pinched me. Kicked me."

He glanced at her. "That's horrible, Paisley."

Her face was set in stone. "Actually, it's pretty common. If a foster couple has their own kids, they naturally come first in the parents' eyes. They can be really mean to foster kids. Even jealous of them. And then there's a pecking order among foster kids. Who's been in the home the longest. Or sometimes who's the oldest foster kid. A lot of abuse goes on in these homes, Sawyer," she said, that last sentence barely a whisper.

Instinctively, he reached out for her hand. Even though the July day was warm, her hand felt like ice.

"How badly were you hurt, Paisley?"

"No sexual abuse, thank goodness. Although two guys tried. You should've seen them after I was done with them."

He squeezed her fingers and then released her hand, regretting that he couldn't hold it longer. But Sawyer knew this woman was fragile and probably sharing something which she hadn't spoke of in a long time.

If ever.

"Anyway, the son knew I was afraid of the snake. I wasn't supposed to go into his parents' bedroom, but he would force me to go in with him and stand in front of the glass cage. One night, the parents went out. It was cold. I remember that. I think it might've been New Year's Eve. There was an older teenage boy who came over to babysit us. I didn't like the vibe he gave off, and so I'd gone to bed really early."

"What happened?"

"The son—I still can't remember his name. Probably because I don't want to. He woke me up. Immediately, I knew something was awful wrong. I looked down, and the snake was next to me in the bed. I remember screaming so loudly. I don't know where the other foster kids were, but the babysitter was also there. He had a nasty grin on his face. He grabbed me as I tried to scamper off the bed and took me to the bathroom. He dumped me in the tub, and the son brought the snake, tossing it into the tub on top of me."

Sawyer glanced to her and saw a faraway look in her eyes.

"I froze for the longest moment. Looked at the snake. It looked at me. It had the coldest, blackest, deadest eyes. And then somehow I found the courage to push it away and jump out of the bathtub. I ran to the door, crying, but it was locked."

She shivered. "I can still hear them laughing outside the door in the hallway. But I went and closed the lid on the toilet. It was always open since that was the bathroom I shared with the three other boys. I climbed up and stood on it. I don't know for how long. An hour. Two. Time seemed frozen. I watched the snake slither out of that tub and onto the floor. I remembered constantly screaming until nothing came out. I'd used up all my voice."

Paisley fell silent, and he didn't push her to continue the horrifying story.

After a few minutes, Sawyer said, "I'm sorry I brought it up. I didn't mean to make you relive something so terrifying."

"It's okay," she assured him. "I haven't ever told anyone that story. In a way, I take pride in it. It shows how brave I was. How resourceful. That's actually a good feeling."

She sighed. "By the time the parents came home, the door had been unlocked and the snake had been removed. I stayed in the bathroom, though, standing on that toilet. The foster mom came in and asked me something. I couldn't answer her with no voice left. I couldn't talk for a couple of days. The dad came in and started yelling at me. He knew the snake had been taken out of its home. His son lied and told him that I'd been the one to do it."

Paisley snorted. "Like a four-year-old could somehow reach that tall, open the lid, and lift that big a snake. A couple of days later, a caseworker showed up and told me to gather up my things. That I was going somewhere else to live. That kid grinned at me the whole time I walked to the car, thinking he had gotten away with getting rid of me. I didn't care. I was happy to be taken from that home."

She fell silent again, and Sawyer reached out and took her hand again. He laced his fingers through hers, and they drove without talking for several miles, the only noise being the sound of the car's tires on the highway.

"I'm not just afraid of snakes, Sawyer," she told him. "When you asked me what I'm afraid of, the first thing that came to mind was not being able to walk. After I was taken to the hospital, the surgeon who was going to operate on me told me that the goal was for me to walk again. Not play professional basketball. Simply walk. That frightened me more than anything ever has in my life, even that damn snake."

He squeezed her fingers encouragingly. "I can't imagine what you've gone through. Not just the injury and coming back physically from it. The mental aspect."

"They had me see a therapist," she revealed. "I did talk therapy for about four months. It helped some."

"Is it something you should keep doing?"

She shook her head. "I don't want anyone in Hawthorne knowing about this. I've already seen in the short time I've been here how you're right. Everyone knows what's going on in town."

"A therapist wouldn't break a confidence, Paisley. It's like attorney and client privilege."

"I get that, but word would get out that I was seeing someone. My car spotted at the therapist's office. That kind of thing. I don't want to add fuel to any fire, Sawyer. I'm already going to be under a microscope as it is. I don't want to show any kind of weakness. While I know seeing a therapist shouldn't be considered weak, I simply want to avoid the gossip attached to it. Besides, my therapist was winding down her practice. I was one of the last clients she took on, short term. She retired at the beginning of the summer."

"What if you could meet with one online?" he suggested. "Would you do that?"

"I don't know. It would be hard to start from ground zero and try and build a new relationship. Learn to trust a stranger again."

"The reason I'm asking is because West zooms with his therapist. Dr. Linda. He started seeing her after his knee injury. West chats with her a couple of times a month now. Says it's like keeping his truck in good working condition. How you bring your vehicle to the dealership for periodic checkups. Rotating the tires. Changing the oil. He says therapy keeps him grounded and in a good place mentally. Ask him about Dr. Linda. I'm sure he would be willing to share his experience. Even give you her contact information."

He looked to her and saw she worried her bottom lip, lost in thought.

Then Paisley said, "I think that's a really good idea. Thank you for suggesting it. I didn't mean to dampen today's mood, Sawyer. I know you're trying to make it a joyful one for me. Doing something that takes my mind off Team USA and where they're bound."

"It's natural for you to miss being out on the court. Being with your teammates. The chance to earn gold for a fourth time."

"Well, whatever you have planned, I'm game for. And I really do appreciate you taking today off to spend with me. I knew it was going to be a rough one. One of several coming up. The opening ceremony will also be hard to watch. That was so much fun to participate in, everyone wearing their red, white, and blue outfits and marching as a group behind our flag."

"I'll watch the opening ceremony with you. If you'd like. And any games telecast. You don't have to do this alone, Paisley. You've got friends here in Hawthorne, and I'd be honored if you would consider me one of them."

"I really appreciate that. More than you could ever know. So, Mr. Montgomery, tell me what we're going to do today?"

"I asked you about heights for a reason. If you were scared of them."

"Nope. Not a bit."

He grinned at her. "Good. Because in a few minutes, we're going skydiving."

Nine

"We're *what?*" Paisley asked. Then she began laughing. "I guess it won't matter if Team USA is playing without me. I'll be dead—so I won't be worrying about basketball."

"Whoa," Sawyer said. "No one around here is going to be dying. We'll be in the hands of experts, not trying this solo. If you're game, we'll be tandem jumping today."

"It's okay," she said. "I was teasing. Well, mostly teasing. Honestly, the thought of skydiving does scare me a little bit, but I'm more intrigued than anything. And you said tandem?"

He nodded. "It's safest for first time dives. Especially since this is something new to both of us and it does possess an element of danger, I thought we should put ourselves in the hands of professionals. We'll be attached to a certified tandem instructor."

"I like the sound of that." She reached out and touched her fingers to his forearm. Once more that sizzle rippled through her at the contact. "I think it's a brilliant idea. Certainly nothing I would've come up with on my own."

"Let's go talk with Andy. He's the owner of this place and knows that our jump will depend upon what he tells us now."

Reluctantly, she let her hand drop, but the energy still zipped through her from the brief contact.

They got out of his car and headed toward an airplane hangar. A man who looked to be in his late forties and sporting salt and pepper hair and a matching beard greeted them.

"Hey. You must be Sawyer Montgomery and Paisley Roberts. I'm Andy Taylor."

Andy shook hands with both of them and added, "Come on inside. I hear this is the first time either of you have ever jumped, so I want to make sure I answer all your questions."

Inside the hangar, she saw two airplanes, much smaller than the ones she had traveled on during her playing days. They entered a separate air-conditioned office, and the cool felt good to her.

Andy went to a small fridge in the corner and removed two bottled waters, handing one to each of them.

"Sip on these while we're talking. You can never be too hydrated for a jump. Let me tell you a little about me. I was with the hundred and first, an army airborne division known as the Screaming Eagles, a light infantry division. They're famous for their role in Operation Overlord, the D-Day landings in Normandy. Nowadays, they're an air assault division stationed at Fort Campbell, Kentucky. Only about half those who go through training become a member of the Eagles. So, I'm part of a proud heritage of men who fought for this country."

Paisley liked how Andy was giving them background about himself. She found herself relaxing.

"I earned my pilot's license when I was seventeen. Went straight into the army after graduating from high school. Did my twenty and a bit of change before retiring from the military. Bought some land, and now I give flying lessons, for the most part. I also conduct jumps for people, both tandem and individual."

Andy grinned. "One jump—and you'll be addicted. Let me walk you through the process, and if you have any questions along the way, feel free to jump in."

She listened carefully as Andy explained how they would be attached to a licensed, certified specialist in tandem jumping. He said their back would be to the instructor's chest.

That caused alarm within her. If she were the person in front, she would be seeing the ground first. Landing first.

"If that's the case, I'd be hitting the ground first. I can't do that, Andy." Panic swelled within her. "I had a severe knee injury several months ago. I know you're falling in the air and must hit the ground pretty hard. I can't afford a broken foot or ankle, much less the impact to my knee."

"Let me calm your fears, Paisley. In tandem jumping, the novice jumper will raise his or her feet up just before landing. It's the TI—tandem instructor—who's the one touching down. And yes, there have been injuries when people hit the ground in solo jumps, but Jared and I are skilled at what we do. We'll touch down so lightly, you'll barely realize you're back on Mother Earth again. We absorb the landing. Not you."

The fear which had spiked started to evaporate. "Okay. I can do that. Tell us more about the jump itself."

"We'll jump from the plane. Space ourselves out by several seconds so we don't bump into one another. Jared and I have been doing this long enough, though, that we usually line up pretty quickly and fall beside one another. That way, you and Sawyer can experience the jump together. You'll be in each other's line of view. We can even take a few pictures for you."

The TI looked her in the eye. "That's one of my non-negotiable rules. Your pockets have to be empty. No wallet or keys. That kind of thing. And definitely no cell phones. Part of it is a safety thing, so that you'll be paying attention to your instructor and what is said and not clicking away on your phone.

"The other reason? I want you to simply enjoy the beauty of the jump itself. Jared and I will take some photos for you so you can have a remembrance of the experience."

"How fast do we fall?" Sawyer asked.

"Good question. When you first jump from the plane, you'll be hit by the wind and the noise," Andy shared. "I'm glad you took my suggestion and dressed appropriately in snug-fitting clothing. That way, you don't have a T-shirt flapping in the breeze, distracting you as you reach terminal velocity."

"What's that?" Paisley interjected, not liking the sound of the term.

"Terminal velocity is the maximum speed you'll reach. Once we jump from the plane, it'll take about twelve seconds to reach it. We'll then be falling at about a hundred and twenty miles an hour by that point."

She shivered. "That sounds really fast."

"You'll be surprised. Things have a tendency to slow down during a jump. You'll find yourself soaking up the landscape below you and not really notice your speed. You will find your adrenaline spiking. It will flood you with endorphins. Not that I've ever taken illegal drugs, but from what I gather, it's a natural high similar to the rush of cocaine shot into your system the first time."

"Who opens the parachute—you or me?" Paisley asked.

"You're simply there to enjoy the jump. Jared and I take care of all the technical stuff. When to jump from the plane. Turning your body so that your belly remains face down. We maintain that belly-to-earth placement so that a constant velocity is maintained. Whoever you jump with will tap your shoulder to give you a heads up that the chute is about to be engaged. I'll admit there is a jerk when that occurs, and I don't want you to be taken off-guard. Once the chute is engaged, you simply float the rest of the way down to the earth and land gently."

"I'm getting excited about this," she revealed, amazed that Sawyer had thought of something so out of the box. "Could I also get a tap when it's time to pull my feet up? I don't want to be caught up in the moment and forget to do that."

"Sure," Andy agreed good-naturedly. "You don't want to do so too soon and have your legs cramp while you're holding them up." He stood. "If you'd like, I'll give you a few minutes to talk it over and see if this is really something you're interested in doing."

She met Sawyer's gaze and nodded imperceptibly. He looked to Andy and said, "We're in. All in. Ready for the experience of a lifetime."

Andy smiled. "Good for the two of you. Let me go grab Jared. I'll also need to check in with the pilot. The weather is terrific today. Very little wind. You should be comfortable in jumping with what you're wearing. The rule of thumb is if you're cold on the ground, you'll be cold in the air. Same with the heat. If you would feel more comfortable in a jumpsuit, though, I can fit you in one of those."

Sawyer looked to her, and Paisley said, "I'm fine with what I have on."

"Same," Sawyer responded.

"Then let me go arrange everything for your jump, and I'll be back. There'll be a little paperwork to sign before we take off."

Andy went to a folder and pulled a few sheets from it. "You can look this over while I'm gone."

After Andy left the office, she said, "If anyone would have told me that I would be jumping out of an airplane today of my own free will, I would've laughed in their face. We really are going to do this, aren't we?

He grinned at her. "We really are. And we're going to have fun doing so. I promised you wild and crazy, and I hope I've delivered."

"Oh, you've more than delivered. I'm already hyped before we even board the plane. I can't imagine what it's going to feel like, falling through the air."

"I read some accounts about the experience online after I booked it for us. It said even people who are afraid of heights don't seem to mind jumping out of a plane because the ground is so far away. That it doesn't seem real. I also read that it's not so much falling as it seems to be floating. I guess we'll see for ourselves. Let me look at the form now and see if it's something I feel comfortable signing."

Paisley sat as he read, his brow slightly furrowed. He was a very handsome guy with a little bit of a rough edge to him. She thought perhaps it might be because of his nose. It looked as if it had been broken at some point, probably during a game. She glanced to his hands, which held the papers. She liked the look of them. Big, strong hands.

Hands she wanted on her.

Paisley found herself growing hot. She never, ever had

sexual thoughts like this. Had never met a guy who interested her in that way. Her heart never sped up. She never got tingly vibes. Yet those were the very things happening being around Sawyer Montgomery.

Maybe there was more to life than her trusted vibrator. Maybe she could explore some of these new feelings with Sawyer.

"I think we can sign the form," he told her.

"Is that Lawyer Sawyer encouraging me to sign or Wild and Crazy Sawyer who is suggesting that?" she teased.

He gave her a very sexy smile. "Both."

She laughed. "What if I had backed out of skydiving today?"

"I had a couple of other exciting things in my back pocket. Who knows? Maybe we'll try them after we've done this."

"I think one death defying activity a day will be enough for me, Mr. Montgomery."

Andy returned to the office, bringing another guy with him. He introduced himself to them as Jared, and they were taken back to an area which housed the parachutes and harnesses. Andy told Paisley she would dive with him, while Sawyer and Jared would jump together.

"We'll be the first out of the plane. I'll tap you on the shoulder twice. That'll be your signal that we're ready to jump."

"I hope I won't balk," she said. "I've never worried about flying, and I don't have a fear of heights. This is very different, though."

"You're an athlete," he said. "Someone comfortable in her own body. I believe you'll take away a lot from this experience. I'll signal you with taps every time something is about to change. Relax, Paisley. This is going to be fun."

The two TIs gathered what they would need as Paisley and Sawyer put on the goggles Jared provided to them. They were snug against her face.

Then she was placed in the tandem harness, and Andy made the necessary adjustments.

"This may be a little tight, but trust me. You want it to fit that way."

Once the parachutes were retrieved and loaded, they went to the hangar. One of the two planes which had been inside now sat on the tarmac. They were introduced to the pilot, who told them the altitude they would jump from. Once they made their jumps and he returned the plane to the hangar, he would be the one to come and pick them up.

They boarded the plane, taking seats along a bench and strapping in for takeoff. Paisley's heart was pounding rapidly now. Andy told them to take several deep breaths and blow them out their mouths as the plane started down the runway and took off. That seemed to calm her. It was a little unnerving, though, to be climbing in the air with the open door nearby.

Once they began to level off, Andy motioned for her to stand. He connected Paisley to him with four different attachments, one for each shoulder and both legs.

"Last advice, Paisley. Arch your body those first few seconds as we freefall to terminal velocity. You want your belly to jut out toward the ground."

"Roger that," she said, sticking a thumb up.

"Let's head to the door."

They moved slowly toward it. She placed her hands on each side of the opening, hoping her heart wouldn't explode. Then Andy tapped her shoulder twice, and she braced herself. They leaped from the plane, and she was immediately aware of the wind on her face and how loud it sounded.

This must be why Andy used taps to communicate because it would be impossible to hear anything spoken with all this noise.

Adrenaline rushed through her as he guided them so that her belly faced the ground. A sudden calm descended over her. Sawyer had been right. It wasn't falling as much as floating, a sensation of being almost weightless. She took in the landscape below them, blood rushing to her ears. Her senses seemed more heightened than ever before. Time no longer seemed to exist.

Then she felt another tap and saw a phone in Andy's hand. She smiled while he took a couple of selfies of them.

Paisley became aware of Sawyer and Jared now near them. She watched Andy take a couple of pictures of the pair and then saw that Jared seemed to be snapping photos of her and Andy, too. She was on sensory overload now as she rushed through the air.

Another tap on her shoulder let her know something was about to happen. She recalled Andy saying there would be a strong jerk as the parachute opened. That's exactly what happened. Paisley gasped, trying to steady her breathing again as they shot backward through the air. Then they stopped, and a gentle swaying began to rock them. The abrupt descent now slowed considerably. As they serenely glided in the air for several minutes, she soaked up everything happening. The landscape was embedded in her brain.

As they approached the ground, however, a trickle of fear ran through her. They would hit the ground soon. For a moment, all she could think about was her bum knee. Then another tap occurred, with Andy's palm facing up, pushing upward. Instantly, Paisley remembered what to do and lifted her legs high in the air. About five seconds later, they touched down so gently that she wasn't quite sure if they had landed or not.

"Here," Andy called, causing Paisley to set her feet on the ground.

Again, another rush of adrenaline hit her, and euphoria flooded her now that the experience was over.

Andy began unbuckling the harness holding them together, his fingers moving nimbly. Soon, they were separated, and he helped free her from the harness. She removed her goggles, glad she had worn them.

"How was it?" he asked.

"Amazing! The best thing ever!"

She glanced and saw Sawyer was also on the ground, climbing from his harness. Their gazes met. He was wearing a huge smile, making him more appealing than ever before.

"I can't believe what a rush that was," he said, tugging off his goggles. Then he sobered some. "How about you? Are you okay?"

Paisley beamed at him. "It was more like flying than falling. It's hard to explain, but I felt at peace." She paused. "I just had the time of my life—thanks to you."

She turned to the tandem instructor. "And you, too. That was the most incredible thing I've ever done."

"I told you so," Andy replied.

"It'll be about twenty minutes or so before we're picked up," Jared said. "We'll gather the silks. You two might want to walk around and get your bearings again."

She took a couple of steps, feeling wobbly. Then Sawyer was there, steadying her.

"Let's do this together," he suggested, clasping her hand in his. "Small steps at first."

As they walked, she slowly began adjusting to being on solid ground again.

He said, "It's like when you've been rollerblading. You take them off and walk a few steps. It's an odd sensation."

"Yes, that captures the feeling," she agreed.

Paisley stopped walking and faced him. "I can't thank you enough for this experience. I never would have chosen to do something like this on my own, but it'll be something which I'll remember forever. One of the best days of my life."

"Good," he said, starting to walk again, his hand still firm around hers.

While they waited for their ride back to the hangar, Andy and Jared texted the pictures which they had taken to both Sawyer and Paisley. She was glad to have the photos so that she could relive the experience.

The pilot returned in a white van to collect them, and they drove back to the airstrip. Andy thanked them for their business and gave each of them his business card.

"In case you want to recommend us to anyone," he said. "And if you ever think about flying lessons, I hope you'll consider taking them here."

Jared handed them bottles of water. "Drink up. Keep hydrating the rest of the day, too."

They said goodbye and returned to Sawyer's sedan. He looked to her.

"Where to next, Paisley?"

"I'm ravenous. It's as if I haven't eaten in days."

"Then I know just the place. It's time you went to Burger Heaven and met Miss Caroline."

CHAPTER

Ten

They arrived back in Hawthorne a little after one, and Paisley entered Burger Heaven with Sawyer. A few tables were occupied, but she supposed the weekday lunch rush had come and gone.

A woman with a puff of white hair and merry blue eyes greeted them. "Hello, Sawyer. Always good to see you." She turned her focus to Paisley. "And you must be Coach Roberts, the new basketball coach. Boy, are we happy to have you here in Hawthorne."

She was finally getting used to people already knowing who she was. She remembered Sawyer saying that he liked the fact that he could walk down the street, and people in Hawthorne knew his name.

Paisley was beginning to understand that feeling.

"It's nice to meet you," she said, offering her hand. "Paisley Roberts."

"I'm Miss Caroline. Well north of eighty and still going strong. I pretty much know everyone in town. At least the ones worth knowing," she said, a mischievous look in her eyes. "Come have a seat. We'll get you fixed up."

Miss Caroline led them to a booth, and she and Sawyer faced one another.

"Do you like burgers, Paisley?" Miss Caroline asked. "I've got the best griller west of the Mississippi. You look like a Swiss and mushroom kind of girl to me."

"How did you know?" she asked. "Yes, that's exactly what I'd like to order. With some fries, please."

Sawyer spoke up. "We can share the fries, Miss Caroline, since there's plenty of them. You know what I want."

"A double bacon cheeseburger. What to drink?" The old woman glanced at Paisley. "I make a damn fine strawberry lemonade."

"Well, then, I'd better check it out."

"Make it two," Sawyer said.

"Be back in a flash."

"Miss Caroline is quite the character," Paisley said once the older woman was out of earshot.

"She's a sweet soul. This used to be the place I took dates when I was in high school. Miss Caroline would always give me extra fries because she liked me."

"I've never known that kind of continuity," she told him. "Growing up, going to the same place. And here you are, a grown man—and still coming to Burger Heaven."

"This was my dad's favorite place to eat, so I do have fond memories of coming here with him, Mom, and Darby."

"Do your parents still live in Hawthorne?"

She saw a shadow cross his face. "No. We lost them several years ago. They went to see Darby graduate from UT and were struck head on while they were on their way home from Austin. Drunk driver."

Paisley heard the hurt in his voice—and she hurt for him.

"I'm so sorry, Sawyer. I know you were an adult by then, but it didn't make it any easier for you."

"You would have liked my parents," he predicted. "They were good people. My mom and West's mom were sisters. Aunt Meg and Uncle Joe really stepped up afterward. Darby and I had practically grown up between our two households, but they made certain that we understood we always had a place to stay and could come to them whenever we needed advice or a shoulder to cry on."

"I think I'm going to like working for Dr. Sutherland."

Miss Caroline returned with their lemonades and placed them on the table. "Give it about seven more minutes," she told them, leaving again.

During the time she was gone, Sawyer told Paisley about a few other people in the town whom she might encounter. It seemed everyone in Hawthorne was a sports fan and that the Lady Hawks games would have a lot of spectators cheering for them, not just students from HHS.

"I met with Hope Sewell yesterday, I heard how the team began to fall apart. West didn't say a word to me about that."

"He would never do that. West is someone who wants you to form your own opinions and not be influenced by others. He wouldn't color your view of the team by saying anything bad about it or Coach Finnerty. Hopefully, though, Hope did tell you a little bit about how things went south. Her insight will be valuable as you begin to put your own mark on the team."

"I know I have my work cut out for me."

When the burgers and fries arrived, Paisley's stomach growled noisily, causing Miss Caroline to cackle.

"Dig in, kids."

The first bite of her burger made Paisley a believer.

"This is the best cheeseburger I've ever eaten. It's really juicy. And the mushrooms are so plump."

"Told you so. Try some fries."

She dipped a fry into the ketchup and took a bite, chewing thoughtfully.

"These are as good as the burger." She smiled brightly. "The perfect post-skydiving meal." Shaking her head, she added, "I still can't believe we did that."

"I'm glad you enjoyed it."

They finished their meal, and Sawyer drove Paisley back to her house. He pulled up at the curb, and she didn't want their time together to end. She didn't know how to keep it going, though. She supposed she could ask if he'd like to come in, but she already felt guilty for taking up so much of his day as it was.

"Thank you for one of the best experiences I've ever had."

"I'm glad it was something we both wound up enjoying." He hesitated. "If you need someone to watch the opening ceremony with you, give me a call. Or that first game."

"The game will actually be broadcast when we're over at West and Kelby's. Kelby invited me. Said that a group of you get together a few times a month."

"The game will be on," he said. "There's always a TV tuned to sports in that household. Do you think that you'll want to have it on?"

"Honestly, I'm not sure," she replied.

"Just say the word, and I'll make sure something else is on if you feel uncomfortable."

She liked how protective he was. She liked how easy things were between them. Paisley didn't know if this could be called a date.

Wanting to clarify that, she asked, "Was this a date, Sawyer?"

He grinned. "Only if you want to call it that. It was planned as an outing between new friends, but I'll tell you that I'm interested in seeing you again, Paisley. As more than a friend," he added."

"Oh!"

His own honesty gave her a bit of a scare, yet she thought if she ever might try to date a guy, it should be Sawyer.

"I'm going to be busy with my team. My new role as a coach. But I wouldn't mind seeing you. As more than a friend."

He reached out and took her hand. That same electricity shot through her again. Having never held a guy's hand before, she didn't know if this was supposed to happen every time or not.

Something told her it was unusual.

"Then let's go to West's house together on Saturday," Sawyer suggested. "Would you mind if people know we're seeing one another?"

She replied instantly. "Not at all," feeling good about her response. Withdrawing her hand, she added "We'll talk soon."

Paisley got out of the car and went inside the house, wondering exactly what she was getting herself into. She already had so much on her plate. Moving to a new town. Holding a teaching job for the first time. Making a career switch from player to coach. She didn't want to shortchange her professional life, but she was eager to see what might happen between her and Sawyer.

And she might have found the perfect person to help her navigate these new, deep waters.

She made a decision based upon what Sawyer had told

her and texted West Sutherland, asking him to call her at his earliest convenience.

The text barely had time to go through when her phone rang. West's name lit up the screen.

Answering, she said, "Hey, West. Thanks for calling me."

"How are you settling in?" he asked. "I hope Hawthorne is treating you right."

"Well, I've eaten at both Dizzy's Diner and Burger Heaven. I've met with Hope Sewell. We plan to meet again, hopefully with Marsha Zelman, later this week."

"I'm glad you're making such a good start, Paisley. What can I do for you?"

"I saw Sawyer today. He told me that you zoom with a therapist."

"Dr. Linda is the best," her new boss said with enthusiasm. "She specializes in working with athletes. Have you ever done any talk therapy before?"

"I did for a few months after my injury. That therapist retired, though. I might be in the market for another one."

"I'll text you Dr. Linda's info. She's tough but compassionate. She uses zoom or FaceTime to work with patients all over the country. She's based in Dallas. I began seeing her in person after my own knee injury. I've kept it up because I see how valuable therapy is to me."

"Thank you, West. I appreciate it."

West sent her a text with the therapist's phone number and told her to add it to her address book. He said he would check in with Dr. Linda now and have her contact Paisley.

She went to the kitchen and claimed a bottled water from the fridge, remembering that Andy said to continue to hydrate throughout the day. She'd only taken a couple of sips when her phone lit up with a FaceTime call. Paisley answered it, seeing a pretty Asian woman who looked to be in her mid-forties on the call.

Smiling, the woman said, "Hello, Paisley. I'm Dr. Linda Tomahacheouli. You can see my last name is pretty complicated, so I just go by Dr. Linda. West Sutherland asked me to give you a call. I hear you might be interested in a new therapist."

Paisley explained how she had been seeing someone after a sports injury but that the therapist retired from her practice a few months ago.

"Let's chat a bit and get to know one another, "Dr. Linda suggested. "Then you can take some time to think about whether this is something you wish to pursue, whether with me or another licensed sports therapist."

Already, Paisley was drawn in by the woman's warm manner and knew if she did decide to continue with therapy, it would be with Dr. Linda.

"I'll start," the therapist said, surprising Paisley. "I have two teenagers. I'm a rabid Green Bay Packers fan, which irks West to no end."

She laughed. "I'm sure it does."

"My husband is an engineer. He's the reason we moved to Dallas about ten years ago. With technology advancing as it has, I'm able to see patients across the country, as well as some in person in my Dallas office. I focus solely on clients who play sports. I see players from all sports. Football. Hockey. Soccer. Men and women."

Dr. Linda bent down and lifted a tiny Chihuahua into view. "This is Tiki, who rules our household. My husband and I are avid runners. Our daughter plays soccer, while our son is into lacrosse and track. My favorite place in the world to relax is Maui, but I wouldn't pass up any opportunity to visit Paris again and nibble on chocolate croissants."

Paisley liked the therapist's open manner. "Thank you for sharing about yourself. My previous therapist didn't tell me squat about herself, and yet I was supposed to bare my soul to her."

Dr. Linda shrugged. "It's a personal choice. Most therapists share nothing about their lives with their patients. With those I see being in sports, however, many of them are in the spotlight. People know everything about them. Or think they do from what they read online. I find there's a level of comfort when I share something of myself with a patient. I do know a little about you since I follow the world of sports. You've had a remarkable career, Paisley. Championships. Gold medals."

The therapist paused. "And I'm sure the next couple of weeks will be some of the hardest of your life."

Her eyes welled with tears, spilling down her cheeks, and she apologized. "I usually don't cry, but you're right. Not being in Osaka is killing me. I've had months to prepare myself to not be there. I thought I had. I guess I did a lousy job."

"No, don't belittle yourself. You may have tried to prepare yourself, but no one can truly know how they'll react in any given situation. Don't be so hard no yourself."

"My whole life seems topsy-turvy right now, Dr. Linda. Obviously, I can't play professionally anymore. I've just taken a job in Hawthorne, and West is my athletic director."

"I assume you'll be the girls basketball coach?"

"Yes. I'm learning the team has been on the skids for a while. Hardly any girls are currently playing. I've got to turn the program around—fast—as well as convince more girls to play on the team."

"You may get a few who'll commit to doing so merely because they're curious about you. What it's like to be around a former Olympian," Dr. Linda pointed out. "But it will be the culture you create which will truly make the difference."

For the next ten minutes, they talked about that idea of culture. What Paisley valued and the lessons she wished to impart to her athletes.

"This is a time of great change for you, Paisley. You're going to be facing new challenges. Beginning a new career. But you do have the perspective of an adult. You're not some green kid, fresh out of college, with no life experience. You know your sport inside and out and should feel confident as you teach young ladies the ins and outs of it. Some will simply want to learn the basics and skate by with that knowledge. With others, you'll be able to get into more intricate things, such as strategies they should use on the court. How to make quick decisions under pressure."

The therapist smiled at her. "I think we would enjoy working together, but I will give you time to assess that."

"No time is needed, Dr. Linda. As it is, we've been talking so long, I'd say I've already attended my first session. I'm very comfortable with you, more so than I was the entire time with my previous therapist. I can tell you aren't going to put up with me trying to weasel out of anything. I'm willing to do the work necessary, but I will need your guidance. And I want to pay for this session."

Dr. Linda laughed. "I have two teenagers whose feet seem to grow every week, so I'll go ahead and bill you for our time together today. I think we should talk at least once a week at this point. Twice would be better. Do you have a schedule in mind?"

Paisley explained that she had a few weeks before teacher training started and that she could make herself available day or night during that time.

"Once I start school and see what my routine will be like, I'll have to let you know about appointments."

"I can work with that. You have my phone number. I'll text you my email, and you should do the same for me. I'll also text you my website. You can view the hours I'm available and what I charge per session. I doubt you'll want to drive into Dallas to see me, so we'll continue our work on the phone unless you request an in-person session. Sound good?"

Relief swept through her. "It's sounds really good. I don't know how busy you are. I suspect very much in demand, but I appreciate you taking the time to add me as a patient."

"I'll be honest. If West hadn't given me his personal recommendation, I don't know if I would have offered to squeeze you in." Dr. Linda smiled. "I already like you a lot, Paisley. I've seen you play and how you put your heart on the line with every shot. I think we'll do some very good work together. You can schedule all your appointments online via the website. I'm looking forward to our next session."

"Thanks again, Dr. Linda. I am, too."

When Paisley got off the phone, she felt a calm descend upon her. She knew she had some big challenges ahead of her, but her support system was growing by the day. She would have Dr. Linda to bounce things off of. A growing friend list. Her new assistant. Sawyer. Everything was shaping up for her.

Now, all she had to do was manage to make it through the next couple of weeks of the Olympics. That was going to be a huge test.

And then the rest of her life waited on the other side.

CHAPTER
Eleven

Paisley put down the pen she used to scribble new plays and closed the spiral notebook as her phone alarm went off. It was almost time for her call with Dr. Linda. She had arranged three weeks' worth of appointments online, all before school started. This would be her second session with the professional.

She remained at the kitchen table since Jen was still at work. Moments later, her cell rang with a FaceTime call. A good feeling washed over Paisley, knowing she was going to talk with her therapist again.

"Hey, Dr. Linda. You're right on time."

"Punctuality is my blessing—and sometimes, my curse," the older woman said, laughing. "But a busy practice and having to get two teenagers who still aren't old enough to drive places makes me lean toward the blessing side of things. How have you been since we last spoke, Paisley?"

"I've been busy with school stuff. Mostly coaching. I met with Marsha Zelman, who's the head girls basketball coach at the middle school. She actually has a daughter who'll be a junior on my team this year. Marsha said Tessie is a fierce competitor and will do a good job for me. My assistant coach and I have been working on the playbook. Hope was only in her first year last year, and the previous coach relegated her to a bystander position. Hope has a lot of great ideas, though, and I want her to be a full part of this team and my coaching staff."

"I'm glad you're meeting those you'll be working with and becoming comfortable with your new duties," Dr. Linda said. "Okay, gonna sound stereotypical now, but let's go back and talk a little about your childhood."

Her belly tightened hearing those words.

"If it's not something you wish to discuss, I respect that, but understanding who we were as children can help us understand more about who we are as adults. It's a good place for us both to see what you were like and how far you've come." The therapist paused. "But the decision is yours."

It made sense. And she did trust this woman. Trust had never been something that came easily to Paisley. Because she did trust Dr. Linda, she decided to run with it.

"I've never thought about it that way before. I'll tell you right off the bat, it wasn't a great childhood. No dad ever in the picture. Not even named on my birth certificate. I hadn't realized that until I started playing professionally. After my first WNBA season, I decided to play overseas and needed to apply for a passport. That's when I saw there was no record of my dad."

She opened up to her therapist, detailing as much as she could recall about her mom and then her time in the foster care system. Dr. Linda listened, occasionally interjecting a question for clarification, and Paisley finally wound down.

"Since we first spoke, I've done a little research about basketball and the different positions, just to understand better where you're coming from, Paisley. Do you feel a point guard is the heart and soul of a team?"

"Yes. Each position has its own special responsibilities, but as a point guard, I functioned as the leader of my team on the court. Directing players where to go. Hoping they'd know what to do when the ball was placed in their hands."

"That goes back to the beginning with you," Dr. Linda observed. "You talked about even as a small child, you had to do things for your mom. Bring her a can of Coke. Fetch her cigarettes and lighter. Covering her with a blanket when she'd fall asleep on the couch. You were nurturing her even then, almost in a role reversal. That pattern continued the entire time you played point guard. You looked after others. You were the player who was closest to your head coach on the team. Because you were the conduit for the offense. It ran from the coach, through you. You were the one who looked out for all the players on the court."

"That's a little mind-blowing," she respond. "But it definitely hits the nail on the head."

"You'll step into a new role now, but you'll still be the head of a team. Of course, you'll have some of your players who will do what you did. Step up and be leaders at practice and on the court during games. But these are still very young women. Teenagers are mercurial, changing constantly. You're going to want to impart lessons that go beyond athletics."

"Yes," Paisley agreed. "You're exactly right. I want to teach them about a game I love, but I want to teach them even more. Give them life skills. Help them learn how to deal with tough situations and even tougher people they encounter throughout life."

"Tell me about your philosophy," the therapist encouraged.

She spoke for several minutes about the culture she

wished to establish with her program. The therapist didn't interrupt her. When she finally finished detailing her ideas, Dr. Linda nodded approvingly.

"You've had a chance to learn from the best at all different levels of the game. I can see you've cobbled your own philosophy from the stops you've made along the way and made it your own. Your team—small or large—is going to benefit from your experiences. What you pass along to them. Now, we have about five minutes left. I think we need to address the elephant in the room. The Olympics."

The opening ceremony was this evening, and Paisley had yet to ask Sawyer to watch it with her.

"TV will broadcast the opening ceremony tonight. I thought I might tune in and watch a little of it. See Team USA as they parade into the stadium."

"Will you be watching with anyone?" Dr. Linda asked.

"No. I hadn't planned on it. The first game is tomorrow, and I'm going to be eating with some new friends during it. I'm sure we'll have it on in the background."

Dr. Linda regarded her with kind eyes. "For so long, it's been you against the world, Paisley. You might want to call upon one of those new friends to watch tonight's opening ceremony with you. It's not a sign of weakness to want someone beside you. More like a sign of solidarity."

She swallowed hard, knowing the therapist was right.

"I haven't really had a lot of close friends. No, I've never had any close friends," she corrected. "I've always been the one who looked out for others. I've never bothered looking out for myself," she admitted. "I do have one friend who offered to watch with me tonight."

Paisley hesitated, not sure what else she wanted to say. Dr. Linda kept quiet.

Finally, she said, "This is a guy I met through West. His

cousin. Sawyer played basketball in college, so we have that in common. He's talked about wanting to be my friend. And possibly more than a friend."

"How do you feel about that?"

"Terrified. Excited. I know we don't have enough time to go into it right now, but I'm going to drop a bombshell on you, Dr. Linda. I've never had a date. I'm thirty-two years old and devoted my entire life to basketball. I haven't even been around men much."

"What about this man?" Dr. Linda nudged.

"I like him. He's a calm, steady type. He took me skydiving the other day."

"Skydiving?" Dr. Linda burst out laughing. "What a fun thing to do. And not an activity I would associate with a calm kind of man."

"It was the day I was supposed to be on the plane. Flying to Osaka. He knew I was upset. A little down. Sawyer told me he wanted us to do something pretty wild to take my mind off things."

The therapist nodded sagely. "Then I would say he is a good friend. Someone who has insight into you. I'm not here to dictate what you should ever do, Paisley, but you need to seriously consider exploring this relationship to see where it goes. At worst, you've made a very good friend who seems to understand you. At best, you might have found someone you can trust and open up to."

Dr. Linda was right. She would be doing herself a disservice if she tried to handle tonight alone. Sawyer had volunteered to watch with her. He had offered because he wanted to be with her.

And Paisley really wanted to spend more time with the attractive attorney.

"Thank you," she told the therapist. "I feel I've accomplished more in two sessions and learned more about myself than I did during the months I spent under my first therapist's care."

"It's okay to lean on others, Paisley. You're embarking upon a new life with this change of career, so you're also going to have to develop some new and different skills for how to cope with situations you encounter. Depending upon friends is something good, especially for a loner such as yourself. Being in a new place, you're lucky you're already finding friends so quickly. We'll talk more about this next time."

Dr. Linda glanced down and back to Paisley. "I see we're scheduled for next Tuesday at ten-thirty."

"I'll see you then," Paisley said, ending the call and placing the phone on the kitchen table.

She knew Jen would be home in a little while. Her new roommate would be happy to watch the opening ceremony with her. Jen was a very positive, upbeat person. While Paisley liked that about Jen, she wasn't certain that's who she wanted to be around tonight.

Picking up her phone again, she texted Sawyer.

> Hope it's not too late to see if you'd like to watch the opening ceremony together tonight.

Paisley waited for a reply and was disappointed when she didn't immediately get one. Then doubts began to plague her, and she sent another text to him two minutes later.

> Don't worry that you can't make it. I'll see you tomorrow.

She swallowed the lump forming in her throat, forcing it down. Paisley decided she would have to depend upon herself. It was a familiar thing to do. All she had ever known.

Dejectedly, she opened the spiral notebook again, no longer in a mood to work, but wanting to keep busy. Five minutes later, she jumped when her phone rang, seeing it was Sawyer.

"Hey."

"Hey, yourself," he said breezily. "Sorry I couldn't text you back right away. I was with a client. He's having a dispute with his neighbor over the boundary between their properties." He paused. "If the offer's still good, I'd be happy to watch with you tonight."

She found herself speechless, a lump in her throat.

"I'm glad you reached out to me, Paisley. You don't know how many times I've started a text to you and deleted it."

Finding her voice, she asked, "Why did you delete it?"

"Because something told me it was important for you to ask me about being together tonight. It's something that you probably thought you had to do on your own. But I want you to know this. You're not alone. You've got me—and a whole lot of others."

"I'm starting to realize that," she said softly.

"Would you like to come to my place? We could grill some steaks. Have a baked potato with it."

"I'm afraid you'll have to be the one doing all that. I don't know how to boil water. I am fairly skilled at pouring a bowl of cereal, however, should you change your idea about the menu."

He laughed. "Then tonight will be your first cooking lesson. Rib eye sound okay?"

"Just hearing rib eye makes my mouth water," she revealed.

"Okay, I'll pick up what we'll eat and then you."

"No, I think I'd rather drive to your place," she countered. "Text me your address and tell me what time to be there."

"Ceremony kicks off at seven. Why don't you come over about five-thirty? I'll light the grill. We'll have plenty of time to eat and then get settled in."

"I'll see you then. Thanks, Sawyer."

"You know I'm here for you," he assured her.

This time, Paisley definitely knew it was a date, but she wanted to keep things as causal as possible. She did shower and put on a fresh T-shirt and pair of shorts, though, before heading to his place an hour later. When she pulled up in front of his house, she saw him getting out of his car in the driveway. He carried two grocery bags in his hand.

"Perfect timing," he said, giving her a smile.

She liked his smile because it reached his eyes. Too many smiled and didn't mean it.

That wasn't the case with Sawyer Montgomery.

They entered the house, and he said, "Don't judge my taste in décor by what you're seeing. None of this dilapidated furniture and bad carpeting belong to me. I put what I had into storage since this house came furnished. Everything's mid-century modern, but I think it's all been here since the early fifties."

Paisley laughed. "What is your style?"

"I like a clean look. Not cluttered. Although my desk at work does have a lot of piles on it, I know exactly what's in each of those stacks."

"Do you have a home office here?"

She watched as he began unpacking the groceries.

"Nope. Work stays at work. That's my new rule of working here in Hawthorne. I was an assistant district attorney in Dallas. Usually, I toiled fourteen-to-sixteen hour days. When a big case came along, the days got even longer. I decided when I moved here, I'd definitely separate work and my personal life. If I do need to put in extra time, I can always go back up to the square to my office there. Home, as sad as it looks, is the place where I get away from work."

"That makes sense. I'm afraid I'm always scribbling new plays down wherever I am."

"I'd love to hear about the offense and defense you're going to run this year, but right now, I'm going to go light the grill and then change. Make yourself at home. Grab a beer from the fridge if you'd like. Or I can open some wine if you'd prefer that."

She wandered around, looking at a few photographs sitting out. One was with Darby and what had to be their parents. Another was with West and a guy in a cowboy hat whom she hadn't met yet.

Then she came across a photo of Sawyer with a beautiful woman. She was slender, with gorgeous strawberry blond hair and light blue eyes. He had his arm around her, and they were both laughing. Sawyer looked so happy. Paisley wondered who this woman was to Sawyer. For a moment, she felt the sting of jealousy, something unfamiliar to her.

She returned to the kitchen, and he joined her there, now wearing a black Led Zeppelin T-shirt and a pair of tan shorts.

"Okay, first thing we'll do is light the grill. Then I'll show you how to put an easy dinner together."

Sawyer taught her how to season a steak using salt, black pepper, and a bit of garlic, doing one cut himself and having her season the second one.

"I'm going to trim a bit of fat from them to prevent a flare-up on the grill," he explained.

After he'd done that, he said, "We're going to cheat a little and microwave the baked potatoes."

He showed her how to scrub the potatoes and then patted

them dry with a paper towel, sticking a fork into them multiple times, saying it would help steam escape as they cooked.

"You set them on a plate to nuke." He put the potatoes inside the microwave and started it. Then he tore two large pieces of aluminum foil. "Here's the important part in this cheat. When the potatoes are done, you roll them up in the foil. Shiny side has to be facing up. We wrap them tightly, and being next to the shiny side, it reflects and assists in the baking a little more. While I prefer ones made in the oven, it's too dang hot to light it now. Besides, we're both hungry, and this is much faster."

Sawyer took her and the steaks outside, placing them on the grill and closing the lid.

"We'll flip them in about five minutes. Usually, five on each side is good, and then we let them rest five to ten minutes."

"Why rest if they're done?"

"Well, they are and they aren't. If you let them rest, they'll be juicer. It also locks in the flavor better. And they don't go cold in such a short amount of time."

"Good to know, Chef," she teased.

They returned inside, and he wrapped the potatoes which were now done in foil, setting them aside.

"Another cheat now," he said, grinning at her as he opened a bag of salad. "All the work is done for you. Just cut open the bag. I like Caesar salad. Just seems to go better with a steak."

He dumped the salad into a bowl and opened the packet which came with it, tossing both together and setting the bowl in the freezer.

"This'll help it get a little cold."

They checked the steaks again, turning them over, and she inhaled. "Smells wonderful."

In less than fifteen minutes, they had the meal on the table, and Sawyer had poured each of them a glass of wine. She wasn't much of a drinker, but she decided tonight was a night to relax a little and enjoy being together.

The table was pretty rickety, but Sawyer assured her it would hold up.

"Everything's delicious," she told him after she'd sampled each item. "And it's actually something I could do. I like the baked potato trick. That's smart."

"There's a place in Dallas I used to go to. All they had on the menu were baked potatoes, but you could get them prepared any way. Plain. Dressed with the usuals, from butter to chives to grated cheese and sour cream. Then they went the extra mile and loaded them with chopped brisket. Ground taco meat. Even sliced steak. It was a terrific meal, all in one."

He chuckled. "I think I knew every to-go place around me."

"You didn't cook in Dallas?" she asked.

"No time for it. I was either working or sleeping. No, I take that back. I did make time to work out, even if it meant sacrificing sleep. That helped keep me sane. I would get up around four-thirty, after three hours of sleep, and go lift weights. Do a few machines to work my lats or abs. Then jog a little. I have a tendency to baby my bad knee, so running's out for me."

She wanted to ask him about the woman in the picture but decided not to. He had his life in Dallas before he came back to Hawthorne. Even though he was talking about what a workaholic he was, he still must have dated some.

"Let's get things cleaned up so we can catch the beginning of the ceremony," he suggested. "The announcers always share a lot of interesting facts with viewers. I like all that trivia."

Paisley helped him clear the table and load the dishwasher, and Sawyer poured them both a second glass of wine, which they took with them into the small living room.

"That's a very large TV," she commented.

"This was my splurge when I left Dallas," he explained, turning it on. "I never had time for TV. I wanted to be able to catch games. Watch the news. West and I moved back to Hawthorne right at the same time, and he bunked with me for a while."

Sawyer chucked. "Of course, he and Kelby became a pair pretty quickly. From what I know, they had dated at the tail end of high school after being friends forever. There'd been a spark between them then, but they were headed to separate colleges. Actually, enemy schools. She cheered for the Longhorns, while he played for the Aggies."

Even though Paisley was rooted in basketball, she knew of the long-standing rivalry between Texas and A&M.

They turned their attention to the TV and the sweeping shots of Osaka. As the coverage continued, the announcers gave background about the Japanese city, as well as each of the teams which paraded by. Paisley found herself enjoying the evening.

And the arm which Sawyer had casually draped around her shoulders.

He smelled divine, the faint trace of some woodsy cologne he must've put on this morning still lingering. She liked feeling the heat from his body against hers. It caused her heart to speed up a bit.

As the broadcast continued, though, she knew Team USA would make its appearance soon. She began to stiffen as the alphabetical appearances of countries drew closer to the US. Even though his arm was around her, Sawyer now reached for her hand, taking it in his. She drew comfort from that.

His gaze met hers. "I know this is the start of a really rough couple of weeks for you. Thank you for letting me be here for you. I want to share whatever you feel, Paisley. If you're upset. Lonely. Vulnerable. If anguish is running through you, I want to absorb it."

Sawyer lifted their joined hands and brushed a kiss along her knuckles. "I'm here for you."

"Thank you," she whispered, lost in his hazel eyes, which were greener than usual.

Then she heard the announcer say, "And here is the moment Americans have been waiting for. Team USA in their red, white, and blue outfits designed by Ralph Lauren."

Suddenly, she had no interest in anything but Sawyer. The words on the TV faded as his mouth moved toward hers. A thrill shot through her.

Her first kiss was about to happen.

His lips touched hers, soft and yet firm, pressing against her own. She'd lived her entire life by instinct, both on and off the court, trusting her gut. She knew it wouldn't let her down now. Paisley might not know exactly what to do, but she trusted her lips would know how to respond to his.

And she was right.

CHAPTER
Twelve

Sawyer worried he was really out of practice and would make a mess of things, but the moment his lips touched Paisley's, his fears vanished.

It felt right ...

He slowly grazed his lips against hers, giving her the chance to pull away—or accept the kiss. She didn't reject him. Instead, she put a hand on his shoulder to steady herself. He took that as a good sign.

As much as he wanted to devour her, he kept things tame. Sweet. He hadn't kissed a woman since Elizabeth. He couldn't even recall what that had been like. All he knew was this woman interested him. Drew him to her in some inexplicable way. He would take his time.

Because he hoped something lasting might form between them.

His hands moved to frame her face, needing to touch her. His thumbs caressed her smooth cheeks, and for the first time in years, he had hope. Hope that he might move forward in his life and not be a hamster on a wheel, constantly in the same spot.

He brushed his lips against hers, breaking contact, and then kissing her again. He was desperate for a taste of her but hesitant to move to a more intimate kind of kiss.

His kisses became a little harder, demanding more from both of them. For a moment, it seemed as if Paisley hesitated, but by now, both her hands were on his shoulders. Her fingers tightened, and he felt encouraged to keep moving forward.

He couldn't wait any longer. Need drove him. Breaking the kiss, he allowed his tongue to sweep slowly along her full, bottom lip. He felt her stiffen with this contact, but she didn't pull away. Instead, she leaned into him a little more, encouraging him. He wondered what kind of relationships she had been in. The depth of her feelings toward others who came before him. But he pushed aside those thoughts now. If she didn't want to keep kissing him, she would break the contact between them.

He outlined the shape of her mouth with the tip of his tongue, sensing the shivers running through her. Then ever so slowly, he ran the tip of his tongue along the seam of her mouth, urging her to open to him.

She didn't.

Disappointment flooded him, but he understood that she wasn't ready for what he offered. He kissed her lightly and as he started to pull away, surprise filled him.

Paisley ran her tongue along his lower lip, setting him afire. If this was what she wanted, he would let her be in charge. Set the pace. He opened to her—but nothing happened. She wasn't denying his invitation, but she certainly wasn't accepting it.

A thought struck him, one which was unbelievable and yet possibly very true.

Her hesitancy wasn't due to wanting to cool things between them.

He suspected she had never kissed someone in such an intimate manner—and it was up to him to unlock the door to that new experience and show her the way.

Taking charge again, he pulled her toward him, his palms still cradling her cheeks, his tongue moving again, swiping along her bottom lip. When she parted hers, he eased his tongue inside. Her startled reaction let him know he had guessed correctly. She stilled, much as an animal being stalked, thinking if it didn't move, it wouldn't become the prey. But he saw her, this wonderful, beautiful, intriguing woman.

Sawyer swept his tongue along hers, caressing it. Desire exploded within him. She remained stock-still, as if she were assessing the situation. Then her tongue responded, moving against his, and the sensations running through him were like a flame racing at lightning speed.

They explored one another leisurely, taking turns. She tasted unlike anyone else. Eventually, the slow exploration heated up, and they fought for control of the kiss. By now, her arms were entwined about his neck, while his encircled her. The heat of their touching bodies felt like two fires which had met and danced with one another, their kisses hot and passionate.

He wanted more. Much more. But small steps were obviously what Paisley needed. He gentled the kiss, giving her a series of soft, lingering ones before finally breaking contact.

Sawyer rested his forehead against hers. They both breathed unevenly, worn out from their kissing and the intense feelings it had brought about. Her body was still against his. Warm. Welcoming. He was determined to give her as much time as she needed before he asked her to become more physical with him, but he knew what he wanted.

And Sawyer was a man who always saw his mission through until the end.

He raised his head, and she opened her warm, brown eyes. Instantly, he was drawn into them and the unique circle of amber which ringed them.

"That was some kiss," she said softly, a hint of amusement in her voice.

"Yeah. It really was. Paisley, I need to tell you something."

"No, I need to tell you something first."

She wet her lips nervously, causing need to rise within him.

"I ... that was ..." She cursed, surprising him, because she had never done so before.

Her eyes misted with tears. "That was the first time I've ever kissed anyone, Sawyer."

Shock reverberated through him. Yes, she had seemed inexperienced, but he had no idea he was the first to kiss her.

"Why did you wait so long to kiss someone?" he asked.

She shrugged. "I think a lot of it goes back to being a foster kid," she explained. "Not being loved. Not loving anyone. I learned to be very self-contained with my emotions. Keep my feelings inside, never letting them show. In high school, all I wanted to do was go to college, and I knew that athletics would be my route there. I studied like crazy and focused on my sport. Foster kids don't go on dates, Sawyer. They don't have parents who buy them pretty dresses for homecoming or prom. I kept to myself, my nose buried in a book when I wasn't out on the court.

"College was the same. I spent most of my time around other women. Again, I focused on making myself the best point guard I could be, honing my skills. At the same time, I studied like a demon, wanting my degree, and was all-conference academic all four years. Twice, I was an all-American academic player. I was just as proud of that as any sports accolade I'd earned."

He wanted to interrupt and ask her questions, but she was opening up in a way he believed she never had with anyone else. Just like when they were in the car, and she had told him the story about the snake. Because of that, he kept silent, listening intently.

"I know you never played in the NBA, but the schedule for pros is brutal. Intense practices, followed by even more intense games. Then road trips where you're gone ten days, moving from city to city. You get home and try to get your body clock to adjust, all while you're still attending meetings and practices and playing high-stakes games. And that doesn't even take into account the media coverage and what social media is spewing about you."

Paisley fell silent, as if she were exhausted just talking about everything. Then her gaze met his.

"After the WNBA season ended, I would go overseas and play in the European league, doing it all over again. I barely had any personal time for myself, much less an opportunity to meet guys and date anyone. I know you must think I'm a real oddball."

He shook his head. "Don't claim to know what I'm thinking, Paisley. You're way off-base. I can see you were dedicated to your sport and your studies. You attained your goal of earning an athletic scholarship and graduated with your college degree. Then you stepped up into the ranks of the pros. How many women have done what you've done? You focused on your priorities, which included being the best player at your position, leading your team to countless victories. I don't judge you because of that. In fact, I'm a little jealous of you. Dating at any age can be confusing. I haven't dated for years. I threw everything I had into the law. Every waking moment was devoted to the case I was trying."

"But you *have* dated," she insisted.

"Not as much as you would think. A little bit in high school. A little bit in college. Like you, I was more focused on basketball than anything or anyone while I was playing at UNT."

He fell silent and made a quick decision he hoped that he wouldn't regret.

"When I was in law school, I met a fellow student. A woman I fell in love with. We became friends and were in the same study group before we ever began dating our final year in law school. Elizabeth was amazing. Brighter than anyone in our class. Poised. Beautiful."

Sawyer released Paisley, clasping his hands to steady himself as he spoke of the past, something he never talked about.

"We dated a few years and decided to get married. Our careers were devoted to opposite kinds of clients. I worked in the district attorney's office, trying to bring criminals to justice. Elizabeth was a public defender, named to represent those accused of a crime who couldn't afford representation. My job was to put them in prison. Hers was to keep them out."

"That must have been hard," she said. "On both of you."

"We both believed strongly in what we did. Our jobs were all-consuming, however. We decided sometime after we

got married, we would open a joint practice." He smiled wistfully. "Montgomery & Montgomery."

"It has a nice ring to it."

"We didn't know exactly when we'd step away from our
jobs and form our own firm, only that we would need to for
our marriage to survive. Especially if we had kids. Kids need
both time and attention. I had that from my folks. I wanted to
be the kind of dad my own dad was."

"What happened?" Paisley asked quietly. "It's obviously
you loved Elizabeth a great deal."

"I did," he confirmed. He swallowed, memories of that
awful day flooding him again. But they didn't hurt quite as
much as they usually did.

And he had Paisley to thank for that.

He reached for her hand and laced their fingers together.

"Elizabeth was killed in a hit-and-run when she was out
jogging early one morning. They never found who was
responsible. That was a bitter pill to swallow."

She squeezed his fingers. "It had to be. You loved one
another. You'd planned a life together, and it was cut short."

His gaze met hers. "I answered all my hurt by burying
myself in work. For years. Then I finally hit my breaking
point. I totally burned out. I didn't care about anything. I
knew to save myself, I had to make some changes."

Sawyer paused. "That's why I decided to return to
Hawthorne. I wanted a fresh start, but in a familiar place, a
place where I had a support system. I had family here. I
didn't associate Hawthorne with Elizabeth or my career as an
ADA. I was tired of living as a shadow of myself. Elizabeth
may have died seven years ago, but I acted as if I had died
with her."

He looked at Paisley intently. "I've been healing in the
time I've lived in Hawthorne. I enjoy my practice, but I know

when to walk away from work. I've been able to cultivate friendships again. I finally started feeling like myself."

Smiling, he added, "And then I met you, Paisley. You've given me hope that I can have a future. I know it's way too early to declare anything to you, but from the moment we met—on the phone—I came alive. You interest me. You intrigue me. That's why I'm hoping you want to explore a relationship together."

"I'm pretty broken myself, Sawyer," she told him. "An injury undid the career I'd worked so long and hard for. I'll admit that I floundered after it, trying to wrap my head around the fact that I'd never be paid to play basketball again, but I've found steady footing here in Hawthorne."

She met his gaze. "Are you sure you want to get involved with someone like me? I feel I'm emotionally immature, especially compared to you. In you, I see someone who has a lot of life experience. A man who was deeply in love and had that love yanked away from him for no good reason. I'm just a super-tall virgin who doesn't know much about anything outside of basketball."

"Tell me if you're not interested in seeing if there can be more between us, Paisley. If you do, I'll back off right now. We can be friends. I enjoy being around you. I think it would be fun to watch games together."

He watched her worry her bottom lip, fighting the urge to take her in his arms and kiss the life out of her.

"I don't want to do that," she finally said. "I don't think I'm that interesting, but I'm way interested in finding out more about you. I don't know if I could ever replace Elizabeth in your heart, but—"

"No," he insisted. "I'm not looking for a replacement. Yes, a part of me will always love Elizabeth. Love what we had together. Mourn the fact that our time together was cut short.

But I've lived in the past too long, as well as ignoring the present. I want to enjoy the present—and look to my future. I want what my family and friends have, Paisley. Love. Happiness. I want to build a home and life with someone. The question is, are you willing to take a chance and see if that's something we might do together?"

Sawyer held his breath, waiting for her to answer.

"I would like to try," she said softly, determination in her eyes.

Happiness washed over him. "That's great to hear, Paisley. I expect total honestly between us, though. If it's not working, speak up. Don't keep me around because you feel sorry for me."

A smile lit her face. "I could never feel sorry for you, Sawyer. I think you're going to be teaching me a lot."

He settled against the couch again, draping an arm about her as she did the same. For the first time, he heard the TV playing.

"I'm sorry I made you miss Team USA march out."

She chuckled low, causing desire to pool in his belly. "You think I would trade my first kiss for seeing a bunch of strangers walk into a stadium thousands of miles from here? Maybe you're not as smart as I thought you were, Montgomery."

He laughed and reached for the remote on the coffee table in front of him. "Let's back it up. I don't want you to miss your friends and former teammates."

Sawyer rewound to the moment Team USA entered the stadium. Paisley had him pause a few times, pointing out various athletes to him. He didn't know the names she spoke of since he hadn't watched basketball for a long time. What he didn't hear was any sign of sadness or depression coming from her.

They finished watching the end of Team USA's entrance, and she turned to him.

"I'm okay not being there, Sawyer. Because I know I'm exactly where I'm supposed to be."

Paisley's hand went to his nape, and she pulled him down for a long, lingering kiss.

Thirteen

Paisley spent most of Saturday at school, going over the UIL handbook. The University Interscholastic League governed all sports in Texas public schools, dictating everything from when practices started and how long they could last to the dates and location of the state's tournament, where a state champion would be crowned in every division. Divisions were based upon student enrollment at each high school, with schools being placed into a district every two years. Updated enrollment figures were then submitted to the state, and the UIL would assign new districts based upon those numbers, trying to place schools with a similar enrollment and in close proximity of one another in the same district.

She printed out the upcoming year's UIL manual, highlighted dates, and then placed those in her cell phone and on a personal desk calendar. While her JV team would meet the first period of the day and varsity would be last period, she could extend practice outside the school day starting in mid-October. Ten days later, she could begin scrimmaging with other teams. Less than a week after that, non-district play would begin.

She brought up the Lady Hawks basketball schedule now, inputting all non-district games into her calendars. District play started in mid-December, and she also placed those games onto her calendars. Putting dates for the playoffs into her calendar seemed pointless. Already, she knew she had an uphill battle with the team she had inherited. Maybe making the playoffs would be a goal for next year's varsity team. Right now, she was merely hoping they wouldn't embarrass themselves and have to forfeit any games because of the size of their squad.

Hope had drawn up the requested list of returning play-ers, listing the girls by the jersey numbers. The profiles included height and weight, along with their position. Hope had then added the skills each girl possessed and the things that particular player needed to work on. While she had also listed the number of points and assists each player averaged, Hope had also provided a box score for each game last year. Paisley poured over all this information, determining that free throws was an area which needed special attention.

West popped his head in. "You look like you're busy."

"Just familiarizing myself with UIL rules and dates," she replied. "I don't want to be in violation of any of them. I've always been a stickler for details, and so every date is going into my calendar."

"The Sunday Prohibition is a big one," her AD said, referring to the rule in which schools couldn't participate in athletic contests or conduct any practices or meetings on a Sunday. It was prohibited to have players gather and teach them any plays, formations, or skills, much less review any tape of previous games.

"Of course," West continued, "I'm sure you know that

rule doesn't apply to coaches meeting on a Sunday. The unofficial rule in Hawthorne is to let your staff go to church and have lunch with their families, then call a meeting for one o'clock on a Sunday. It's the best time for you and your staff to review film, both of your team and your upcoming opponents. You can plan practices for the upcoming week based upon what you see."

"Got it." Paisley made a note. "Any more advice?"

"Not really." West studied her a moment. "I know you've already met with Hope and Marsha. I talked to both of them, and they really think you'll be great for the program."

"You didn't tell me in my interview how bad things were." She said this neutrally, not wanting to accuse her new boss of hiding anything.

"Each team is different, especially under the leadership of a new coach. Were there problems last year? Absolutely. I didn't think Coach Finnerty was getting the job done and was going to let her go. She's lucky she had some connections and was able to move to a new school. But this team is yours, Paisley, all the way. I didn't want to influence you one way or the other. I wanted you to make the decision to coach here because you *wanted* to be here."

West leaned against the doorway. "I'm not expecting miracles. I know it takes time to create a new program. Form a new culture—and have kids buy into it. Yes, you've got challenges ahead, but nothing I didn't think you couldn't handle."

"Thank you for your faith in me. That means a lot." She paused. "And for giving Sawyer my phone number."

Her AD looked innocently at her. "He told you I did that?"

"He did. And I'm really glad you did, West."

He gave into a smile. "I'm happy to hear that. Sawyer is the oldest of the five cousins. I always looked up to him. He was the best athlete I'd ever seen before I went to A&M. Yes, he had some physical gifts, but Sawyer wasn't just all talent. He had a tremendous work ethic. *That's* what I came to admire most about him. He transferred that work ethic to law school and then his career as an attorney. You won't find a more solid, steadfast guy than my cousin."

"We'll see you tonight," she said.

West gave her a lopsided grin. "Sounds good."

He left, and Paisley continued reviewing all the UIL rules and regulations until she thought she could repeat them in her sleep. Then she returned to drawing up plays based upon the team she would put out on the court this year. They were thin, but Hope had indicated that several had solid ball handling skills. She only hoped she could convince a few of the players who had left to come back.

Paisley had gone online and pulled up stats from last year's district games. Hope had given her current player and team stats, but she wanted to review information about some of the players who had left the team. Four players had refused to enroll in basketball again. One, who had run cross country in the fall, chose to run track in the spring. She had been a track star her first two years at HHS and had only played basketball last year. Paisley doubted she could convince the girl to return for her senior year.

Another had decided to stick solely with softball. Hope told her the athlete was an adequate forward on the basketball court, but she really shone as a center fielder, so Paisley wouldn't try to talk her into returning to the team.

Instead, she would see if she could persuade Desiree Sonato and Sheila Briggs to change their minds about not playing their senior year. Both had been starters their sophomore and junior years. The team needed their experience. Hope said Sheila was a born follower and did whatever Desi told her to do. Desi would be the one Paisley would need to approach. If she could talk the former point guard into returning to the team, Sheila would most likely join in again, as well.

Her phone rang, and she saw it was Sawyer calling. She felt her face flush, immediately thrown back to those heady kisses from last night. Paisley was glad he wasn't Face-Timing her because she could feel the heat filling her cheeks.

"Hey, Sawyer," she answered, hoping he didn't hear the quiver in her voice.

"Hey. Hope you don't mind a call instead of a text."

Actually, she thought it was sweet. Her cell rarely rang since she silenced unknown callers and had a spam call filter on her number. She liked the fact that he called her. It was thrilling to hear his deep, rumbling voice.

"I didn't know phones could do this," she flirted, realizing for the first time that she *was* flirting.

He laughed. "Yeah. They're not just for texting and scrolling through Instagram. You can actually talk to real people. Pretty old-fashioned, right?"

"I like talking to you," she responded. "That's the truth. Texting is great. Quick and easy. But I like the sound of your voice."

"I like the sound of yours. What are you doing?"

"I'm at school. In my office. Working."

She told him how she'd spent her day, and he asked her a few questions which let her know he was truly listening to her. That was a wonderful feeling. She'd held so few conversations that didn't revolve around basketball. It was nice talking to a real person. Even if she was talking basketball. This just felt different. He *was* different. Even though she had very limited experience around guys, Paisley's gut told her Sawyer was a rare man. She didn't want to blow her chance with him.

"Think you can break away for dinner with the gang?" he reminded.

She glanced at her watch. "I'm done here. For now, at least. I'll head home and change."

"Why?"

"I'm wearing school issued shorts and T-shirts. I don't want to be dressed like West and twin with him," she retorted, causing him to laugh again. Paisley loved the sound of his laughter. It was rich. Vibrant. And he laughed as if he thought something was really funny.

"Keep it casual, Coach," Sawyer said. "Kelby had said something about having people wear red, white, and blue. Probably in honor of the Olympics. Do you have something in that color scheme?"

"An old Team USA jersey. Or something from the past."

"Then you'll be a celebrity tonight. People will line up for your autograph."

"I should charge. Then again, that probably would violate some obscure UIL rule. Maybe you can represent me when I go on trial."

He laughed again, and her heart sang.

"Go home, Coach. I'll pick you up in half an hour."

She said goodbye and headed to her SUV. When she got home, she passed Jen, who wore a dress and heels, something Paisley had never seen Jen in.

"Going somewhere?"

"Yes. I've got a date," her roommate said. "I was working on a new website for the local florist. Went over to walk her through it and see if she wanted any changes. Her delivery driver came in, and he was hot. I mean, really hot. He's her brother. A fireman who helps her out on his days off. We got to talking, and we're having dinner together tonight."

"Must be a nice place. You look fantastic."

"Thanks." Jen placed her palm to her belly. "I'm excited. Like butterflies exploding in the belly excited. We're meeting at Great Steak."

"Do you always meet your dates?" she asked out of curiosity.

"I started doing that when I moved to New York. I like the freedom to be able to come and go." Jen grinned. "But if things go well tonight, I'll be happy for him to pick me up next time. Oh, I hope there's a next time!"

"There will be," she assured her roommate. "You're a fun, interesting person. Also, those heels are killer. They make your legs look very sexy."

"Good. I jog for a reason. Toned legs should be noticed," Jen quipped.

"Have fun."

Paisley went inside, deciding she had time for a quick shower. She toweled off and put on one of her last Olympics shirts, the blue polo one with white piping, a red Team USA logo emblazoned above her heart. She had thought she would never wear it again but hadn't wanted to part with it. Glancing in the mirror, she decided she liked it. She looked good in blue. The shirt was a part of her past. Just because she'd been injured didn't mean she had to wipe away all those memories.

She pulled on some denim shorts and opted for white Keds. They weren't stylish, but they were comfortable. She didn't think Sawyer would judge her based on her shoe choice tonight. She brushed her teeth and applied a coat of lipstick before pulling out her hair tie and brushing her hair, leaving it down for tonight.

The doorbell rang, and she hurried to answer it. Sawyer stood on the porch and gave her a long look from head to toe.

"I appreciate what I see," he said, leaning in and dropping a light kiss on her lips. "Your legs are a mile long."

"That's because they are. I was the tallest kid in elementary school, taller than even some of the teachers. Believe me, I know I've got long legs."

He caught her by the waist. "It was a compliment, Paisley. You have beautiful calves. Ones I want to run my tongue along."

His outrageous words caused a ripple of something to run through her. "Would you really do that?"

Sawyer looked at her longingly. "I'm dying to do that. And lick a few other places while I'm at it."

She felt her face flame. "Seriously?"

"I'm dead serious. But that's for later. Let's go."

She locked the front door, and he took her hand, leading her to his car. Even holding hands was a new experience for her, one she really liked.

Once they were in the car, she asked, "Who'll be there tonight?"

"Obviously, West and Kelby. Darby and Jace. Eli, Jace's brother, is Autumn's husband. Probably Chance and Summer."

"I've met all the women, but only West and you from the guys."

"You'll like them. Jace was West's agent, while Chance is West's best friend. Eli only came to Hawthorne when Triple H opened. Or actually before. He had a lot to do with getting it ready to be opened. He's the medical director."

"And what does Chance do?"

"He runs the Blackstone Ranch. They raise cattle and some horses."

"A real cowboy then."

"I think Summer's broken him of wearing boots with his shorts," Sawyer said drily, causing her to giggle.

"I like being with you, Sawyer. I never knew how fun it was to laugh. I've been so serious my entire life, always concentrating on basketball."

"Then you'll like this group. They're fun—and they're funny."

He was right about that. Paisley liked the four women already, and she quickly felt at home with their spouses.

Darby handed her two big volumes.

"What are these?"

"Hard copies of the last two yearbooks. I think I told you I sponsor the yearbook. These editions of *Horizon* will be good for you to look through. It'll help acquaint you more with the school. You can also look up your players. While they'll be younger than they are now, it'll still give you a chance to become familiar with them."

"This is fantastic. Thank you. I'll take good care of these and return them to you."

"No rush."

They gathered outside. Although it was still July and hot, the patio was covered and had ceiling fans turning, creating a slight breeze. There was also an outdoor kitchen and a TV with lots of comfortable furniture. West and Sawyer manned the grills, while Kelby and Darby worked in the kitchen. Paisley volunteered to help, but they shooed her outside, telling her they had everything down. She joined Summer, Chance, Autumn, Eli, and Jace.

"I hear you own a ranch," she said to Chance. "What's that like?"

"Come by and I'll give you a tour," he drawled. "If you're interested in riding, I can teach you."

"Or I can," Sawyer said, looking over his shoulder, a spatula in his hand.

Chance looked from Sawyer to her and then back to Sawyer. "So, it's like that?"

"It's definitely like that," Sawyer said, before looking back at the grill and flipping a burger.

Summer touched Paisley's hand. "You and Sawyer are a thing?"

She bit her lip. "I guess so. I mean, yes. We are. This is really new to me. I'm not sure exactly how to handle it. Or questions about us."

"You won't find a better guy than Sawyer," Autumn said. "If he weren't my cousin, I would be madly in love with him. He's the most reliable guy in the world. Everyone in Hawthorne adores him."

"He took me skydiving," she revealed.

"What?" Summer and Autumn said in unison.

"This is something I've got to hear about," Jace said, leaning forward. "I've never been. Is it as amazing as they say?"

Paisley beamed. "It's way better."

"Don't tell us about it now," Eli warned. "Otherwise, you're just going to have to retell it at dinner when everyone's here."

That's exactly what she did, with Sawyer chiming in, adding more details. Everyone had questions, and they answered them as best they could, recommending Andy to the group.

Darby, who had come outside to hand her husband another beer, patted her belly. "Maybe that's how I'll celebrate after having Sam." She looked to Paisley. "Sam is my dad's name. I really wanted it for our baby."

"I wanted it, too, but my little sister beat me to having the first boy," Sawyer said. "Maybe I'll reserve Andrew since that was Dad's middle name."

"We're going with Sarah Elizabeth for our baby," Autumn told Paisley. "That's the names of our two grandmothers."

As the conversation drifted from babies, she fell silent. It was way too soon to think about babies—and babies with Sawyer—but the name Andrew really stuck with her.

Andrew Montgomery.

That would be a wonderful name for a baby boy.

Suddenly, she felt eyes on her and turned, seeing Sawyer looking at her. He winked, causing her to blush, and she wondered if he had any idea where her thoughts had traveled.

Jace yelled at the TV, forcing Paisley's thoughts to other topics. Others also started cheering, and she saw a swimming event was coming to a conclusion. An Australian and American swimmer were vying for the win, and the American touched first, causing everyone to cheer. She supposed this is what it was like all across America—and the world. People cheering for the athletes representing their home countries. Paisley had been a part of the Olympics for so long that she hadn't really thought about fans at home, at gatherings such as these, watching and cheering.

"That was amazing," Summer said. "What a finish!" She looked to Paisley. "Could you tell us what playing in the Olympics is like?"

Sawyer caught her eye, but she shook her head imperceptibly. "I'd be happy to."

"Burgers are ready to come off the grill," West called.

They gathered in a large dining room inside the house, and she happily shared some about her Olympic experiences.

"I hope you don't mind if we have on the game later," Eli

said, empathy in his eyes. "I know you should've been there, repping the US."

"I'm actually looking forward to watching and not playing," she said honestly. "I had my time in the sun. It's time for others to shine."

After dinner, they moved to the great room, large enough to easily seat them all. Sawyer took a seat beside her, his arm going about her, claiming her as his. As they watched Team USA beat Brazil in the first round, Paisley decided that while she had enjoyed her Olympic days, she was also enjoying this new life in Hawthorne. The food. The fellowship.

And the man next to her.

If anyone would have told her that she would prefer sitting on a love seat and watching the first game being played rather than being a player in it, she would have thought them crazy. It was funny how fast things had changed. Contentment filled her as she shouted at the screen, yelling at the refs, and cheering as former teammates of hers made basket after basket.

Paisley had discovered a home in Hawthorne. She was also learning things about herself, thanks to Dr. Linda and her relationship with Sawyer.

This second chapter in life might just become her favorite one.

CHAPTER
Fourteen

Despite it being the first day of school, Paisley already felt comfortable at Hawthorne High School. She had spent countless hours in the weeks leading up to today in her office and the gym. She had met the new hires during their orientation sessions and had also been introduced to the entire staff during the past week of teacher training for the upcoming school year.

Darby had been great, easing the way for Paisley by introducing her to so many others. West had also been gracious, making certain she felt comfortable in coaching staff meetings. He'd also spent several hours with her, going over her specific responsibilities as a head coach, covering everything from what was expected when traveling to away games to budget requirements to how concessions were handled at home games.

She felt confident today because of Darby and West's help. Paisley also had met a few of her players at a park last week when she and Sawyer had been out walking after dinner one evening. A pickup game took place on one of the public courts, and they had watched it for a few minutes, with Sawyer pointing out a couple of girls who would be playing for her this year. She recognized them from the yearbooks Darby had provided.

The two players who stood out the most, though, were ones who had decided to walk away from the team. Paisley watched Desiree Sonato and Sheila Briggs in action and practically salivated at their ball skills. If she could convince even one of them to return to the Lady Hawks, her job would be much easier, and the team would have a better chance at notching more than a couple of wins.

When the game ended, she had introduced herself to some of the girls on the court. Desi and Sheila avoided her, quickly retrieving their water bottles and walking away. Others, though, were nice enough to stick around and talk with her and Sawyer. While she ached to get out on the court and start teaching them, Paisley knew she couldn't cross the line drawn by the UIL and told the teenagers she would see them when school started.

That day had now arrived.

First period was her JV team. These girls were mostly freshmen, new to the high school and eager to play. She had borrowed last year's team photos from Marsha so that she knew all of these players by name. Paisley talked about what it meant to be a team. A team player. She told them the skills they would be working on this year. Then she turned things over to Hope. Her assistant would take more of an active leadership role with these players.

While Paisley would still be their head coach, she would leave many of the daily decisions in Hope's hands, from how practices were run to play calling during a game. She wanted her assistant to stretch her wings and grow under Paisley's tenure. Every assistant dreamed of becoming a head coach one day, and she wanted to prepare Hope for when that opportunity arose.

The school day was divided into six periods. After first period with her JV, Paisley had a girls PE class second period, followed by a boys PE class third period. These were students who didn't play a sport, march in the band, or participate in drill team or cheerleading, all activities which earned a PE credit. She didn't expect any of these students to be great athletes, but she wanted to give them an appreciation for various sports, along with instilling in them that activity at any age was good and made for a healthier life. She explained to both PE sections how they would cover various sports, learning the rules and playing everything from volleyball to soccer to basketball during this school year. Her PE classes would also do units where they performed yoga and Pilates, with a little meditation thrown in for mental well-being.

After those two PE classes, she had her teacher conference period during lunch and a coaching conference period she shared with Hope and other coaches. It would be good to be free at the same time other coaches were. She hoped to learn from them. Although they coached sports different from hers, they had common ground in wanting to do their best for their student athletes.

Her last period was when she and Hope met with the varsity squad. When the bell rang ending fifth period, she felt the nerves flitting through her. They were the good kind, though, not something she dreaded. Paisley looked forward to this first official meeting between her and her players and hoped she wouldn't disappoint them.

She had the girls assemble in the bleachers and noticed other students scattered about. Hope had explained that seniors who had enough credits to graduate had the option for a senior out, where they didn't have a class scheduled during the first or last period of the day. It allowed them to sleep in or leave early in case they had a job they needed to get to. Hope said some students shared rides with others who had to be here during those classes, though, and they would hang around the gyms, cafeteria, or library, catching up on homework or simply relaxing.

Desiree Sonato and Sheila Briggs were two of those seniors who were in the bleachers now, far enough apart not to be mistaken as members of her varsity team—yet close enough to hear what Paisley would have to say to them.

Ignoring the two former players, she smiled as the bell rang and her team stopped chattering, focusing their attention on her.

"It's nice to finally meet the varsity Lady Hawks. I'm Coach Roberts." She indicated Hope. "You already know Coach Sewell. She'll be taking on a larger role in the program this year."

"What was it like, playing in the Olympics?" asked Effie Compton, a junior who played center.

"I don't want to dwell on me," Paisley said, even as she read the disappointment on the faces of her players.

Then she realized she should share more of herself with them, just as Dr. Linda had done. That had made Paisley want to be more open and trusting of the therapist. The same lesson could apply here with her players.

"But I'm happy to spend a few minutes answering your questions before we get started."

Looking at Effie, she said, "There's nothing that compares to the Olympics. I played in championship games in both high school and college, and the Olympics are simply magical."

Paisley went on to describe the feeling of entering a stadium in a foreign country, the rest of Team USA marching alongside you. What it felt like to live in the Olympic village. How competing in an Olympic game drove you to new levels.

"It's a true honor to play for your country," she concluded. "Your teammates are the best athletes in your sport from your home country, and you're playing against others of the same caliber from around the world. When you notch a win, you see a sea of faces cheering you on. Not just from the US, but from other countries. People who are merely fans of the sport. Who relish seeing the best players on the planet competing against one another."

Paisley smiled. "And a lump comes to your throat when you witness those USA flags waving in the stands. You realize you're part of a team, but you're also part of the bigger picture. You're an American, proud to be one, representing your country on the world stage."

She saw every eye round with wonder.

"But playing in the Olympics is just one stair step in a list of goals. Very few athletes have that as an objective, but every athlete should set goals. That's what we're going to do now."

Nodding to Hope, her assistant started passing out note cards and envelopes. As she did, Paisley continued speaking.

"You're going to write down your goals for this year. Putting something in writing always makes it seem more real. Makes you more accountable to that goal. Do we reach every goal we set? Of course not. But the journey to those goals is what's really important."

She looked around, seeing everyone had a card now.

And that Desi and Sheila were trying not to look interested.

"On your note card, I want you to list three goals for this school year. One academic. One regarding basketball. And one personal. We'll seal the note card inside an envelope, and I'll pass them out to you at the spring sports banquet."

"Why are we doing this?" asked Roberta Gaffen, a junior point guard, looking confused.

"To learn more about yourself," she replied. "To make you think about what's really important to you. Believe me, we'll be setting goals each week for our play on the court. You might aim to hit half your shots one week. Set a goal to bring up your number of assists per game the next. Want to learn how to execute a certain play better. Every week, I'll meet with you individually, and we'll discuss what your goal—or goals—are for that week. As I said, reaching for a goal doesn't mean you'll always attain it, but it can make you a better player. And a better person."

Paisley took a deep breath. "Okay. I want everyone to think now and then list an academic goal for this year. Yes, you're an athlete, but you're a student first. Set an academic goal for yourself. Maybe it's making the A or B honor roll. Getting into National Honor Society. Think. Write it down."

She gave them adequate time to do so, seeing the girls really thinking before they wrote.

"Next, your basketball goal."

"Is it for the team or us as an individual player?" asked Ashley Phillips, a senior forward.

"Why don't we do both?" she said.

Ashley looked at her blankly. "You mean ... we can?"

"It's a good suggestion, Ashley. I like input from my team."

Paisley heard a snort coming from the direction of where Desi and Sheila sat. She ignored it.

"I think collaboration is key," she continued. "I'll talk more about that in a minute. Right now, ladies, write down a goal for the team and a personal goal for you as a player."

She gave them much longer this time since they were

thinking about two separate goals. Finally, Paisley said, "Okay. Last goal is personal."

"I'm confused," Tessie Zelman said. "I just wrote down a personal one."

"No, you set a personal goal as a player," she said. "As an athlete, maybe you're aiming to become a starter. Or make the all-district team. Those are athletic goals for you as an individual. What I want you to think hard about now is a personal goal."

"Like?" Tessie pressed. "I still don't get it."

"Let me give you an example or two." Paisley paused, collecting her thoughts. "Personal goals are to make you a better *you*. Your objective could be to listen more than you speak. Read a book—once a week or once a month. Decide to take over a responsibility at home. Maybe do your own laundry or take out the garbage on trash days. It could be to spend thirty minutes a week with a little brother or sister. Limit yourself to an hour a day on social media. You could set a goal to learn something new. It's better if your goal isn't generic like that. Instead, say what you want to learn to do. Is it learn how to make a chocolate cake or French braid your hair? Maybe it could be to cut out soft drinks or say a prayer of gratitude each day.

"This is about you. Not academic or athletic. Just you."

Paisley watched her team really think about this one. Slowly, each girl began writing. She glanced and saw Desi and Sheila seemed more than interested now.

Good.

"Okay, when you finish writing, place your cards in the envelope Coach Sewell gave to you. Put your name and date on the front and seal it. As I said, you'll get these back next spring."

"You won't look at them?" Effie asked.

"No. They're your goals. Not mine. I did mention, however, I would meet with you weekly about that week's goal. Mostly, those will be sports-oriented. Specific to what you wish to accomplish that week in practice or in an upcoming game. Your goals will fluctuate as your skills improve. That's why we'll chat each week for a couple of minutes."

Roberta suggested, "I think after we talk with you, Coach Roberts, we should talk as a team each week. See what we want to accomplish as a group. If we're united in our goal as a team, we'll be better on the court."

Paisley beamed. "I like that, Roberta. That's awesome. We'll definitely do that. And that leads into what I have to say next." She looked to Hope. "Coach, will you collect the envelopes?"

As Hope started gathering the envelopes, Paisley said, "I know you're coming off a rough time with Coach Finnerty."

"She was—"

"Nope. Not going there, Ashley," she said firmly. "I don't deal with negativity. I've heard a few stories. I know how you were punished for things which weren't infractions. For some of you, the love of the game was sucked from you. It led to some of your teammates leaving the team."

Paisley paused. "I can't change yesterday. But I can help you today—and tomorrow."

She let that sink in a moment, knowing that Desi and Sheila were also listening as closely as her players were.

"You aren't going to trust me off the bat. And you shouldn't. But know I have both the varsity and JV teams' best interests at the heart in everything I do. I want to prove myself to you, and I hope you'll give me the benefit of a clean slate, because that's what you have with me. Besides trust, I believe in collaboration. Coach Sewell and I already have a fantastic working relationship. I'm also working closely with Coach Zelman at the middle school."

She set a foot on the bottom bleacher and leaned forward, her forearms on her thigh, seeing Tessie's pleased smile at the mention of her mom.

"I want to collaborate with each of you, as well. If you have an idea for a play, bring it to me. If you have an exercise you do which is a better stretch, let me know. We'll incorporate it into our workout. I want your suggestions and will build on those. As I learn more about you as players—both your physical skills and your mental toughness—I'll design plays which are tailored to your talents."

Paisley paused, looking out at her team, already so proud of these girls.

"We're going to come to know one another very well. We're going to build trust. Learn the basics. Develop the skills you have and add new ones to your repertoire. Push you to perform better than you ever have. I promise that I'll listen to you. If you come back to the huddle during a time-out and tell me something's happening on the floor, I'll want you to share it with the team. You're out there in the thick of things. You'll see things I'll miss. You're my eyes and ears on the court. Time-outs are not just for me to share the next play with you. It's for you to communicate with me and your teammates about what we need to do to win."

She stood again. "I believe in winning. On the court and in life. I want you to walk away from this program feeling good about yourself. About your contributions to this team. I want you to be a good basketball player, but I also want you to be a good person. I hope we'll teach each other some lessons that go beyond the court. Life skills which you'll use in the near and far future. We're in this together. No one will be blamed for a loss. We are a team. We stand as a team. We win and lose as a team. The culture of Lady Hawks basketball is one in which we ask ourselves to be better today than we were the day before. To be better people. Better players. Better teammates. And I guarantee you, when you do that, you will shine, as will everyone around you."

Warmth filled Paisley as she saw the genuine smiles on her players' faces.

"Our culture is one of learning. Of respecting ourselves and others. Our objective is to be the best version of ourselves today. We aren't going to get caught up in what happened yesterday or last month or last year. We'll focus on today. We'll set our goals for the future. And by being a little better each day, it will add up. I guarantee you that by the end of this year, you'll like who you are—and what you've accomplished."

It touched her when the team broke out in spontaneous applause. She waved it away.

"I'm here for you. Coach Sewell is here for you. And you're here for each another. Tomorrow, we'll dress out and begin practice. You know UIL rules. We'll practice as a team during sixth period each day until mid-October, when we can start holding practices outside school hours. We'll talk more about that later. I want to emphasize that my door is always open to you. If you want to share something you've learned. Ask me about something. Or if you just need an ear. I'm a pretty good listener."

Paisley named the star player from the most recent Olympics, one who had led Team USA to another gold medal.

"I've listened to her for years. Even she has doubts sometimes. Everyone needs a friendly ear." She smiled. "I hope we're not just a team. I hope that we'll feel like family. Now, go see Coach Sewell. She's got the list of lockers and codes to assign. You'll also receive your workout clothes from her, and she'll issues shoes, too. I'll see you here tomorrow, same time. Be ready to work hard and play hard. Dismissed."

As the girls climbed down the bleachers, every one of them stopped to speak to her. Paisley felt grateful that she would spend many hours of school year with this small group of teenagers. There weren't a lot of them, but they would form the core she would build on.

"Nice job, Coach," West said.

"Thanks," Paisley said. "I didn't see you here."

"I wanted to check in. Heard your talk with the team. Damn, but you're a great motivator. I'm already afraid I'm going to lose you. That you'll be a one-and-done and head to the next division level."

"Nope. You've given me a great opportunity, West. I plan to make Hawthorne home for as long as you want me here."

He placed a hand on her shoulder and squeezed. "Good to know." Then more quietly, he said, "I think you might've hooked a couple of big fish with your inspiring words."

West told her goodbye, and Paisley saw Desi and Sheila studying her. Desi leaned over and spoke to her friend, and Sheila nodded. Both teens stood and climbed down the bleachers.

"Hey, Desi. Sheila. You must have senior out this period," she said, trying not to get her hopes up.

"We do," Desi said coolly, studying Paisley for a moment. "Did you mean everything you said, or was all that just rah-rah, make everyone feel good shit?"

She didn't call out Desi for cursing because she knew the senior was testing her.

"I spoke from my gut—and my heart. I stand by everything I said."

"You actually want to have players suggest plays to you?" Desi pressed.

"Of course. Doesn't mean I'll use all of them, but I'll use as many as might help the team. That's why I also want to create plays which let players shine." She paused. "I've watched film of you." She glanced to Sheila. "You, too. You're both talented players. It's a shame you aren't playing this year because we could certainly use you."

Paisley walked a fine line now. She wanted to convince these two to return to the Lady Hawks but didn't want to appear too eager.

"I don't know if either of you intend to go to college, but there's the chance you could earn an athletic scholarship if you decide to play."

"My mom and dad definitely want me to go to college," Sheila volunteered. "Money's tight, though. I'll probably stay home and do some online courses." She hesitated. "But if I had a chance for an athletic scholarship, that would be great."

"They don't come easy. Sometimes, it's not a full ride but a partial scholarship," Paisley said. "But I will do everything in my power to help you reach your full playing potential, Sheila." She looked back at the other girl. "You, too, Desi."

Desi's mouth hardened. "My mom died last year. Lung cancer. She worked in the cafeteria here. My dad's the custodian at HHS. They don't pay him enough for all the work he does. We don't have a lot left over."

"So, if you want to go to college, it's either on an academic or athletic scholarship then?'

"Yeah."

Desi still seemed hesitant to commit, so Paisley said, "While I believe in discipline, I don't believe the kind of discipline doled out last year was beneficial to anyone on the team. If that's keeping you from playing this year, don't let it, Desi."

Paisley took a deep breath. "I was a foster kid. I grew up in the system and was never adopted. I knew I could only depend upon myself if I wanted to make it to college. So I studied like crazy and spent the rest of my time in the gym, perfecting my basketball skills. College was my way out. I earned my degree. I also got the chance to play professionally. Now, I'm putting my degree to use by teaching. You're really talented, Desi. You have basketball smarts. I've watched film on you and can see how quickly you make decisions on the court. You also back up those decision with superb ball handling and leadership skills.

"I'd be proud to coach you and Sheila."

The two girls looked at one another. Both faced her again.

"We want to come back, Coach Roberts," Desi said firmly. "But if you aren't the real deal, we walk."

"I can accept that," she said. "Go get your locker assignments and practice clothes from Coach Sewell. I'll go to the office and talk to your counselors about changing your schedules. You'll need to get your physicals and be cleared to play before you can officially be a part of the team, though. You'll also have some paperwork to fill out. I'll get that for you now."

"Coach Sutherland will help us schedule the physicals," Desi said.

For the first time, she saw excitement on the teenager's face.

"Thanks for handling that, Desi. I appreciate you and Sheila wanting to be a part of this team again. I know your teammates will be happy you're ready to contribute."

Paisley went into the office and pulled copies for the two returning players to fill out and sign.

She leaned in and quietly told Hope, "Desi and Sheila are at the end of the line. They've decided to be a part of things."

Hope played it cool. "Got it, Coach. Next."

Once she had given the former players the paperwork, she headed to the office. As she did, she pulled out her phone. Her first instinct was to share this news with Sawyer.

And that told her everything she needed to know about how she felt about their relationship.

Things had been heating up with them physically since that first kiss, but they hadn't made love yet. She had been hesitant. Not because she didn't have feelings for Sawyer. She definitely did. What she worried about more was commitment. Her only commitment had been to basketball and her studies. Yet suddenly Sawyer was taking up more room in her heart.

It was time to do something about it. Not just tell him she cared for him.

Show him.

She had already called him during her lunch break to thank him for the bouquet of flowers he had sent to celebrate her first official day at Hawthorne High School. Now, she dialed his number again.

He answered on the first ring. "Has a riot begun at school? Are teachers angry their boyfriends and husbands didn't think to send them flowers for the first day of classes? More importantly, will I get any clients out of this?"

She laughed. "No riots. No clients. Just one very grateful girlfriend with some good news."

"Spill."

"Nope. I want to see your face when I share it with you."

"I guess that means we're having dinner together tonight."

"I'm in the mood for barbeque. How about I stop at BBQ Bliss and bring something over?"

"I say yes, to you and the barbeque. I'm meeting with a client at four-thirty. It shouldn't take long. Just to be on the safe side, be at my place at six, okay?"

"See you then," she said.

Paisley put her phone back in her pocket. This first day of classes had been a good one. Way better than she'd thought. The idea of sharing how her day had gone with Sawyer over dinner made her glow inside.

And then she was ready to kick their relationship into high gear.

CHAPTER
Fifteen

Sawyer locked up his office at four-fifteen and drove to Bill Packman's place. It had been a good couple of weeks for him professionally. He had gained several new clients and been to court twice. Most of the law he practiced now was family law, dealing with things related to a family and domestic issues. He handled the creation of things such as wills, pre-nups, adoptions, and child custody issues.

He hadn't found any paperwork in Isaiah Smith's files regarding Bill Packman. He had met Bill several months ago at Dizzy's diner. They were both eating alone and sitting at tables next to one another, so Sawyer had invited Bill to join him. They gray-headed older man was full of interesting stories, including several about his wildcatting days in oil. He had seen Bill a few other places around town, usually at lunch, and had always taken a moment to speak with him. Sawyer supposed today's meeting was to discuss writing a will.

It had surprised him when Bill asked if they could meet

at his house instead of Sawyer's office, but he didn't mind making a house call. Bill lived only a few blocks from the house Sawyer was now renting, so he would be even closer to home.

And Paisley.

He was glad she had appreciated his gesture of sending flowers to her on her first day of school. He hadn't been sure if it would go over well with her or not. Although they were seeing each other exclusively, he still felt she was a bit tentative about their relationship. The fact that she had referred to herself on the phone as his girlfriend had bolstered his spirits, though.

Once he arrived at Bill's house, he noted it was a modest brick with a neatly manicured lawn and lush flower beds. Bill was standing in front of one of the flower beds, a hose in his hand as he hand-watered marigolds and zinnias.

Sawyer climbed from his car and called a greeting.

"Just giving my babies an extra drink," Bill said genially as Sawyer approached. "Let's go inside and have ourselves some lemonade."

Bill turned off the water, and they entered the house. To the left, which would usually serve as a living room, was an office. To the right, the dining room stood empty of furniture, which he found a bit curious.

He followed Bill into the kitchen and took a seat at the table while his host poured tall glasses of lemonade for them.

Setting the glasses on the table, the older man said, "Crushed ice in here. Makes everything taste better, in my opinion. I buy a bagful of it at Sonic each week. Best money I spend."

"Lemonade is always good in the summer," Sawyer agreed. "It can make a hot day better."

They spoke for a few minutes about things going on in

Hawthorne, and then he asked, "Why am I here, Bill? What do you need a lawyer for?"

"I need a good one and think you fit the bill. I've researched you on the internet, and you'll do."

He bit back a smile at the backhanded compliment. "Well, I'm glad to hear that, Bill. What services are you interested in me providing to you?"

"I'm seventy-two. In good health. But that can change quickly. A fall where you break a hip. A sudden heart attack. I need to make some end-of-life arrangements and get my finances in order. Tie a bow on everything, if you will. I shouldn't have let it go this long without doing anything, but I'm ready to finally get started."

Sawyer opened the briefcase he had brought, pulling out a yellow legal pad to take notes.

"You're going to need a will. We can also talk about a general and medical power of attorney. Who would be in charge of making those decisions if you're incapacitated. Even a living will, if you're interested in that. I can explain each of these things to you. Do you have your beneficiaries in mind? Someone to serve as the executor of your estate? Your executor acts in the best interests of you, the deceased, to settle your estate as efficiently as possible. That being said, they can also be a beneficiary. It's more common than you think."

Bill gave him a sad smile. "There's no one but me, Sawyer. I never married. Never fathered a child. A long time ago, I fell in love with a pretty little thing. I was young and immature, though, and didn't think I was ready to settle down. She was. When I told her I wasn't ready for marriage, she moved on. Married a solid guy. Had three kids."

A faraway look came into Bill's eyes. "She's gone now. And I regret every day that I was fool enough to walk away and not make her mine. No one came close to touching my heart after her. I concentrated on my career. Making money. Lots of it. I told you some of my stories about the old days and oil. I became rich off that."

His words surprised Sawyer since the house was so unpretentious. He didn't know when Bill had come to Hawthorne or why and asked that now.

"If you have money, Bill, why did you settle here?"

"I moved around a lot over the years. Made myself and others quite a bit of cash. Lived in Houston a while. Ft. Worth. San Antonio. Big cities never were for me. I came from a small town in West Texas, and I was drawn back to one five years ago. I was driving through Hawthorne after I sold my business, and my gut told me this was the place I'd end my days in."

"Since you don't have a will drawn up, that'll be where we start. If you would like, I can serve as the executor of your estate."

"I like what I've seen of you, Sawyer. If you'd be willing to step up and hold the power of attorney for my financial and medical needs, as well as act as executor of my estate, it would give me peace of mind. I know I do want one of those DNRs. Do Not Resuscitate. There's no sense in prolonging my time on earth when the end comes. Nobody's going to miss me."

"Don't sell yourself short, Bill. I see you at lunch and around town with others. You always have a smile on your face, brightening someone's day. You enjoy others' company, and they enjoy yours."

"I have made some friends here in Hawthorne. I like this town. I like living in a small town. I do want you to talk to me about the difference between a will and a trust, though. Been reading about trusts on the internet."

Sawyer explained how both were ways to acknowledge who would receive Bill's assets, with the chief difference being when they went into effect.

"Nothing happens with a will until you pass. Then your executor notifies the court, and the probate process can begin. With a trust, it goes into effect immediately, the moment you sign and fund it. With a will, your estate is required to go into probate. That's averaging about nine to ten months in Texas, which means it's almost a year before your affairs can be settled. If we set up a trust for you, it's slightly more complicated than a will, but you can avoid probate altogether."

He paused, letting Bill process what had been said.

"Under a trust, we can set it up for future situations. For example, what should happen if you become physically or mentally unable to make decisions for yourself. It specifies what your wishes are during your lifetime *and* when you're gone, so the guesswork is removed entirely."

His new client nodded thoughtfully, asking a few questions, which Sawyer answered.

"I think I've given you plenty of information for you to think about." He reached into his briefcase and pulled out a manila folder, passing it to Bill. "This contains written information about what we've talked about. I know a lot of people are visual and need to see things to truly understand them. It also gives some examples of situations. If you'll read through what I've included, I think it may help you decide what best suits your needs."

Wrapping up their time together, he said, "Take your time. Review these papers and what your goals are. When you're ready, make another appointment with me. If you have sizeable assets, let's do an entire day together. We can go over things in the morning. I'll have some general templates, and we can adjust them according to your needs and the decisions you've made about your estate. We could take a break and have lunch together. Come back and finish up in the afternoon. How does that sound?"

"I would like some time to mull things through," Bill agreed. "Not too long, though. I've dilly-dallied enough as it is, and I want my money to go to some good causes, especially ones right here in Hawthorne."

Curious, Sawyer asked, "Do you have a ballpark figure of how much your estate and its assets are worth?"

Bill rubbed his chin thoughtfully. "Depends upon where the stock market closes today. I've been investing for years, buying and selling stocks on my own. I'm damned good at it, and pretty lucky, as well. I invested early in things such as Apple. Amazon. I would say probably somewhere between forty and fifty million."

Shock rippled through him. He couldn't believe Packman hadn't planned better. Then again, it sounded as if his new client was a self-made man and had never depended upon financial advisers or attorneys. "We're talking serious money, Bill."

The old man shrugged. "I know. When I lost my girl, every thought I had went into making money. Foolishly, I thought I might even win her back if I became rich. By the time I had enough money to offer her the sun and the moon, she was pregnant with her second child. I knew she was happy, and I wasn't going to tempt her or fate by dangling my worldly goods in front of her. She'd made a good life for herself with a good man. I never contacted her."

Bill sighed. "I do want the money I've amassed to go to good causes, Sawyer. I've been thinking on my own, but I'd like to bend your ear about that. What's your calendar look like?"

He opened his phone and consulted his calendar. "I'm in

court tomorrow. Have two appointments on Wednesday, but Thursday is wide open. Want me to reserve that day for you?"

"Do it," Bill said. "I'll have decided between the will and the trust by then, and we can get those written up. Then discuss which worthy causes need an injection of mad money from old Bill Packman."

The old man rose, a bit unsteadily, and Sawyer did the same, offering his client his hand.

As they shook, Bill said, "I want us to do some great things together, Sawyer. My life doesn't have a legacy of children or good deeds, but I can leave something of myself behind by pouring money into people and places which need it."

"I'll see you at eight o'clock on Thursday, Bill," Sawyer said, closing his briefcase and heading back to his car.

He had heard of people who had made huge fortunes but lived frugal, ordinary lives. He recalled one woman in her nineties who had been the chair of a medical school board in New York. Upon her husband's death, she donated over one billion dollars, and it allowed students to attend that medical school for free. When Melinda French Gates had divorced her husband, she had become a philanthropist in her own right, advocating globally for women with donations of hundreds of millions of dollars to causes, especially ones regarding women's health. Mackenzie Scott had done the same after her marriage to Jeff Bezos dissolved, donating billions to various charitable causes.

What Bill Packman wanted to do was similar in nature. He was a man without family, willing to give back to his community and beyond. It was incredible—and inspiring. The kind of money Bill possessed could seriously change the lives of so many people. When he wasn't busy in court or with clients during the next few days, Sawyer would research some different ideas to present to Bill on how to spread out his client's generous donations, as well as keep the money working for as long as possible.

He arrived home and went inside, changing from his work clothes into a T-shirt and pair of shorts. His attention now went to Paisley and spending a couple of hours with her.

She showed up twenty minutes later, carrying a brown paper sack with handles, the BBQ Bliss logo stamped on the side.

As she set it on the counter, Sawyer reached for her, snagging her by the waist and pulling her to him for a long, slow, heated kiss. Her arms entwined about his neck as she kissed him back.

"I could get used to coming home to something like this," she told him.

Immediately, his thoughts jumped to a future with her, where that very thing happened.

He kissed her again and released her. "I'm starving," he said. "What did you bring us?"

"I couldn't decide, so I got two different sandwiches," she said, pulling them from the bag as he retrieved plates from the cupboard. "One is pulled pork, and the other is sliced brisket. You can have your choice."

"Or we can split them in half and enjoy both."

"You think like a lawyer, Sawyer," she teased. "Sounds good to me."

Paisley removed four different sides from the sack, and they worked on plating the potato salad, mac and cheese, baked beans, and creamed spinach.

She pulled the final container from the bag and held it up. "Banana pudding. If we have room for it, that is. I'll put it in the fridge for now."

"We could always start with it—and go from there," he suggested, waggling his brows, causing her to laugh.

"Dessert first? That's a great idea. We'll have to try it sometime."

All he could think about was having her for dessert.

Paisley took both plates to the table, while he claimed a pitcher of iced tea from the fridge and poured them tall glasses from it. Where he liked a lot of ice, she wanted no more than a fourth of her glass to hold ice. He set the glasses on the table and put the pitcher there, too, knowing he'd drink more than one glass.

"I want to hear your news," he said. "And I've got some of my own."

"You go first. We've talked so much about school stuff for weeks. I want to hear more about your practice."

Knowing he could only speak in generalities because of attorney/client privilege, he said, "I landed a new client today," not giving her Bill's name. "I'm going to be writing up his will and acting as the executor of his estate. He doesn't really have anyone to leave things to, so he's decided he wants to do some good with the money he has."

She placed her hand over his. "I always thought that would be me," she confessed. "Coming to the end of my life and having no one special in it. You've changed that for me, Sawyer. You and Hawthorne." Paisley's eyes misted with tears.

"I'm glad you've found a home here," he said huskily. "I hope you'll stay for a long time."

They gazed into one another's eyes, and Sawyer sensed things shifting between them. Becoming more serious. He wanted to pick her up and set her in his lap and kiss her for hours, but he had learned to take his cues from her. Paisley was surrendering to him in small increments, and he wasn't going to jeopardize things by pushing her too hard or fast.

"So, what's the big news coming out of HHS?" he asked, trying to lighten the mood as he took a bite of the brisket sandwich.

"With it being the first day, none of my classes dressed out. I met with JV first period. They're a bright, eager bunch of girls. My PE classes are going to be fun. They seemed appreciative of the different units I'm going to cover with them. It surprised me, but several of the boys said they were really interested in yoga when I included that in my overview of the course."

Her eyes sparkled now. "And then came last period and the varsity team."

Sawyer listened as Paisley told him she had addressed the team sitting in the bleachers.

"I talked to them about the culture I want to create. I had them set goals for the year. Guess who was listening the entire time?"

She beamed at him and answered before he could reply. "Desi Sonato and Sheila Briggs."

He frowned. "Why were they there? I thought they'd left the team."

"They had senior out—and just happened to be hanging around the gym, close enough to hear everything I said to the team."

Sawyer had taken advantage of senior out his last year of high school, sleeping in and not reporting to school until second period started at nine-thirty. It had been especially nice when the basketball team had a road game the night before and he'd gotten in late. He remembered that other students with senior out had gone in sometime during first period, sitting in the cafeteria or the gym, leisurely eating breakfast as they talked and finished up their homework.

"I'm assuming they liked what they heard by the look on your face," he said.

"They did. Just watching film of those two girls, they are true players at heart with a love for the game. It must have killed them to walk away from a team and sport they love. I could see in Desi's eyes, though, that she was interested in what I want to build with this year's Lady Hawks. While Sheila is a talented player in her own right, she is very much a follower. If Desi hadn't wanted to come back to the team, Sheila wouldn't be there."

Paisley smiled. "But they're both a part of it now. I made it official, talking to their counselors and having their schedules updated to reflect the change. It's not as though they needed the extra credit they would receive, but I need everything to be above board for UIL purposes. I don't want to have to forfeit a single game. Now, Desi and Sheila are officially members of the team."

"How did their teammates react?"

"I don't know this firsthand because I was in the office, but Hope issued lockers and athletic practice wear to the players. She said everyone was thrilled to have those two seniors back on the team. More importantly, both Desi and Sheila asked Hope for note cards so they, too, could record their goals for the year, just as their teammates had done. That lets me know they really bought into what I said."

They finished eating and cleaned up the kitchen, and then Sawyer said, "I guess since it's a weekday, we need to make an early night of it."

Paisley's gaze met his. "No. I told you I was coming over to celebrate. Not just my first day of school and reclaiming two star players for my team. I want to celebrate *us*, Sawyer."

His mouth went dry. "Exactly how are we going to do that?"

"By doing something I've been longing to do ever since I met you."

She reached out and took his hands in hers, gripping them tightly.

"I want to make love with you, Sawyer."

CHAPTER
Sixteen

Paisley watched surprise flash in Sawyer's hazel eyes, but almost immediately, they turned green.

Hot with desire ...

Still, he didn't leap into action. His fingers squeezed hers gently. "This is a big step, Paisley. Huge. I don't want you to have any regrets about this decision. I'm happy to wait."

"I'm ready," she assured him. Then, speaking from her heart, she told him, "I've been waiting for you my entire life, Sawyer Montgomery."

What she didn't say was that not only did she want to experience lovemaking with Sawyer as her first partner—she wanted him to be her last. Though they hadn't known one another long, her gut told her this man was for her. That together, they would make an incredible team.

But first, they had this hurdle to cross. They were compatible in every way, but Paisley knew a physical relationship was something important in a lasting one. She only hoped Sawyer could look past her inexperience and that they would click.

He leaned in, his hands still holding hers, and gave her a long, sweet kiss. In it, he promised her that she would be all right. That he would take good care of her as she crossed into something unknown.

Paisley couldn't think of a better person to introduce her to sex than this tall, handsome, caring man.

Breaking the kiss, he smiled at her. "I guess it's a good thing I recently invested in a box of condoms."

"Did you buy them here?" she blurted out. She shouldn't care if people in Hawthorne knew she was having sex with her boyfriend, but she still worried. Just a little bit. Gossip thrived in a small town.

He released her hands and framed her face. "Actually, I was in Decatur on business when I stopped at a Walmart." His thumbs caressed her cheeks. "I wanted to be prepared for when this time came."

Sawyer bent, lightly brushing his lips against hers. Paisley stepped into him, bringing her arms around him, wanting to be near him. Touching him. Feeling his heat. Inhaling his scent.

Suddenly, he swept her into his arms, carrying her from the room. Her heart quickened, knowing he headed to his bedroom. Her mouth grew dry. Worry seized her.

As he entered the bedroom and set her on her feet again, she asked, "What if I'm not enough for you? I may not be any good at this, Sawyer. You might not—"

He silenced her with a long, drugging kiss, which caused the blood to rush to her head. She heard her heartbeat pounding in her ears, and she responded, kissing him back with everything she had. Heat rushed through her now, rippling along her limbs.

She broke the kiss and gazed up at him. "We're really going to do this?"

He gave her a boyish grin. "We really are." He brushed his lips against her brow, the gesture comforting her. "It won't be perfect. Not because it's your first time. Because it's *our* first time together. No couple gets it right the first time. We have to learn what the other person likes. And learn what we like to do together. The more practice we get, the better we'll become at pleasing each other and enjoy making love together."

"I guess it's like dribbling," she observed, causing him to chuckle. "The first time you try it, you don't know how hard to push on the ball each time. The harder you push, the higher it bounces. You have to find a rhythm that suits you."

"Exactly," he agreed. "Then when you get good at dribbling, you have to learn how to do it when you walk. Then when you run down a court. A good ballplayer will also learn how to dribble with both hands eventually, so they're comfortable with using either and switching from one hand to another. That'll be us and lovemaking, Paisley. I promise you it will be good this first time, but we'll keep at it. Get better. Find what's enjoyable."

She grinned at him. "I've always liked practicing. Getting better at something. And you will be the best partner to teach me what you know."

His hands smoothed her hair. "I do have more experience at this, but as I said, it'll be different from what I've done before because I'm making love with you. You'll have to use your voice, just like you do out on the court. Tell me what you like. What you don't. We can try anything. What pleases us now may give way to something even better down the line. That's the beauty in a physical relationship. We'll have our go-to moves, as we did on the court, but we'll continually try new things."

He kissed her lightly. "I think we're going to be really great together."

"We are," she said, her confidence beginning to soar, along with desire.

Sawyer kissed her again. While they had kissed a lot, these kisses seemed even more heated, knowing what the end game would be. She had thought they would immediately shed their clothes and get into bed, but that wasn't the case. They kissed for a long time, the heat magnifying between them as they did. His hands ran along her back and then dipped inside her T-shirt, continuing to move against her bare skin. All the while, his tongue mated with hers, causing her heart to race.

She repeated his action, her hands slipping inside his shirt, her palms flat against his chest, moving along his flat belly. His breath hitched, and she smiled, secretly pleased that she could move him. She allowed her palms to rotate in small circles, moving up his chest, brushing against his nipples, which were hard. She realized her own were the same and suddenly longed for his hands on them.

Thinking about what he'd told her, she wasn't afraid to ask him anything and said, "Touch my nipples."

"Gladly."

He unclasped her bra in the back and slid his fingers to her front, raising the bra slightly as they pushed under it. The pads of his fingers traced circles around her nipples, causing them to ache. Need pooled in her belly as he then brushed them against her nipples, back and forth, causing her heart to beat erratically.

"Like that?" he murmured against her mouth, still kissing her.

"Yes," she said, breathless.

Then he rolled her nipples and tweaked them. She gasped, feeling a hot spark.

"Good?" he asked.

"Good. Really good.

"Let's get your shirt off," he suggested, stepping back and lifting the hem up and over her head before peeling away her bra.

Though she stood bare to the waist, she felt no embarrassment, which surprised her.

"Let's get your shirt off," she echoed, causing him to smile as she pulled off his, tossing it to the ground.

Her eyes roamed over his muscular chest, liking what she saw. She began stroking it lightly with her fingers, dancing them up and down before brushing the back of them against his rock-hard abs. He shuddered.

"Good?" she asked.

"Good," he assured her. "Keep talking when you want something. Ask me. Tell me. We're learning about each other's bodies. The more we communicate, the better it will be."

They kissed again, their bodies pressed together, her breasts squished against his hard chest. She wrapped her arms around his neck, pulling him as close to her as she could, reveling as he deepened the kiss. Her core was now pounding violently, and she took his hand, moving it so he cupped her.

"I need you to touch me here. A lot."

Smiling, he said, "I can do that. A lot."

He slipped his hands into the waistband of her shorts, easing them over her hips, letting them drop. He held her as she stepped out of them, leaving her only wearing panties. Her breath now came in spurts, anticipating what was to come.

"Have you ever pleasured yourself?" he asked.

She felt her face flush. "I've got a vibrator. That's all I've ever used."

His grin turned wicked. "You are like a blank canvas. I can't wait to put my mark on you."

The words caused butterflies to erupt in her, their wings beating rapidly, causing her to go lightheaded.

Taking her hand, he led her to the bed, neatly made in a very Sawyer-like fashion. He threw back the comforter and then the sheets before grasping her waist and guiding her to sit on the mattress. Nudging her to her back, her legs now dangled from the bed.

His gaze met hers. "Trust me."

"I do."

He knelt, draping her long legs over his shoulders, pushing her thighs farther apart. She felt heat flood her face, knowing he saw her now as no one ever had. He held her gaze as his fingers parted her folds, running up and down the seam of her sex, causing her to grow dizzy.

"You're going to come. I want to see you when you do," he said roughly, his voice causing shivers to dance along her spine.

He sank a finger deep into her, causing her to gasp. Slowly, it stroked her. His other hand remained palm down on her belly, holding her in place. Soon, she began to writhe, his finger joined by a second one, making magic happen.

"Small, shallow breaths," he instructed. "You'll feel the orgasm coming."

She did as he said, and she did feel something building inside her. Something delicious and wonderful.

He pressed hard, moving the pad of his thumb in a slow, circular fashion. The feeling continued to grow, little mewls escaping her lips.

Then it hit. Hard. Fast. Almost out of nowhere, even

though she knew something had been coming. Waves of pleasure undulated through her, causing her hips to rise. She bucked against his hand, squeezing his fingers, riding the waves.

Finally, they subsided. She felt limp. All her energy had vanished as she languished on the bed. He slipped his fingers from her, licking them.

Tasting her ...

That erotic thought caused her core to tighten again.

"You taste divine," he said. "Did you like that?"

"Who wouldn't like that?"

"Let's try it another way," he said, mischief dancing in his eyes.

Before she could protest, his hands clasped her thighs, parting them as his head disappeared between her legs. She had no idea what was about to happen but had complete trust in him.

His tongue licked up her seam, and she almost came off the bed. In surprise. In shock.

He repeated the action, moving slowly in the other direction, causing desire to scream within her. Then his tongue pushed inside her, causing her to whimper. She began to moan, her head thrashing back and forth, her hips rising to meet him. The now-familiar feeling grew inside her, and anticipation filled her, knowing now what pleasure would soon spill from her. As he feasted on her, it built, coming to a head, and then exploding inside her.

"Yes!" she cried. "Yes! Yes! Yes! Yes!"

Her body was no longer hers. It was his as she moved, the orgasm tearing through her. As it subsided, he slowly kissed his way back up her body until their mouths fused together. She wrapped her legs around him, pinning him to her, never wanting to let him go.

Time meant nothing as they explored one another's bodies. Touching. Tasting. Kissing. He was lean muscle everywhere, and her fingers delighted in touching him. Kissing him. Licking him. She did everything by instinct, and he made appreciative noises, so she knew he liked what she did to him, just as she reveled in the ways he touched her.

She was aware of his cock. It grew larger and larger until she was afraid it might explode. He moved away from her, opening the drawer to the nightstand, removing a foil packet. He tore it open and sheathed himself as she watched in fascination.

"The next time, I want to do that for you," she said boldly.

"Then I'll let you."

He hovered above her now. "Are you sure this is what you want?"

"I want you inside me more than I've ever wanted anything. *Anything*," she repeated for emphasis.

"Good." His look of satisfaction caused another wave of desire to flood her.

He kissed her deeply, and she could feel his fingers parting her, readying her for him.

"You're slick. Wet. Ready for me," he said, his voice low and possessive.

"Yes. Now," she urged. "Now."

She felt the head of his penis press against her for a moment, and then he thrust deeply into her. Filling her. He stayed still, and she knew he was letting her get used to the feel of him inside her.

Slowly, he began to move. At first, she didn't know if she should also move, but her body responded to his dance. It took a moment, but they found a sweet rhythm. Soon, they danced atop the mattress, kissing, touching, needing, taking.

His finger also entered her, caressing her, circling, even as he drove into her. The tension built within her, and she knew another orgasm was coming. It erupted as he pounded into her, his own hoarse cry sounding with her own as they finished their dance of love in a frenzy. Then he collapsed atop her, and she wrapped her legs and arms about him, holding this precious man to her. She could feel the pounding of his heart, sure he could also feel hers, too.

Gradually, their hearts began to beat more slowly. She threaded her fingers through his hair. He rolled to his side, and they now faced one another. He leaned in for a long, soft kiss.

"How was it?" he asked, his hand now running up and down her bare back languidly.

"Amazing. I don't know how it could get better than this."

"It will," he promised. "We'll learn more about each another. Familiarity will breed an intimacy between us. We'll have our own special love language."

Paisley chuckled. "If it gets any better, it may kill me."

Sawyer scooped her up, his arms enfolded about her. "Then I guess this will be the best way to go. Together," he teased.

Then he sobered. "Paisley. Every kiss. Every touch. This was more than I could have expected."

"I had no expectations going in," she admitted. "Just a little bit of fear that we wouldn't have a spark."

"Oh, we practically burned the bed to the ground," he joked. "We definitely have chemistry. You don't need to worry about that."

"It was good. *We* are good together," she said, knowing in her bones what she said was true. Then without any prior thought, Paisley said, "I love you."

The moment she heard the words, she wanted to take them back.

"I'm sorry. It was too soon to say that. We haven't known one another long enough," she babbled. "Don't feel pressured to say them back. I don't want to force you to—"

His finger pressed against her lips, silencing her. Sawyer gazed deeply into her eyes. A calm descended over her.

"I've wanted to say those words to you, but I was afraid I'd frighten you away. That you wouldn't want to have anything to do with me."

He held her close, her head against his broad chest, her ear pressed so that she heard the loud beat of his heart. He dropped a kiss on the top of her head.

"I love you, Paisley. I cherish you. And I want a life with you. It's not the sex talking. I mean, it was amazing, but my feelings for you have been growing. So fast that it scares the hell out of me. But I can see a future for us."

He tilted her chin up, pressing a soft kiss against her lips. "No promises for now. No heat of the moment declarations about what our future holds. Let's just bask in this moment and know we love one another."

She nodded. "Okay," she said softly, and he kissed her again.

Paisley forced herself to put thoughts of tomorrow aside.

And revel in the here and now of today.

Seventeen

Although they were only a few weeks into the semester, Paisley felt good about everything. For the first time in her life, she was building relationships with many people surrounding her. Her players and students. Other faculty members. Friends she had made in the community.

Most of all, with Sawyer.

Adding a physical dimension to their relationship had definitely changed things between them. It had brought them closer together. The closest she had ever been to anyone was Maggie, during her years at Baylor, but even then, it was a coach/player relationship. What she had with Sawyer was something she was experiencing for the first time. It was hard to use the word love—especially since she had zero experience with it—but that's exactly what she felt.

She loved Sawyer Montgomery.

He was right, though. Their relationship was still new. Both of them were a bit fragile because of their pasts. Hers, from growing up in the foster care system, keeping a wall up to protect herself from being hurt. He had loved before and lost his fiancée in a very tragic way. Sawyer hadn't allowed himself to get close to anyone ever since Elizabeth's death. Paisley should be glad that she was the first, but she worried that he still might not be ready to move on.

She had gone online and looked up Elizabeth. Found that her last name was Pope. Read about the hit-and-run and how Elizabeth was respected by her colleagues in the public defender's office and beyond.

Paisley worried that she wasn't good enough for a man such as Sawyer. She did her best not to compare herself to a dead woman, but it was hard. Elizabeth Pope had been bright. Beautiful. Going places. Next to such an accomplished woman, Paisley wondered if she truly fit with Sawyer because she was so different from Elizabeth.

She had talked about these demons with Dr. Linda this past week, sharing with her therapist that she was in a relationship with Sawyer and that they had gotten serious. Dr. Linda had pointed out that it had been several years since Sawyer had gone out with other women, much less committed to seeing one exclusively. The therapist had told Paisley that she needed to live her life and let Sawyer make his own decisions. Not to push him away because she felt inadequate. Dr. Linda said their relationship would hinge on honesty and communication, and Paisley had finally agreed she would try to keep thoughts of Elizabeth Pope to a minimum.

Especially when she was with Sawyer.

He was going over to West's house at noon to watch the Cowboys play the Eagles, along with a few other friends. Autumn had asked Paisley to have lunch with her, just the two of them. She liked all the women in the circle of friends she had made outside of HHS, but she felt Autumn had a little more insight into her than the others did.

She called in the pizza order they had agreed upon and picked it up on her way to Autumn's house. Her friend greeted her at the door, looking a little tired—and very large.

"I'll take that for you, Paisley."

"I don't want you even carrying a pizza box," she joked. "You look like the baby will be here at any moment."

They went into the kitchen, where Autumn got plates and Paisley poured iced tea for them.

"Ironically, tomorrow is my due date," Autumn informed Paisley. "It would be interesting to be laboring on Labor Day."

The two women sat at the kitchen table, and she asked a few questions about what it was like to be pregnant.

"They say each pregnancy is unique. Kelby and I had different experiences. Same with Darby. Morning sickness may vary from literally occurring in the mornings to suffering it late at night. Some women never experience it at all. Supposedly, every woman's pregnancies can vary from baby to baby. I know my mom said that she was so sick that she couldn't keep anything down for the first four months when she was pregnant with West. Yet when she had Summer and me, she didn't experience a day of nausea."

Autumn sipped her tea. "No one seems to remember to tell you about the awful heartburn, though. I had experienced heartburn before, but I've had it several times in these last few months. They say that's a sign your baby will come out with a headful of hair. It's hard to wash your feet when you get as large as I am. Sleep has also gotten harder the last couple of months. I just can't seem to find a comfortable position. Also, I have to get up and pee three times a night. Minimum. I suppose that's good practice for getting up to check on Sarah Elizabeth."

"I think it's great that you're naming the baby after your two grandmothers."

"I checked with Summer—and West—before I did so. They didn't have a problem with it. Eli and I settled on Sarah Elizabeth instead of Elizabeth Sarah. It just seemed to have a better flow to it. We plan to call her Sarah."

Paisley couldn't help but be happy at hearing that. The less she heard the name Elizabeth, the better.

"It's nice that your baby will be close in age to Kate. And Darby's baby. She told me they're going to name him Sam, after her dad."

Autumn smiled. "Uncle Sam was one of the kindest souls you could meet. It's a shame he won't be here to get to know his grandson. Mom and Dad will do their best to step in and serve as a kind of grandparent to Darby and Sawyer's kids." She eyed Paisley with interest. "Speaking of Sawyer, the two of you seem pretty cozy these days."

She felt herself blushing. "We're seeing one another exclusively."

"Do you see a future with my cousin?" Autumn asked.

"We're trying not to take things too fast, but if I did ever marry, I would want it to be a man just like Sawyer. No," she corrected. "I would want him to be Sawyer."

"Well, it's obvious that he's crazy about you, Paisley. My cousin is cut from the same cloth as his dad was. He's the full package. I'm so glad Sawyer came back to Hawthorne."

Sawyer had told Paisley that he had burned out from the job he held in Dallas. She knew it was because of how Elizabeth's death had affected him. He'd poured so much of himself into his career—and it had almost broken him. She suspected he had come back to Hawthorne, not only to heal emotionally and physically, but to try and leave memories of his fiancée behind. Though insecurity still filled her, she needed to trust that Sawyer was ready to move on, else he wouldn't have asked her out to begin with, much less gotten as serious as they had.

They placed the remainder of the pizza in the fridge, and Autumn took Paisley upstairs to see the nursery. It was large and inviting, done in light pinks and soft grays. She learned that Kelby was responsible for the artwork, which included a mural of animals from Noah's ark on one wall. On another wall, Kelby had stenciled *Sarah Elizabeth.*

They returned downstairs, and Autumn put her hands on her belly, pausing.

"Are you all right?"

"I'm not sure," her friend said. "I had some Braxton-Hicks contractions this past week. They were irregular, though, and when I moved positions, they would stop. I've been feeling small contractions for a few hours now. I just thought it was more of them same. Now, I think they may actual be real ones."

Autumn winced. "Paisley, I do think I'm in labor."

"We should call Eli," she said quickly. "Get you to Triple H."

"That would be a good idea. Would you mind going to our bedroom? There's a carry-on standing by the dresser, all packed for my hospital stay."

"I'll get it now," she said, hurrying to the primary bedroom and collecting the suitcase.

Paisley was returning to the kitchen when she heard Autumn gasp, "Oh!"

Rushing to her, she saw her friend standing next to the kitchen's island, a puddle of water beneath her.

Autumn grinned. "My water broke. I'm officially in labor."

Panic filled her, but Autumn placed a hand on Paisley's

forearm. "Don't worry. We've got plenty of time. First babies usually take their time coming, unlike subsequent kids. I'm going to get out of these damp clothes before we go anywhere."

"Where's your mop?" she asked. "I'll clean up the floor while you do so."

Ten minutes later, they were in Paisley's SUV. As she drove Autumn to the hospital, her friend called her husband.

"Hey, Eli. What's the score? Are the Cowboys winning?"

Paisley couldn't believe how calm Autumn sounded. Then again, it seemed to be in Autumn's nature to be serene and nurturing.

"Ten points? That's great. Listen, I hate to pull you away from the game, but you need to meet me at Triple H. My water just broke. We're going to have our baby today." Autumn laughed. "At least I hope so. By tomorrow, for sure, though."

She couldn't make out what Eli was saying, but it was obvious he was very excited by the noise coming from Autumn's cell.

"No, don't go home. I'm with Paisley. She's driving me to the hospital now." Autumn paused. "Yes, she got the suitcase. I'll see you soon."

"I couldn't help but overhear you saying the baby could come today or tomorrow."

Autumn nodded. "First babies take their time. I could be in labor ten, twenty hours. At least I'm not having to bring two at a time into the world, like Mom did. I still don't know how she managed, especially since West was a toddler at the time, and she already had her hands full with him."

As Autumn fired off a few texts, Paisley pulled up into the circle at ER. A nurse emerged, and Autumn blithely informed the woman that she was in labor, causing the nurse to rush back inside and return with a wheelchair.

While the nurse helped Autumn from the car, Paisley said, "I'll go park the car and bring your bag inside."

She found a parking place and grabbed the carryon, supposing it had not only clothes for Autumn but something for Sarah to wear home from the hospital. She said a quick prayer for both mother and child and then entered through the glass doors.

Autumn was nowhere in sight, so she went to the desk. The receptionist asked, "Are you Paisley?" When she nodded, the woman said, "Autumn has already been taken up to L&D. You can meet her up there."

She gave Paisley the room number, and she went to the bank of elevators, soon finding the room. A nurse asked her to wait outside for a few minutes while they examined Autumn to see how far she had progressed, and then Paisley was allowed inside the room. She placed the suitcase in the corner and went to Autumn, who now wore a hospital gown and thick, cotton socks.

"Shouldn't you be in bed and not in a chair?" she asked, worry filling her.

"I'm able to keep walking for a little bit. That will help labor progress. I'm already dilated to four centimeters."

Paisley looked at her helplessly. "What does that even mean? I know nothing about giving birth."

"When your cervix is dilated to ten centimeters, you can begin pushing to ease the baby from you. Labor can slow down if you're lying in bed, so I want to walk while I can. Would you stay with me until Eli gets here?"

"Of course. I'm here as long as you need me."

She took Autumn's arm, and they walked the length of the corridor. They were heading back toward Autumn's room when Eli came bursting out of the elevator, panic on his face. Then he caught sight of his wife, and it was the warmest smile Paisley had ever seen.

Eli rushed to Autumn and enfolded her in his arms. Paisley stepped away, knowing they needed a private moment.

"Are you all right?" Eli asked. "How many centimeters?"

"Four when they checked," Autumn responded. "I want to do another lap. More if they'll let me. It's helping with the pain to keep moving."

By now, West and Sawyer had joined them. She went to Sawyer, who slipped an arm about her waist.

"You okay?" he asked, brushing a kiss against her hair.

"I'm a bundle of nerves," she admitted. "Autumn is completely cool and collected, though. It's as if she's had a dozen babies before."

"She has worked as a nurse in labor and delivery," Sawyer explained. "I'm just glad you were with her when her water broke and got her to the hospital."

They looked to the couple, and Autumn said, "You don't have to stay. It's going to be hours before the baby comes. We'll let you know."

West stepped to his little sister and kissed her brow. "I definitely know how long this can take. Kelby's at home. Kate just went down for a nap."

"It's Labor Day weekend, West. Go enjoy the time off with your wife and baby," Autumn encouraged. "You'll be buried during the rest of football season."

West kissed his sister's cheek. "Have you let Summer know?"

"I texted her in the car on the way here," Autumn replied. "She said she and Chance are leaving the horse auction and will be back by tomorrow morning."

"What about Jace and Darby?" Eli asked his wife.

"I thought you'd want to be the one to text your brother and let him know."

"I'll call him now," Eli said. Looking to her, he said, "Thanks again, Paisley, for bringing Autumn to Triple H."

"Happy I was there and could help," she told him.

"I guess we'll head home," Sawyer said. "Let us know if you need anything."

"Thank you," Autumn said.

As they got into the elevator, Sawyer asked, "Do you want to come back to my place for a while?"

"That sounds good. Jen and her firefighter are at the house watching the game now."

They returned to Sawyer's house and put on the Cowboys game, but Paisley didn't really watch it, her thoughts still on Autumn and what her friend was going through.

After the game ended, Sawyer turned off the TV. They sat on the couch, talking quietly, until she took his hand and led him into the bedroom. They disrobed without speaking and made love slowly, drawing comfort from being with one another.

As they lay with limbs entangled afterward, he asked, "Do you want kids?"

"Before I came to Hawthorne, I hadn't thought much about it. Since then, I find that I really do. It's been fun holding Kate and listening to her babble. And being around all my students, seeing how unique each of them is, has let me realize that I do want to be a mom in the future."

He kissed her softly. "I've always wanted kids. It was another reason I came back to Hawthorne. Not that there's anything wrong with raising kids in a big city, but Hawthorne is that proverbial village that helps raise a child. I'd like for my kids to grow up here and have the kind of childhood I did, with everyone looking out for them the way they did me."

They held hands, talking about other things, but in the back of her mind, Paisley could see having children with Sawyer. He would be an ideal father, modeling himself after his own dad. She, on the other hand, worried about the kind of mother she would be, having had no good role models in her life.

Around eight, they got out of bed and dressed, both hungry. Sawyer made grilled cheese sandwiches, while Paisley heated a can of tomato soup for them to split.

While they were eating, her phone buzzed. Then his did. Quickly, they reached for them, and Paisley saw a picture of a sleeping baby. She had tufts of auburn hair, the same shade as Autumn's was. Her mouth was in the shape of an O. She read the text message below the picture.

> Sarah Elizabeth Carson arrived at 7:15 tonight. She weighs 8 pounds exactly, is 21 inches long, and she's the most beautiful baby on earth. Both Sarah and Autumn are doing fine.

They both replied to Eli's text, as did others on the text chain. Sawyer asked if they could come to the hospital tonight, but Eli suggested they visit tomorrow, after Autumn had gotten some rest.

He took Paisley's hand in his. "Would you like to go together to meet Sarah?"

"I can't think of a better way to spend Labor Day," she replied.

The next day, Sawyer took her to breakfast before they went to Triple H. Autumn was sitting up in bed, holding her sleeping daughter in the crook of her arm. They asked how she and the newborn were doing, and Autumn said everything had gone well.

"Mom and Dad came last night. They couldn't stay away. They should be here in a few minutes," she told them.

"Then I better ask to hold my new cousin now because Aunt Meg will monopolize her," Sawyer said. "If that's okay."

The new mother smiled gently. "Of course, you can, Sawyer."

He scooped the tiny bundle from Autumn's arm and cooed down at the baby. Sarah was awake now, carefully listening to what Sawyer was saying to her. He looked at Paisley, grinning from ear to ear.

"Want to hold her?"

"Absolutely."

Though she had never felt maternal before this moment, something washed over her now, a sweet tenderness as she took the baby in her arms and looked down into Sarah's inquisitive eyes. Sawyer put an arm about her, bringing a warmth with the gesture.

In that moment, Paisley knew she wanted to marry this man and have his children.

No one else would ever do.

CHAPTER
Eighteen

Sawyer welcomed Bill Packman to his office. They had already met for an entire day, going over various options for the multi-millionaire and how he could make the most of his estate, possibly by establishing a nonprofit organization. Today, Sawyer was going to talk with the older gentleman about forming a private foundation, which he believed would make the most of Bill's money and help a wider variety of those in need.

"Good to see you, Bill. Let's take a seat in the conference room. Want some coffee?"

"No, thanks. I'll pass. Caffeine and I aren't getting along these days."

His client accompanied him to the small conference room, where Sawyer had copies of various documents set out.

"You know my expertise is in criminal law, but I've practiced a lot of family law since coming to Hawthorne. You've kept me busy though, ever since we met. I've been researching corporate law. How organizations and business are formed. How corporations deal with their investors, shareholders and directors. How everyone interacts with one another. Yes, I had some law school classes on these topics, but I've really hit the ground running, refreshing myself on financial matters and how best to make your money work for you—and keep working—after you're gone."

He paused. "I hope you don't mind, but I contacted a buddy of mine from law school who's in the corporate world. With my research and advice from him, what I believe best in your situation is to form not simply a nonprofit organization but a private foundation."

"Why private?" Bill asked. "I'm wanting to help the public."

"Nonprofits consist of a cycle of three things. Donor acquisition. Fundraising efforts. And mission-driven work. As the money runs out, the cycle starts over again, continually looping. If we create a private foundation, we can support many other organizations—and individuals—of your choosing. Basically, it's a private charity which allows you to take community service to a higher level for long after you're gone."

He explained how a foundation was sustained by private donations, securities, and other financial funds and didn't solicit public donations, although they were allowed to do so if they chose that as an option.

"A private foundation basically grants funds to charitable activities. They don't directly get involved with the programs or services the grants fund. They allow that organization to handle things since they know their needs better than anyone else."

Bill nodded thoughtfully. "What about taxes? I know they can eat up things fast. And administrative costs, too. That's a consideration."

"A private foundation is exempt from income tax, like any nonprofit would be. It is responsible for up to a two percent excise tax on any income generated by investments, however. Your foundation would need to give a minimum of five percent of the net assets via grants every year to be functioning correctly. More if the board chooses, of course."

"And you say the grants can be to a charity group or an individual?"

"That's right. Your board of trustees would vote on who receives the grants, and those can vary in amounts from small to very large."

Sawyer spent a good hour explaining the legal structure they would set up, including naming the foundation, registering it, and creating articles of incorporation and bylaws which would specify how to name a board of trustees and manage the foundation's funds.

"I can do all that for you and serve as the attorney for the foundation if that's your desire."

"Absolutely," his client said. "I can't imagine proceeding without you at the helm, Sawyer. I know I've already put you on retainer and that you've billed me for the legal documents you've already created for me, but this sounds as if it'll take a good deal of your time. I'd like to have a salary set aside for you because of the amount of time you'll be involved with the foundation."

This would be a godsend. While he had saved a portion of his salary while an ADA in Dallas, the savings were slowly eroding. He paid Isaiah Smith to rent his offices each month. He took on most every client who came to him, but family law didn't pay nearly as well as corporate law did and wasn't steady. His earnings were hit and miss. Having a guaranteed income and all the work the foundation would bring meant he could save more. Buy a house.

Make a life with Paisley.

"I won't get into the particulars with you now, Bill, but I'm assuming you'll want a big chunk of your investments liquidated and placed into an endowment. Basically, the principal would remain untouched, and we'd invest in various assets. The earned income from investments is what we would use for the grants we issue. We'd also pay a salary to any employees hired by the foundation. At the beginning, I can handle everything. Eventually, though, you'll need someone to manage some of the day-to-day operations. Review grant requests. Meet with prospective clients. Make presentations to the board. That kind of thing."

"Let's talk about that board of trustees," his client said.

"They'll guarantee the foundation is operating correctly based upon its mission statement. They'll vote on the various grants. They act not only as stewards but ambassadors for the foundation."

He paused. "Does this sound like how you'd like to have your money working, both now and in future decades to come?"

"I've always trusted my gut from my wildcatting days. It's telling me now that this is the right thing to do. That I could make a big difference with the money I've accumulated by having you draw up the necessary documents to create this foundation."

"The advantage of doing so would be that you could help the town of Hawthorne and still go far beyond that. You might want to pick three to five causes which interest you and concentrate on helping those in need through a variety of organizations. Or you let the board be the guiding influence on the groups and individuals you invest in."

"Let's talk more about that board," Bill said. "It's important to me to keep it local. I don't want it to be the kind of thing where bigwigs from all around the country fly in for a board meeting. I want locals who will truly be invested in it. First of all, because it'll make Hawthorne a better community, but I also want likeminded people who are average Joes and want to simply do good with the mad money I'm providing. Do you have any suggestions on who we could approach?"

"Since I'll be acting as the organization's attorney, I wouldn't feel right about taking up a slot on the board. The first person who comes to mind, though, is my uncle Joe. He's Dr. Joe Sutherland, superintendent of Hawthorne ISD. He's lived in Hawthorne his entire life and dedicated himself to public service the last forty years. More importantly, Uncle Joe has told a handful of people that he'll be retiring at the end of this school year. In my mind, he's still young and has many years left ahead of him. He's already talked to me about ways he could act as a servant leader in this second chapter of his life. He would be ideal to serve on the board, maybe as its president."

"I like that idea, Sawyer. I've never met your uncle, but I read about things in the newspaper, and I've talked to people who've worked with him. I think Joe Sutherland would be a brilliant choice to head our foundation's board. Any other suggestions for board member?"

"My cousin Autumn is married to Dr. Eli Carson. Eli came from nothing and has made himself into someone really special. He came through the foster care system and is a medical doctor as well as an administrator. He currently serves as the medical director at Triple H, which has become a vital part of the Hawthorne community in a short amount of time. I think Eli is a solid choice."

Bill wrote down the two names Sawyer had suggested and then looked up. "Anyone else you can suggest?"

"It would be good to involve someone from the community with a different perspective. There are still a lot of farmers and ranchers in the area. My cousin Summer is married to Chance Blackstone, owner of the Blackstone Ranch. Chance would not only bring a rancher's experience to the table, but he's also a businessman since the Blackstone is the largest ranch in the county. He's quiet. Reflective. But when Chance does speak, others listen because he has something important to say."

Once more, Bill scribbled the name next to the others. "That's three men. I would like a female perspective. Can you think of anyone who would be qualified?"

"The woman who has her finger on the pulse of the community is Marge Bliss. Shorty handles all the food prep at BBQ Bliss, from smokers to grills. Marge is the brains. Handles all the bookkeeping and menus. She's on practically every committee in the community, from Parks and Rec to president of the women's club at her church. Marge is likeable and has great ideas."

"Sold," his client said, adding Marge's name to their growing list. "One more woman."

Sawyer thought. "I think Mischa Sabbatino would be good."

Bill frowned. "The gal from Pizza Palace?"

"Yes. She and Mario came here probably twenty years ago or so from Brooklyn. Mischa is friendly. She doesn't put up with nonsense. And it might be nice to have the perspective of someone who has come to Hawthorne and made themselves a part of the community."

"I'll put her down."

"That would make for five board members, Bill. I

wouldn't go much larger than that. At least in the beginning. I'm sure you'll want a seat on the board as well."

His client shook his head. "No, I need to step away."

The older man hesitated a moment, and Sawyer's gut told him that Bill had something important to announce.

"When we started this process recently, I told you that you never know when something could go wrong. Although I was feeling fine, except for a few headaches lately, I decided to have a physical done at Triple H." Bill swallowed. "I've got a brain tumor, Sawyer. The inoperable kind."

He sucked in a quick breath, surprised by this news. "I'm so sorry to hear this, Bill."

"I'm not. I've had a good run, and I'm ready to see what the afterlife holds for me. It does mean, though, that we better get a move on things. Get this foundation set up and legally approved. Make certain the trustees are in place, with all the T's crossed and the I's dotted."

"I understand the necessity for speed, Bill." He paused. "Did they give you any indication of how long you might have?"

His client shrugged. "They're doctors. Not God. They said probably six months to a year. No longer than that. The tumor's location and how soon it begins pressing is going to make a difference with when I'll need to stop making decisions for myself and let you do that for me. So if we can move quickly on putting this organization together, I'll be grateful to you, Sawyer. I'd love to meet with the people we've talked about serving as trustees by next week."

He made a note. "I'll contact all of them today. Do you have a day or time in mind? I don't want to interrupt any medical treatments."

"I'm not having any. Just a lot of tests and follow-ups, which won't change anything. Time is of the essence."

Sawyer thought a moment. "We're going to need some help in creating this foundation. My cousin West's wife, Kelby Sutherland, would be someone good to bring in on this. She works with businesses, creating their mission statements. Designing their websites. Helping brand them. She also handles social media posts. Kelby would be a vital part of getting the foundation off the ground quickly and helping give it direction."

He studied Bill, worried the older man might be tiring. "Do you feel good enough to hang around a while longer? I can give Kelby a call. If she's not tied down with a client, I'm betting she would be willing to meet with us now."

"Call her," Bill urged.

Sawyer did so. When Kelby answered, he said, "Hey, Kelby. You're on speakerphone with me and my client Bill Packman. Do you have a minute to chat?"

"You've caught me at a good time, Sawyer. I just finished a zoom with a client in Tulsa. While I've work to do today, I definitely have time to take a meeting with you and Mr. Packman."

"Would it be easier if we came to you, or would you rather stop by my office?" he asked.

"I've got to go to the post office to mail a business package. Let me come to you. I can be there in fifteen minutes."

While they waited for Kelby's arrival, Sawyer went over some details of the power of attorney documents he'd drawn up for Bill. These covered both medical decisions, as well as legal and financial ones.

"Guess I'm glad we also drew up that DNR," his client said. "Just in case."

Kelby joined them, introducing herself, and Sawyer explained how Bill had amassed a good deal of wealth and was ready to establish a foundation to distribute it and give back not only to the Hawthorne community but other causes.

She took charge after that. "You'll need a name for the foundation. If you have an idea for it, we'll need to research and see if it's being used in any form or fashion in that capacity. If not, we'll claim that domain. I'll build a website using it."

Kelby sat next to Bill and opened her iPad, showing the older man various websites she had built. They talked about colors and content tabs to use, with Sawyer interjecting some ideas, as well. Bill didn't have many preferences, saying he would defer to Kelby's judgment on visual items.

"I'll come up with the mission statement for the foundation, based upon what we've talked about. Naturally, you'll need to create a board of trustees to make the decisions as to where the grants will be awarded. I'll create a tab for the board members with their pictures and bios. One more important tab will be where to contact the foundation for consideration. Be it an individual or group, they need to know how to apply for funding their request."

She looked to Sawyer. "Will you be the one who monitors the website for that? Or is that something you want SSC to handle?"

"We can decide on that once you've created the website. I'd like for the board to meet first and have Bill talk to them about his vision for the foundation."

"Could I come to that meeting?" Kelby asked. "I'd also like to bring Jen, too, since she'll work with me closely on this project."

Bill and Sawyer agreed to this request.

Kelby pitched a few ideas regarding the name of the foundation. While Sawyer liked the direction her thoughts went, he couldn't help but think how Bill had never had a family. How his name would die with him.

"Bill is a modest guy, but I think the foundation should bear his name," Sawyer said. "After all, it's his money which will fund it. We'll eventually see about taking charitable contributions even though I'll set up an endowment, but Bill's name should be a part of the organization's name."

Though the older gentleman looked embarrassed, Kelby jumped on the idea. "I agree, Bill. You're unselfishly giving everything you have to make this world a better place. The grants the foundation hands out will range from small to multimillion dollar ones. I like the idea of this being The Bill Packman Foundation."

Sawyer provided the names of those they would like to ask to sit on the board of trustees, and Kelby seconded their choices.

"You're touching various aspects of the Hawthorne community. I also like that you have men and women sitting on the board, but if you also take a seat, Bill, that means six members. Ties could come up in voting matters. Are the bylaws going to reflect that you'll have the deciding vote?"

Bill shook his head. "I don't plan to sit on the board, Kelby."

"You should," she encouraged. "You need to have a say in the projects your money will fund."

"I've only found this out, and I'm still trying to get used to the news. I have a brain tumor, and I won't be around this time next year."

Tears misted in Kelby's eyes, and she covered Bill's hand with hers. "I'm so sorry to hear this, Bill. I was looking forward to working with you for the next twenty to thirty years." She smiled gently. "But the work will go on in your name for decades to come. Thanks to your philanthropy, lives will be touched in a positive way."

"I'm going to tell the board my news," Bill said. "I'd like to keep it quiet beyond that small circle, though. At least for now."

"We'll respect your wishes," Sawyer told his client. He looked to Kelby. "I'm going to contact prospective board members and see if they can meet this coming Monday at nine o'clock."

She consulted her phone. "I can be there. Jen, too. Where are we going to meet? Your conference room won't hold all of us. I'd be happy to host something at the house. We've got the room. That way, we could keep it a bit informal."

"I like that idea," Bill said. "I want those who choose to serve on this foundation's board to be comfortable with one another and enjoy the work they do on its behalf."

Kelby chewed on her bottom lip a moment and then said, "Can the three of us meet again on Friday? I'd like to have portions of the website's pages built by then, plus I'd like to show you the mission statement and get it approved. If you like it, we can show everything to the trustees on Monday. I can also draw up a plan as to how we'll be using social media to support the foundation. If there's anything you don't like, I'll have time to make some tweaks over the weekend."

"I like this plan," Bill stated. "I knew I was doing the right thing when I came to see Sawyer." He smiled at Kelby. "You'll be a great addition to the team."

She told them goodbye and left the conference room. Since it was lunchtime, he asked Bill if they could grab a bite to eat at the diner, where they'd first met. His client readily agreed, and soon they were seated at Dizzy's Diner, eating the lunch special of pork chops, butter beans, fried okra, and mashed potatoes.

He paid their bill. As they left the diner, he asked, "Are you still driving, Bill?"

"Not anymore. That's something the doctors told me I better give up right away. There's a chance I could have a seizure. I don't want to be behind the wheel and hurt anyone if that happened. They suggested that I hire some help. Someone to either run errands for me or accompany me on them. I'll also need someone to take me to my doctor appointments."

Sawyer thought a moment and said, "I have someone in mind. She might be open to working for you. I just settled a divorce case for her and know she's at loose ends. She's looking for work and needs a place to live."

"I've got a spare bedroom," Bill said. "Do you think we'd get along?"

"Ginny is very kind. A bit reserved. I think you would be helping each other out with this arrangement."

"Let's call her up."

He learned that Bill had walked to their appointment this morning, and so he drove the older man home. On the way, he dialed Ginny's number.

"Hi, Ginny. It's Sawyer Montgomery. I wanted to check in and see how you were doing."

"I'm just happy the divorce is behind me, Mr. Montgomery. I've applied for a couple of jobs. I'm hoping to hear back from Walmart in the next day or two. You know I've been staying with my aunt, but I think she's tired of me sleeping on her couch. I need to find a place to live. Maybe just rent a room for now."

"I may have a job for you, Ginny," he shared.

By now, they had pulled up in front of Bill's house, and he cut the engine.

"I'm with one of my clients now at his home. He's going

to be needing some help. Do you think you could come over and meet with us now?"

Sawyer provided the address, and Ginny said, "That's only two blocks from Aunt Mindy's. I could walk over now if that's okay."

"Head our way. We'll see you in a few."

They went into Bill's house, and a few minutes later, Ginny Freeman arrived. They sat at the kitchen table over a glass of lemonade, and Bill explained his recent diagnosis.

"I can't drive anymore, so I'll need someone to drive me places. I'm not much of a cook. If you are, I'd appreciate you making meals for me. I've got a spare bedroom you could stay in. No furniture in it now because I've never used it, but we can order us some. I'll let you pick out what you might like."

Bill looked at Ginny hopefully. "Think you might stay with an old man while I'm dying?"

Tears sprang to Ginny's eyes. "You would be helping me as much as I'd be helping you, Mr. Packman. I got married straight out of high school, even though I graduated near the top of my class. My husband didn't want me going to college or even working. He didn't want me to do much of anything. He was mean, Mr. Packman. Really bad to me. He liked hurting me. It's taken five years for me to come to my senses and stand up for myself. Your offer would change my life."

"Then let's do it," Bill said genially. "I think we'll get along like peas in a pod."

He offered Ginny a salary, which made her eyes go wide. She looked to Sawyer, who nodded, and Ginny accepted.

"I'll leave you two to work out the rest of the details," he said. "Right now, I need to contact those people we talked about, Bill. We'll meet again with Kelby on Friday, and I'll also make sure Ginny has the Sutherlands' address for the board meeting on Monday."

Sawyer left, feeling good about the work he would be doing with Bill and the foundation, as well as happy at the monthly income he could now count on to supplement his regular earnings.

He couldn't wait to share everything that had happened today with Paisley.

Maybe it was time to start thinking about putting a ring on her finger. He would start saving for one now.

CHAPTER
Nineteen

Paisley watched as various students took shots at the basket from different areas on the court. She had her students in PE, both girls and boys, working on a basketball unit now. They had already completed ones in volleyball and yoga and were now learning how to dribble with either hand, as well as make different kinds of shots. Some of the teens were easily able to bank a shot, while others preferred to try for a basket which was all net.

She glanced at her watch and then blew the whistle, bringing things to a halt. Immediately, students began collecting the basketballs they had been using and setting them on the rack, returning to their assigned spot in the gym where they gathered for roll. She closed each PE class with five minutes of meditation. It allowed the students' heart rates to come down from the activity they had been participating in, as well as helped to clear their minds to be fresh for the rest of their school day. Although several had been skeptical when she started the practice, she could tell they now eagerly looked forward to winding down this way.

"Good session today," she told the group. "Steve, Robbie, and Jameson were the most improved in your free throws today. And special shout outs to Marcus and Nathan for your consistency with three-pointers."

The teenagers in the gym clapped, another practice she had implemented. When students were recognized by her, she also wanted their peers to acknowledge their progress. Paisley had recalled what a surly teen she had been at times, but her PE students had wonderful attitudes. They were supportive of one another.

"Let's take it down, guys. Clear your minds and breathe."

As a group, they sat on the floor cross-legged, placing their open palms on their knees and closing their eyes. She set her watch for five minutes. While it was five fewer minutes to work on a sport each class period, Paisley believed the benefits of those five minutes of mediation outweighed losing a brief time of physical activity.

She truly enjoyed the life she was leading now as the end of the first semester approached. Teaching her PE classes had been more fun than she had anticipated. The prep was easier for them than if she had been in an academic classroom and had papers to grade. As for basketball, she had a talented team, thanks to Desi and Sheila's return.

At first, Desi had hogged the ball. Since she was the most skilled player on the team, her teammates wanted to continually feed it to her. Paisley quickly broke them of that habit, pulling Desi aside for a private conversation. She let the senior know that while Desi was a great shot, she needed to work on other facets of her game. That a point guard who exercised true leadership was going to get the ball to many of her teammates. It was more important for Desi to learn how to run the offense than it was for her to continually shoot as the others looked on.

When Desi seemed unsure, Paisley even offered the teen the opportunity to move to shooting guard, but Desi decided she was up for the challenge of learning more about being the best point guard she could be. While Paisley couldn't guarantee the girl would earn a scholarship, she was sending highlight reels to several different coaches. Consequently, Desi was receiving interest from three different colleges.

The only problem that Paisley had these days was seeing so much less of Sawyer. She had never been in a relationship with anyone, much less during basketball season. As a player, the season was time consuming. As the head coach, she put in double the hours her players did. When she did see Sawyer, they spent a lot of their time together discussing basketball. She drew on his wealth of knowledge and experience, and they worked together in designing different offensive and defensive plays for her team. If the Lady Hawks won district this year, Sawyer's contributions would be no small part of that process.

Paisley missed being able to spend more time with him. She loved him and knew he loved her, but she didn't know what basketball season would do to their relationship each year. Already, Sawyer was working more than usual, thanks to his role with The Packman Foundation. Bill Packman had become a close friend to them both in the last few months, even functioning as a father figure to Paisley. The older gentleman came to games with Ginny, who chauffeured him about Hawthorne, and they sat with Dizzy, being three of the more vocal fans cheering on the Lady Hawks.

Between Sawyer's work with the foundation and the hours at his law practice, along with her crazy hours with weeknight games and weekend tournaments, they barely saw one another. While she spent more of her nights at his house than she did hers, they didn't have nearly as much time together as she would have liked.

Her watch buzzed, and she said, "That's it for today, gentlemen. Thanks for a great class."

The students rose and returned to the locker room to change for their next class. Paisley went into the small office off the gym. Her cell rang, and she saw it was Bill calling.

"Hey, Bill. You called at the perfect time. I think you know my schedule better than I do," she teased.

"I know we're playing the Trojans tonight in our first district matchup of the season, but you need to take time for lunch because I know you won't take time for dinner."

"Guilty as charged," she admitted. "Are you bringing me something to eat?"

"Ginny and I just pulled up outside the gym," he told her. "I have sandwiches from BBQ Bliss if you're interested."

She laughed. "Oh, I'm more than interested. I might even eat yours and mine. I'll come open the door for you."

Bill had gotten into the habit of bringing Paisley lunch once a week. It only took half an hour out of her schedule to eat with him, and she truly enjoyed their time together. Bill had told her dozens of stories of his days in the oil fields, as well as sharing about the various businesses he had begun and then sold over the years. In turn, Paisley had opened up about her rough childhood, telling Bill more than she had told anyone else, even Sawyer. Bill had been orphaned at a young age, and she could tell that he looked upon her as the daughter he'd never had. Especially with his time limited, Paisley was happy to serve in that capacity.

The bell rang as she went to the gym doors, which remained locked for safety reasons. Usually, a visitor would need to sign in at the office, but she had cleared it with

Blanche so that Ginny could drop Bill at the gym and keep him from having to walk such a long way.

Paisley opened the door and grinned. "Come on in, Handsome," she said, taking his arm and guiding him to her office. He looked more tired than usual, which concerned her.

In her office, she took the paper bag and placed it on her desk as he took the seat by the desk. Opening her mini-fridge, she pulled out two bottled waters for them.

"I'm glad you had time to talk with me today," Bill said.

"What have you got Ginny doing while we're visiting?" she asked, removing the sandwiches and bags of chips from the brown paper sack.

"She's going to pick up a couple of library books for me. I've really gotten into reading Nora Roberts. She's got mystery and romance together. It's a good combination."

"Do you know that Summer is writing a romance trilogy right now."

Bill grinned. "Chance has told me all about it. He's very proud of his wife. I'm hoping I'll be around long enough to read it."

Paisley knew nothing could be done about his brain tumor. It was why Bill had pressed so hard to get The Packman Foundation off the ground quickly. Bill had met with his board and told them his vision, explaining the types of individuals and groups he wished to assist. Then he had stepped away, allowing the trustees to begin making decisions on their own. Their first grant had been awarded to the City of Hawthorne to add on to the public library. The additional space would include having several social areas with comfy furniture for people to gather. It also included a dozen rooms which could be used for conferencing with others or students to meet in small study groups. The addition would also expand the children's area, where there would be a playroom, furnished with toys and books, and space for story hours for toddlers and preschoolers during the week and on Saturdays.

The best part was a large meeting room, along with a kitchen. The room would have space for up to one hundred people. Local groups, such as the Hawthorne Women's Club or Rotary Club could assemble there to hold their meetings and hear guest speakers.

For the upcoming holidays, the board had been working with Meg Sutherland so that a book would be ordered for every student in Hawthorne ISD. Bill had said that reading had been something which had taken him places he had never gone before and that books had been a good friend to him over the years. He wanted the students in the school district to enjoy reading and owning books of their own.

Paisley bit into the chopped barbeque sandwich. "This definitely hits the spot. Thanks for stopping by with lunch, Bill. While the food is appreciated, I'm always happy to see you."

"Happy to do so. You know how much I enjoy our talks."

She hesitated a moment, and he encouraged, "Talk to me, Paisley. Seems as if you have something on your mind."

"My entire life has been centered around basketball. You know that. Basketball saved me when I was a kid. It helped me earn a college degree. It's how I earned a living for over a decade. I think I've done a pretty decent job transitioning from player to coach. I'm proud of the team I've put on the court this season, and I believe they're learning a lot under me."

Bill looked at her expectantly. "But?"

"I don't even know how to say this. I came to Hawthorne for basketball, but I can see there's so much more to life now. Sawyer and I are committed to one another, but I worry about how little I've seen him since my season began. And when we get married and throw kids into the mix? I don't know if I can be the kind of wife and mother I want to be and continue coaching at the level I wish to. I keep wondering if maybe I could do something beyond basketball."

"That would be a big change for you. What are you interested in doing?"

She laughed. "I have absolutely no idea. Basketball is all I've ever known."

"Let's think about the skills you possess. Things you've learned, both as player and coach."

Paisley had never thought how her basketball skills might transfer to the real world.

"I'd say being organized would be at the top of my résumé," she began. "I couldn't get everything I need done unless I was organized. I believe I have good leadership qualities, having led teams as a player and now a coach. Despite the fact that I've held others at arm's length most of my life, I've really learned to click with the kids here at HHS. The faculty, too."

"Okay." Bill nodded thoughtfully. "We've got organizational and leadership skills. People skills, which we give the fancy name interpersonal skills in the business world. What about communication?" he asked.

"Definitely that. I've never been one to throw out a lot of fancy words. I communicate on a very basic level, but I'm comfortable speaking to students or adults."

"As a business owner, I know it's more than that, Paisley. Communication involves listening as much as speaking. You're a good listener. Both your players and your other coaches speak, and you truly listen to them. Communication is also giving and receiving feedback."

"There's plenty of that in coaching," she agreed, thinking

of her team meetings, as well as time spent with individual players, addressing their goals and performance on the court.

"And don't forget decision-making," Bill added. "During games, you have to analyze situations quickly and think of the consequences. Act upon what you've evaluated. The plays you send in and advice you give your players about how to handle what's happening on the court results in progress, if not downright success."

"I'm going to add adaptability," she told him. "Adapting in game situations. Changing things up when the game plan isn't working or an injury occurs." She brightened. "I believe I have more to offer than I previously thought. That's thanks to you, Bill. You're not only a friend to me. You're a mentor. Thanks for helping me add to this imaginary résumé. I may actually have to create it now."

Then Bill asked, "Would you consider stepping away from coaching if a new opportunity arose?"

"That would be a hard call. I don't know what I could do in Hawthorne besides coach. I'm just frustrated. I really like what I do, but I see how much time it takes me away from Sawyer. We both have talked about how having kids is important to us. With basketball, I have to be all in. Pretty much ignore everything and everyone else so that I can focus on my team. I can't be a mom—or wife—part of the time and ignore my family for months on end."

"You could always coach the teams of the children you and Sawyer have. The local Y has basketball teams. Volleyball. Softball. It would be a way to stay connected with sports, with a bonus of getting to spend more time with your own kids."

"I never thought of that," she said, the idea intriguing her.

"I understand your concerns, Paisley. I let work absorb my every waking moment. It cost me the one love I had—and it kept me from ever looking for anyone else. I don't want to see that happen with you."

His gaze met hers. "I have an idea. You don't need to make a decision right away. In fact, I wish you wouldn't."

His words intrigued her. "What are you thinking about, Bill?"

"You and Sawyer are very committed to one another. You have a heart for people, Paisley. It's not all just revolving around basketball."

He took a sip of his water and then added, "Right now, The Packman Foundation is just getting started. Ginny is helping coordinate with Meg Sutherland on the books which will be gifted to students. Sawyer is handling meetings with the architect and will work with the construction company regarding the library's expansion. Eventually, though, the foundation will be involved with more than these two projects. I'm going to need someone to keep things on course after I'm gone. Sawyer will maintain his role as The Packman Foundation's attorney, but there will need to be someone who can head the organization. Be the face of it. Look through the grant requests and bring the most promising ones to the board, then go from there after the board has voted.

"Would you be interested in being that person, Paisley?"

Excitement filled her. This was a once-in-a-lifetime opportunity. It would give her a chance to spread her wings. Challenge herself. Do something entirely new, away from the world of sports. Yet she had come to Hawthorne for the chance to coach basketball. She couldn't leave her team in the lurch. Resigning mid-season would be unthinkable. She could see, though, finishing up the year and then turning the reins over to someone else. Maybe even Hope, who was proving on a daily basis just how good a coach she was.

Paisley looked at Bill. "I won't give you an answer now.

It's definitely food for thought, however. I'm excited by the opportunity you're presenting, but I do owe a lot to Dr. Sutherland. West. My players."

"I get that," Bill said. "Stepping away from coaching would be difficult. Sports is all you know." He grinned impishly, looking like a young boy for a moment. "Or all you *think* you know. I think we've proved otherwise as we've spoken. I believe you would offer quite a bit if you spearheaded The Packman Foundation, Paisley. As I said, though, I won't take an answer from you now."

"I will share this with Sawyer. I want his input in such a big decision. I don't know when I'll do that, Bill. Could we keep this conversation between the two of us for now?"

"You betcha."

By now, Paisley had finished her sandwich. Bill had barely touched his.

"Are you not hungry?" she asked, concerned.

"I think I'll wrap this up and take it home for dinner," he told her.

It took him a moment to stand, and she realized he was growing more frail. His loss of appetite also worried her. Bill was going downhill. She felt helpless, knowing there was nothing anyone could do for him.

"Let me walk you out to the car. Ginny should be back from the library by now."

"I don't want to put you out."

"Not a problem. I'll head to the field house once I see you safe and sound in Ginny's hands."

She locked her office and took his arm, guiding him across the gym and out the door. As she suspected, Ginny sat behind the wheel of his Lincoln Continental. Paisley opened the passenger door and helped Bill into the sedan. She handed him the sack.

"He didn't finish his lunch," she told Ginny. "Get him to eat the rest of it for dinner if you would."

Ginny nodded solemnly, and Paisley knew the young woman also understood that Bill's time was coming to an end.

She waved goodbye as Ginny pulled away and then crossed the parking lot, heading inside the field house. Paisley tweaked the game plan for tonight, adding in one play between Effie and Ashley, which would allow each athlete to shine. She hoped her players would take down their biggest rivals in district tonight.

When Hope arrived after her last class of the day, she told Paisley that she had an idea for a new play and walked her through it on the whiteboard. Paisley loved Hope's unbridled enthusiasm and had watched as the younger coach had blossomed and come into her own during their time together. It struck her that if Hope succeeded her, the program would be in excellent hands.

At that moment, Paisley already knew what she was going to do. She couldn't wait to share news of this opportunity with Sawyer.

Twenty

Sawyer wrapped up the meeting with his client, eager to head to the high school. It was mid-December, and district play started tonight for the Lady Hawks. They would be facing the Thatcher Lady Trojans, the team which had won district three years in a row and made it to the state semi-finals last year. Paisley had shared that she was equal parts excited and nervous for her team to take on the reigning district champs.

He was proud of her. She was a natural coach, giving critical feedback when needed and knowing exactly when a player's spirits needed to be bolstered. Her creativity in drawing up new plays continued to amaze him. He also appreciated her collaborative spirit. Together, they had worked on the playbook, and Sawyer hoped he had contributed a few plays which would help Paisley's team play to the best of their ability. They had won over eighty percent of their nonconference games and walked away as tournament champions in the annual Thanksgiving classic held in Caldwell. Expectations were running high in the Hawthorne community. Even West had told Sawyer that he was surprised by how much Paisley was getting out of her underdog team.

Since he hadn't eaten, he stopped at the concession stand, picking up two hot dogs and a Dr Pepper. Not the most nutritious dinner, but these days, both he and Paisley were eating more meals on the run. As much as he liked her being the head girls basketball coach, Sawyer couldn't help but feel a little sorry for himself. Once the schedule kicked in, Paisley had been consumed by basketball and her myriad of responsibilities. After school practices occurred throughout the week, and she coached varsity games on Tuesdays and Friday nights. She also attended every JV game. While Hope Sewell was the head coach for those games, Paisley made certain she was on the bench with her assistant at each of those games, guiding Hope in game decisions.

And that didn't even take in the weekend tournaments.

Sawyer was discouraged. He knew Paisley was living her new dream as a coach, but their relationship now took a backseat to basketball. He, too, was much busier than usual, with not only his caseload growing but in handling things for The Packman Foundation. He loved being a part of Bill's foundation, but their busy schedules had helped to put a damper on what had been building between Paisley and him.

And that included finding the right moment to ask her to marry him.

He told himself this would be a yearly occurrence. That October through February would be the time when Paisley's job took precedence. They would simply have to work around her schedule. Most likely, they wouldn't celebrate Thanksgiving and Christmas like a normal family because of basketball. He decided he would need to talk with West about this. As head coach of the Hawks football team, West also spent a good chunk of time away from his family. Maybe it would be better to talk with Kelby and see how she dealt with being a football widow with a baby. He could relate more to her situation.

It worried him that when he and Paisley did have kids, childcare would be challenging. He wanted to be at her games, but he would probably be the parent who missed them in order to feed and bathe their children and put them to bed at a decent time. He chuckled to himself as he made his way into the bleachers. They weren't even engaged yet, and he already worried about a mountain of things.

"Sawyer!" Bill called.

He joined Bill, Ginny, and Dizzy in the bleachers. They had been sitting together for the non-district games, and he got a kick out of the two older men screaming at the refs and cheering on the Lady Hawks with such passion. Sawyer was glad that Bill had become a close friend to both Paisley and him. He wanted Bill's last year to be a good one. Bill and Paisley had taken to each other and almost seemed like a father and daughter now to one another. He hoped it filled a part of them which had been empty.

"Think the girls are ready to trounce the Trojans?" Dizzy asked, shoveling popcorn into his mouth.

"Paisley says they are. No girl on the team has ever beaten the Trojans."

"Desi's looked good in warmups," Ginny said.

"Sheila and Effie have been hitting threes well the past two games," Bill said. "And Tessie's been on fire."

Sawyer thought Bill looked a little pale. Quietly, he leaned in and asked, "You feeling okay?"

Bill shrugged. "Okay. Haven't had much of an appetite lately, though."

Darby and Jace appeared at the bottom of the stands.

"Hold this," Sawyer said, handing his hot dogs to Bill and rushing down the stairs to meet them.

"Hey, big brother," Darby said.

"What are you doing here?" he demanded. "You should be at home resting."

"Duh, I'm here to see us beat the Trojans. And support Paisley, of course."

He looked to Jace, who shrugged. "She's got a mind of her own. The baby already does, too. I'm going to be outnumbered in my own household."

"Where are you sitting?" his sister asked. She glanced up and waved. "I see Dizzy. Come on."

Jace took Darby's elbow and guided her slowly up the stairs. Sawyer took his seat again, with Darby and Jace sitting on the row in front of them.

"When's the baby coming?" Dizzy asked.

"Soon. I'm due in two days," Darby told him. "On Thursday. I'm hoping I can finish the semester on Friday and then have Sam. That would be more convenient, but I know babies come when they want to."

"You're naming him Sam?" asked Bill.

"Yes. It was our dad's name," Darby shared. "Sawyer's fine with that."

"She's having the first baby, so she should get first dibs on a name," Sawyer said.

"You better get started soon," Bill teased.

"I plan to."

He did. Sawyer decided that he'd waited long enough to marry Paisley. If he asked her tonight, they could get married over her two-week winter break. He'd already checked, and though the boys basketball team was playing in a tournament in Dallas, the girls didn't have one scheduled. Paisley was holding a few practices after Christmas, though.

Surely, they could work a wedding around those.

The pregame activities were in full swing by now. A small group of band members played as the cheerleaders performed a dance. Then the buzzer sounded, and the PA announcer, a biology teacher at HHS, introduced the starters for each team and their coaches. It pleased him that Paisley got such a good hand from the crowd. Then again, she had really turned the team around from where they were this time last year. Already, attendance at Lady Hawk games was up, thanks to their winning record.

Sawyer watched Paisley more than he did the game. How intense she was. How the players huddled around her during timeouts as she madly scribbled on a small whiteboard, gesturing with her hands. She wasn't shy during play, hollering at players, telling them where to be and what they should be doing. He realized it was a learning experience for them, but it also was one for Paisley, too, since it was her first year.

At halftime, he went for popcorns for his group, but as he headed back up the stairs, he saw Darby and Jace going down them.

"Heading home?" he asked.

"I'm tired," his sister said. "And I've still got three more days of school to get in."

He passed one of the boxes of popcorn to her. "Snack on this on the way home."

She pulled him down for a hug. "Thanks, Sawyer."

The game had been tied at the half, but the Lady Hawks slowly began pulling away. Effie Compton hit two three-pointers in a row, surprising the crowd and herself. Even though the Trojans matched the Hawks basket after basket the remainder of the game, that lead held. The Lady Hawks won the game, much to the delight of their home crowd.

"It's good seeing Paisley in her element," Bill said. "I think that girl could do anything she wants."

"I couldn't agree more," Sawyer said. "Talk with you later."

He headed down to the court, standing off to the side while Paisley talked with a few opposing players. She even called for her whiteboard, and Hope brought it over. He watched Paisley draw a play and explain it, two Lady Trojans standing nearby. Both slowly nodded their heads and then smiled.

"Thanks, Coach," they said in unison.

As the pair walked away, he came and wrapped his arms around her. "Aiding and abetting the enemy?" he asked, kissing the tip of her nose.

"They had a couple of questions. Things that weren't working for them. I explained it so they would understand where they were supposed to be and what they were supposed to be doing." She smiled at him. "Now, will it come back to haunt me? I sure hope not."

He kissed her lightly on the mouth. "Good game, Coach."

"I was pleased with the way we played. It was a strong outing against the district champs. I'm just hoping we'll be in the running to win district this year."

"You will. I know you need to head to the locker room and address the team. See you back at my place?"

"Yes. Jen's boyfriend started his forty-eight hours off this morning." She laughed. "That means they'll be hot and heavy if I go home."

He touched her cheek. "Well, we can do hot and heavy and raise them a few scorching kisses."

"I like how you think, Montgomery."

"I like you, Coach. See you soon."

Sawyer returned to his car and drove home, turning on

lights and kicking up the heat in the house since the night was chilly. He turned the bed back and even lit a few candles in the bedroom before opening a bottle of wine to breathe.

When Paisley arrived, he was wearing nothing but his robe.

"You look awfully comfortable," she said, dumping her backpack on the sofa.

He handed her a glass of wine. "I know. It's not the week-end. But I thought we needed to celebrate your first district win."

She took a sip of the wine and sighed. "Yum. This was a very good year. You're an extremely thoughtful boyfriend, Sawyer."

He took the wine glass from her hand and set it down, along with his own. Pulling her to him, he slid his arms around her and kissed her.

"I'd like to be more than that."

Understanding dawned in her eyes, but she still asked, "What are you saying?"

He released her and dropped to one knee. Taking her hands in his, he said, "I'm saying that I'm crazy about you, Paisley Roberts. I think about you day and night. I've never been more comfortable around anyone the way I feel around you."

Sawyer brushed his lips against her fingers and then gazed into her eyes. "I love you, Paisley. I want to spend all my days and nights with you. I want to share in all life's big and small moments. I want you as my best friend. My confidant. My lover. My wife. The mother of my children."

She shivered. "I love you, Sawyer. So much it almost hurts. It's like I don't even remember pre-Sawyer Paisley. I like who I am when I'm with you."

He rose, and she wrapped her arms around his neck. "It's a yes, Lawyer Sawyer. Definitely, positively, a big yes."

The kiss went on and on, growing hotter. Needier. Her hands slid down his chest, finding the knot on the robe's belt and working it free. Paisley parted the robe and kissed his chest, causing desire to run through him. With a gleeful noise, he swept her off her feet, carrying her to the bedroom.

Once there, he placed her back on her feet, stripping off her clothes, kissing her hungrily. They tumbled onto the bed, their hands roaming one another's bodies, their mouths fused together. He couldn't get enough of her. She was everything he wanted in a partner for life.

He reached to the nightstand, managing to open the drawer, and pulled out a condom. Tearing the packet open with his teeth, he started to remove it.

"Let me," she said, her voice low and tempting.

She placed the condom over the tip of his penis and rolled it into place. Having her do this for him felt intimate. Right. As he began kissing her again, he thrust into her, hard, causing her to gasp. Their dance was wild. Frenzied. Ending in an orgasm for them both.

He collapsed atop her, totally spent, his hands cradling her face.

"I love you," he said. "I want to marry you as soon as possible."

"My break is only a few days away," she said, her breathing uneven.

"We can apply for our marriage license online. Right now. It'll speed up the process, and then we can stop by the courthouse and sign and pay tomorrow. Can you get away from school during your lunch and conference period? We could go then."

"Only if you drive through Sonic and buy me a Frito pie and slush," she said flirtatiously.

Sawyer laughed aloud, loving her even more. "I can do that. And I'll even throw in some tots for good measure."

"And tots? Well, then it's a date."

He kissed her again, low and slow, finding it hard to believe this woman was going to be all his.

Forever.

When he broke the kiss, though, he saw something in her eyes. Unease settled over him. "What?"

"Maybe we better talk before we buy the license."

"We can have whatever kind of wedding you want," he assured her. "Big. Small. Aunt Meg is a genius at pulling things together on short notice." He chuckled. "She's had some practice at making great weddings happen with very little time."

"It's not that," Paisley said. "There's something serious I want to discuss with you. I don't think it's a deal breaker, but it's a big decision. I want your input, but I think my mind is already made up."

Sawyer rolled to his side so that he wasn't crushing her. A trickle of fear wound through him, but the need to know was even greater. "What do you want to talk about?"

Paisley looked at him a long time and then said, "I might give up coaching."

CHAPTER
Twenty-One

Paisley saw surprise register in Sawyer's eyes. She took his hands in hers, finding strength in them.

"I thought you were happy coaching. Tell me what's changed your mind, love."

She liked that he hadn't flown off the handle or began pestering her with questions. Her man was a steady one, not jumping to conclusions. One who truly listened to her.

And she valued that as much as she did anything.

"I do enjoy coaching. I think I'm actually pretty good at it." Paisley paused. "But I realize since I've met you that there's more to life than basketball."

He looked intrigued, but he kept silent, waiting for her to continue.

"From the beginning, you've seen me. The person. Not the former player. You liked me for who I was, even when I didn't know exactly *who* that person was. I feel I'm becoming more myself with you. That I'm seeing I'm not simply one dimensional." She hesitated. "I feel that I have more to offer than my knowledge about basketball."

He leaned in, giving her a soft kiss. "You're definitely more than just a basketball player or coach, Paisley. And you're right. You have a lot to offer. You have talents which are just beginning to blossom. If you choose to step away from basketball, you have my full support. I'll always be in your corner, whatever you want to do in life."

Tears sprang to her eyes. "How did I get so lucky? You're the best thing that's ever happened to me, Sawyer. Just when I think I can't love you any more than I already do, you go and do or say something, and I fall even more in love with you."

His arms went around her, and Paisley nestled against him, her head on his chest. His steady heartbeat, so reflective of the man he was, gave her strength to face the unknown.

"I talked to Bill about this today," she told him.

He nodded in approval. "I know the two of you have grown close."

"Bill is a good listener. He never had the personal life he yearned for, and I see if I continue coaching, I won't, either. While I appreciate how you've supported me during this first season, I feel as if we've hardly seen one another. I miss that. I miss us, being us."

He stroked her back. "I know. But that's the job you signed up for. You, better than most, know what a huge commitment coaching is. If you're giving up coaching because we don't have as much time together, I'm asking you to rethink things. We can power through any problems that arise."

"That's not why I want to step away," she explained. "Not having much time with you simply got me to thinking about my life and commitment to coaching. And I've decided that while I could continue coaching the rest of my adult life, I would be doing myself a disservice."

She shifted, stacking her hands atop one another on his

chest and resting her chin on them. Gazing into his eyes, Paisley said, "I want a second chapter in my life. One which doesn't involve devoting every waking moment to sports. I want more of a balance between work and my personal life."

"What are you considering doing?"

"I think I'm going to work for The Packman Foundation. No, not just work for it. Head it up. While the trustees will vote on the grants to award, someone has to be in charge. Look over those grants and bring those with the most potential to the board. I understand Bill's vision. I can communicate with the board, present which grants should be considered, and even talk with individuals and groups to coordinate presentations they would make to the trustees."

Excitement began to fill her. "Once the board votes, I would communicate that vote and for those approved, I would start the process of how the grants would be awarded. Work with others, making certain the funds they receive are used to maximum benefit. The foundation is going to grow, Sawyer. It will for years to come. I can make certain we hire the right people to monitor the investments. I can work on fundraising. Keep Kelby in the loop so that our website and social media presence remain constant and constantly refreshed."

His smile caused warmth to ripple through her, and he smoothed her hair. "I can see you in this role. You've got fantastic leadership and communication skills. You would be a natural at this, Paisley."

Sawyer's hands went to her waist, pulling her up just enough so that their lips met. The kiss was tender. It also held the promise of what they might accomplish together.

"We would be working together, too. At least some of the time," she added. "I know you still have your practice here in town, but you'll continue to play a vital role with the foundation. Better yet, no more drawing up plays on napkins when we're trying to have dinner."

He laughed. "But what if I'll miss doing that?"

"Bill suggested that I could always coach our kids if they played sports." She cupped his cheek. "I want more time for us—and the family we're going to have. I don't want to be missing from our kids' lives for months at a time while basketball season is going on. With this job, I could balance my own personal needs with being a wife and mom."

"It would be the best of both worlds," he agreed. "And Bill will be happy, knowing he's leaving his foundation in good hands." Sawyer paused. "When would you resign from HHS?"

"I'm committed to finishing out this season. I owe it not only to my players, but to myself. I plan to give everything I have to coaching, and then I'll step away. For now, the foundation hasn't bitten off more than it can chew. Ginny is also helping with a few of the administrative duties."

"She's really bright," he said. "When Bill passes, she'll need another job."

"I'll talk with Ginny and Bill. Maybe she can become my executive assistant and play a bigger role once her caretaking days are behind her."

"I'll confide in you that Bill made a few changes. He's leaving his house to Ginny. The mortgage is already paid off on it, so she won't have that to worry about."

"That's wonderful. I know she's had a rough patch these last few years. With her divorce and these changes in her life, things should really turn around for her."

He kissed her soundly. "Let's go online and file for our marriage application. Now, back to my original question, what kind of wedding do you want?"

"Small. Definitely, no fuss. I'm not someone who

dreamed of her wedding since I was young and had every detail worked out. I didn't even think marriage was in the cards for me." Paisley smiled. "Until I came to Hawthorne and met you. That was the best day of my life. And every day forward will be the new best day of my life—because I'm living it in love with you."

They kissed, and Paisley's gut told her she was making the right decision. About leaving coaching. Beginning a new career.

And marrying this incredible man.

* * *

PAISLEY HAD two dresses to her name. She much preferred wearing pants, from sweatpants to nicer ones which she paired with blazers. But she didn't want to wear pants on her wedding day. She wanted to feel a little girly.

One dress was her go-to. A sleeveless, black cocktail dress that hugged her figure. She'd worn it to weddings. Receptions. WNBA official league events. The other she had bought on a whim when she'd gone to a Nordstrom Rack. Although it was unlike anything she'd ever worn, something about it had called her name The A-line, V-neck, long dress was champagne in color, with short cape sleeves. A filmy overskirt, which was transparent, had dozens of small butterflies scattered across it. At the time, Paisley thought she had absolutely nowhere she could ever wear it.

Yet she had bought it—and now she knew why. It would serve as her wedding dress today.

They had gone to the courthouse and picked up their wedding license on Wednesday. Sawyer had called his aunt and uncle, and they'd met with them after she finished practice after school that day. The Sutherlands couldn't have been more welcoming upon hearing the news. Meg had asked her a few questions and written down the preferences Paisley and Sawyer had, which included a wedding cake with butter cream icing and using potted poinsettias as flowers since Christmas was the next week.

Their only other request was that they wanted to marry the day after school was released for the holidays, so they could enjoy the entire winter break as a married couple. Meg said to leave everything to her. That meant much of what happened today would be a surprise, a unique kind of wedding, but one which would suit the two of them.

The Lady Hawks played last night, and Paisley had been surprised when just before the game began, Sawyer had appeared on the court, a dozen red roses in his arms. He'd presented the bouquet to her and then slipped an engagement ring onto her finger. It fit perfectly. Hope and all her players gathered around, congratulating her. Desi proclaimed when she got engaged, she also wanted a marquise diamond engagement ring. Paisley hadn't known that was what the shape of the ring was called, but she did know she liked the way it looked on her hand.

Then she had set aside everything to concentrate on the game. Her team defeated the Lady Lions by seven points, so they were off to a solid start in district play with back-to-back wins over two fierce competitors. She'd told her players good-bye, reminding them they would hold practice on January second and third before school started up again on the sixth. Their next game would be played on January seventh, and she wanted to make sure her players' conditioning remained in place.

Paisley finished dressing and was wondering what to do with her hair when the door to the bedroom opened, all her new friends coming in. Autumn, who would serve as her matron of honor, crossed the room and gave Paisley a hug.

"You look amazing," Autumn praised.

"What are you going to do with your hair?" asked Kelby.

"I haven't decided," she admitted. "I usually wear it in a ponytail, but I wanted something different for the wedding."

"Let me play around a minute with it," Summer said. "Darby, you get off your feet."

Darby waddled to a chair and sat. "At least I made it through the end of the semester. Let's hope Sam doesn't decide to interrupt your wedding," she joked.

Summer asked Kelby to fetch some bobby pins and hair ties, and she began brushing Paisley's hair.

"You have a gorgeous mane of hair," she told Paisley. "This rich, chocolate brown color is to die for. Let's hope at least one of your kids gets this shade."

Summer tried sweeping it back and letting the soft waves fall. Then she worked it into a sleek chignon. Paisley liked both styles, but she wasn't certain which to go with.

"Wait, I know," Summer declared. "A fishtail braid."

As Summer's fingers worked, Paisley knew this was it, especially after Kelby presented her with a hand mirror and she used it to view the back of her hair. Her hair was loosely pulled back from her face, and the braid was not a tight one. Instead, it was loose and romantic.

"I love it," she said.

"Tie a ribbon at the bottom," Autumn suggested.

Kelby left again, returning with one, and Summer tied it at the end of the braid. "Perfect," she said, admiring her work as she handed Paisley the mirror again.

"I agree. Thank you, Summer. I know Sawyer is going to like this."

Summer laughed. "My cousin is crazy in love with you,

Paisley. I'm not sure he'll even notice your hair, but you'll have pictures to show him when he comes out of his daze."

She looked to Kelby. "Thank you so much to you and West for agreeing to host our wedding. I know everything is so last minute."

"Not a problem," Kelby assured her. "When love strikes, you want to be with that person as soon as you can so that you can begin your happily ever after right away."

Summer interjected, "That's what happens in all my books. My hero and heroine are so in love and ready to begin their lives together." She smiled at Paisley. "Just like you and Sawyer."

Meg appeared. "It's close to time to start. Darby, honey, let's get you settled. Jace is pacing the floor, worried about you, especially since you're now past your due date."

"First-time dad nerves," Autumn said. "He'll settle down once you've had Sam."

"Did you bring Sarah?" Paisley asked Autumn.

"She's with a sitter in Kate's nursery," her matron of honor replied. "Mom thought to hire a babysitter so Eli and I could enjoy the wedding. I know the reception is going to be low-key, so we may bring her in for a little of it."

Meg and Summer helped Darby to her feet, and they left the bedroom.

"The ceremony will be held in the great room," Kelby informed her. "Luscious Layers delivered the cake a few minutes ago. Since today's turned out to be so mild, we'll let the reception spill out onto the patio. Oh, and Shorty and Marge are set up in the kitchen. They've brought sliced brisket, ham, and sausage links, with plenty of sides."

Tears stung the back of her eyes. "Thank you."

Kelby gave Paisley a hug. "You make Sawyer happy.

You're one of us, Paisley. And family helps out whenever they can."

A knock sounded at the door, and Autumn answered. Paisley saw Bill standing there, looking gaunt but happy. He wore a rosebud boutonniere.

"I've been sent to claim the bride," he announced. "Sawyer's getting antsy."

"I'm all yours," she told Bill as Autumn and Kelby left. "Thank you for agreeing to give me away. I know we haven't known one another for long, but I'm grateful for your friendship. And the new job down the line."

Paisley and Sawyer had both talked to Bill about her role with The Packman Foundation. They agreed that after basketball season, Paisley would start attending the monthly board meetings. Once the school year ended, she would assume responsibility as the CEO of the foundation. Joe Sutherland, who served as the president of the trustees, had been taken into their confidence regarding these plans since Paisley would be leaving HHS. Joe had suggested once basketball season ended that they sit down with West and discuss whom they would like to hire as the next head coach for the Lady Hawks. She already knew she would suggest Hope Sewell for the position.

Bill led her down the hallway, and she paused a moment at the nursery. Kelby's weekday nanny was sitting on the floor, encouraging Kate to crawl toward her. Another woman sat in the rocker, holding Sarah, whose eyes fluttered a few times and closed.

"That'll be you one day," Bill said quietly. "You and Sawyer will be terrific parents." He smiled at her. "And don't wait. You have a lot of love to share. Have your babies sooner rather than later."

She grinned. "We'll work on it. Starting tonight."

They went down the stairs and through the large foyer, coming to the entrance of the great room. It was crowded with others. Besides those she had already seen and their spouses, she saw her entire basketball team present, Hope standing proudly beside them. Jen and her fireman stood next to Hope, and Dizzy and Miss Caroline were beside them. Blanche Biggerstaff was arm-in-arm with her husband.

Happiness filled her, seeing this sea of smiling faces. Paisley had found a home, not only with Sawyer, but in Hawthorne.

Bill led her to her groom now, and she only had eyes for him. His caramel hair looked windblown, and his hazel eyes shone at her with all the love in the world. Bill handed her off to him after kissing her on the cheek and returned to stand with Ginny.

"Hey," Sawyer said, smiling at her.

"Hey, yourself," she answered, feeling giddily in love.

"Ready to get married?" he asked.

She nodded, her smile as her answer.

When Paisley turned to face Judge Stowe, though, the officiant wasn't there. In his place stood Maggie, her coach from her playing days at Baylor.

"Maggie?" she asked, confused.

The older woman beamed at Paisley. "Sawyer thought I might want to be at your wedding. When I told him I was actually licensed to perform them, we agreed that I should officiate. I've got the best seat in the house."

Paisley flung her arms around her former coach, hugging her tightly. "This means the world to me."

Then she turned to her groom, who grinned lopsidedly at her. "Surprise."

She wrapped her arms around him. "The best one yet."

He slipped an arm about her waist, drawing her near, and

Maggie began the ceremony. Paisley felt as if she were dreaming as they spoke their vows and exchanged rings. Then Maggie pronounced them husband and wife, and Sawyer turned to her.

"Hey, Mrs. Montgomery," he said softly.

"Why, hello, Mr. Montgomery."

Her groom turned to those gathered. "I'm going to kiss my wife now. Long. Deliberate. I may kiss her into tomorrow, so you might want to go and grab yourself a drink and even fix a plate. We'll join you. Eventually."

Paisley heard the laughter as Sawyer enveloped her in his arms. His kiss was long. Deliberate.

And the best one of her life.

Paisley finished telling Dr. Linda about the latest grant The Packman Foundation had awarded. She met with the therapist once a month now, liking having that anchor in her busy life.

The past eight years had flown by. She'd become pregnant a month after their wedding, making her and her new husband very happy. Summer also was expecting her first baby, and they compared notes throughout their pregnancies. Summer had Burt and a week later, Paisley gave birth to Megan, who shared her father's caramel hair and hazel eyes. They'd decided to share a nanny, with Gretchen coming to the Montgomery household a couple of days a week and the Blackstone ranch the other weekdays.

As the foundation's work increased and Summer's publisher requested her to write faster, Paisley and Summer added to their workdays. Gretchen bounced between both households. They quickly learned Megan and Burt enjoyed being together, so the nanny kept both children at the same time, switching which house the kids would play at, based upon their moms' schedules.

As a couple, she and Sawyer decided they would like to have four children. They wanted to give birth to two and adopt two from the foster care system, hopefully alternating between births and adoptions. Then an opportunity occurred which changed those plans. They were introduced to Tim, who was eighteen months old, and they fell in love with the blond-haired, blue-eyed toddler. He had been placed in foster care when his mother died after a house fire. The mother had managed to get Tim outside to safety and returned for her baby. She saved Hayley, too, but smoke inhalation damaged her lungs, and the mother had died the following day.

Sawyer said they couldn't adopt the brother without also adopting his sister. Eli and Jace had been separated as children when they'd been placed into foster care, with only Jace being adopted. Paisley agreed wholeheartedly, wanting the brother and sister to remain together. Suddenly, their family of three had increased to five overnight. Megan was three and thankfully potty-trained. Now they had a boy eighteen months younger than Megan, plus a six-month-old baby.

Summer, who was pregnant again, told Paisley she should use Gretchen full time. Summer said she would put Burt in a Montessori preschool in Hawthorne. Megan was having none of that and demanded that she, too, get to go to school with Burt. Gretchen agreed to work only for the Montgomerys, caring for Tim and Hayley. Two years later, they added Andrew to their family, naming him after Sawyer's dad. Their youngest had Paisley's chocolate brown hair but possessed his father's hazel eyes.

All their children got along well and had different personalities and interests. Megan was seven and very outgoing, playing soccer and softball. She also liked to sing. Tim was now five and very tall for his age. He was quiet and smart and spent every moment he could shooting baskets in their driveway. Hayley was very girly and refused to wear anything but dresses. She enjoyed her gymnastics and dance classes. At two, Andrew was all boy. He loved stomping in mud puddles and climbing and swinging. He liked to throw and kick balls, but during quiet time, he also liked to do puzzles and read.

Paisley felt blessed to have such a large, loving family, as well as the friendships she'd made during her years in Hawthorne. It had all been possible because of Bill Packman. Her friend had given her the opportunity to lead the foundation and be the guardian of Bill's legacy. Her career change had led to her being able to experience the kind of family life she wanted.

"Anything else?" Dr. Linda asked, interrupting Paisley's thoughts.

"No. I think I've covered everything," she told the therapist.

"It's Olympics time again," Dr. Linda mentioned. "Any feelings about that?"

"I can look back fondly on the years I participated in the Olympics. I realize how special it was to represent my country and come together with athletes from all over the world." She grinned. "And I do have a former player involved in them this year. That's pretty thrilling."

"Ah, yes. Desi. I know she looks to you as her mentor."

"I've had a blast watching her play in her first Olympics."

The therapist studied her a moment. "And no regrets still about stepping away from coaching?"

"None," Paisley said with certainty. "It was the right decision for me. It's given me the chance to make a bigger impact with my work through the foundation. More importantly, it's given me the kind of time I wanted to have to spend with my family. I am very fulfilled, Dr. Linda."

"I'm glad you're so content, Paisley. We'll talk next month. Goodbye."

"Bye."

She closed her laptop and looked up. Her office had French doors, and she could see Megan standing patiently outside. The children knew not to interrupt her when she was in her office, and they were very good about sticking to that rule. Paisley stood and crossed the room, opening the door.

Megan threw her arms around her mom. "It's almost time to go to West and Kelby's. And we get to watch the Olympics and see Desi again!"

Her daughter knew Desi because the former player was a frequent visitor. Desi had spent college vacations in Hawthorne, stopping by to get advice from Paisley and seeking help with her basketball skills. Desi had even asked Paisley to help her train before the WNBA draft, and she had agreed to do so. The one-on-one coaching worked well, and Desi was selected in the second round by the Atlanta Dream. They didn't see as much of Desi these days, but all of Hawthorne had been excited when the former Lady Hawk had been tapped to be a part of Team USA in the Toronto Olympics.

"We will definitely be cheering Desi on during this final game," Paisley said, kissing the top of her daughter's head. "Let's go round everyone up."

She gathered her children, while Sawyer grabbed several food items from the kitchen for today's cookout. Their group of friends looked forward to these occasions, which occurred about once a month. Since West and Kelby had the largest house, it was easiest to meet at their place each time, especially since the number of kids continued to grow amongst their friends.

They strapped their children into their car seats, listening to them chatter happily during the short ride.

Sawyer reached out and threaded his fingers through hers. "It's like music, hearing them all talking and laughing. We've done good, Paisley."

"We have," she agreed, squeezing his hand. "I don't see how I could be happier than I am right now, in this moment."

He lifted their joined hands and brushed a tender kiss on her knuckles. "Thank you for saying yes all those years ago. I knew you were the one for me from that first conversation we had on the phone."

They arrived at the Sutherlands' house. Sawyer opened the door to the van, unbuckling kids, who spilled out and ran, finding their friends. Paisley looked and saw a volleyball game going, as well as half a dozen children kicking a soccer ball. Andrew ran toward that group and even though he was the youngest, he immediately found the ball and kicked it hard, squealing in delight.

She helped Sawyer carry the bags into the kitchen, greeting everyone. Autumn asked about the latest grant. She now served as the chief human resources officer for Triple H, with Eli still its medical director. They had two girls and had adopted a boy two years ago.

Summer came and pressed a book into Paisley's hands. "The newest. Hot off the press!"

"You know how I love to escape into your romances. Thank you."

Summer had sold her first trilogy to a publishing house in New York. Not the one she had worked for, but an even bigger name in the business. Romance readers took to the small Texas Panhandle town Summer wrote about, and she had now set three other series in various regions across Texas. Chance still managed the ranch, and he was happy to give riding lessons to the children of his friends. Paisley hadn't known how to ride, and Chance had also taken her on as a student. She now rode a couple of times a month at Blackstone Ranch, sometimes alone, sometimes with Megan or Tim. Hayley and Andrew were already begging to learn how to ride, so she supposed that would happen before she knew it.

Darby appeared in the kitchen, Jace leading her to a chair.

With a deadpan delivery, he told everyone, "Darby promised she would not go into labor at this cookout," causing laughter.

"I don't mean to," Darby protested. "Just because I went into labor at Sawyer and Paisley's reception *and* at Flynn and Quinn's christening does not mean that'll happen today." She paused. "Well, maybe not today. We'll see." She looked up at Jace. "Stay close, honey. Just in case."

Kelby leaned down and hugged her best friend. "If you do, West and I will keep the kids for you."

Paisley was still impressed with how West managed to be a great husband and father while continuing to lead the Hawthorne Hawks football team to district championships. He'd even coached the Hawks to two state titles during the last eight years, all while Kelby's business had flourished. It had grown so large that she no longer worked from home. She had an office in Hawthorne and employed a dozen staff members. Paisley used SSC's services, having them manage the foundation's social media accounts and website. Kelby had also been instrumental in establishing the foundation's mission statement.

The next few hours passed happily, burgers and hot dogs

coming off the grill quickly. The adults made certain the children were all fed first, and then they were allowed to play again while their parents ate.

"Are you ready for the fall election, Mr. Mayor?" West asked Sawyer.

"I'm not doing much campaigning," her husband replied. "I've been mayor for two years now. People either like what I've done—or they don't. Based upon that, they'll vote accordingly. I'm making myself available. I'm at community functions and happy to answer questions, but as far as running a campaign like a typical politician?" He shrugged. "That's not me."

Paisley slipped an arm about his waist. "And that's why people will vote for you. Because you're honest. Transparent. Just an all-around, nice guy." She kissed him.

"Or they're voting for me because I have the best wife in the world," he quipped, kissing her back.

"Hey, it's almost four," Jace said. "You don't want to miss tipoff for the gold medal."

Team USA was playing the Chinese national team, and Desi was a starter.

"Thanks for the heads up, Jace," she said. "Honey, will you go find Megan? She really wants to watch Desi play."

"Will do." Sawyer stood, brushing a kiss on the top of her head.

"Dad, can we go swimming?" Kate, who already wore her swimsuit, asked West.

"Okay, need some pool volunteers," West said.

Several of the adults agreed to help. Suddenly, Darby said, Oh, no!"

Every eye turned to her. Her face flamed.

"Jace, people are going to stop inviting us over. Yes, my water broke. Let's go. We need to tell the kids."

"I'll handle that," Kelby said. "They're probably already in their swimsuits or playing. You go take care of business and have a terrific baby. The kids can stay here. Overnight if they need to." She kissed Darby's cheek.

"You're the best friend ever, Kel."

Paisley tried to help in the kitchen, but Summer pushed her out the door, saying, "Go watch Desi. We've got this."

She went to the great room, where the TV was already on the pregame coverage. Megan ran in and sat next to her on the couch. Sawyer came and sat on her other side, draping his arm along the back of the sofa. She leaned into him, still relishing his warmth and scent after years of marriage.

The game began. Several people drifted in and out of the room, but her eyes were riveted on the screen. Her heart raced each time Desi took the ball down the court. Her former player was confident, and it showed. She was running this team like the pro she was.

"Shoot, Desi!" shouted Megan.

Desi did, sinking a three-pointer as the buzzer sounded to end the game.

Her daughter sprang to her feet. "We won! Desi won! USA! USA! USA!"

Those in the great room took up the chant, Megan leading them, a huge grin on her face.

"Quiet!" Sawyer shouted. "Desi's on."

Paisley watched with pride as her former player was interviewed by a sportscaster who had been a player herself on the second Olympic team Paisley had belonged to.

"What does this moment mean to you, Desi? Winning your first gold medal?"

"It means everything, Paula. And I wouldn't be here if not for Paisley Montgomery. She was my coach in high school."

"Mommy! She said your name!" Megan said excitedly.

"You're referring to the former Paisley Roberts, who competed in three Olympic games herself, bringing home the gold all three times."

"That's right," Desi said. "Paisley has been the biggest influence in my life. While I've played under some really good coaches, my work ethic and how I've honed my basketball skills over the years is all thanks to her. She helped a troubled teen become a basketball star. She's worked with me during my college years and my professional career with the Dream. Paisley encourages me. She inspires me. I'm a better player—and a better person—thanks to her."

Desi looked straight into the camera. "And this first gold medal is for *you*, Coach. I'll be bringing it to you in Hawthorne soon. But I'll keep the ones I earn after this."

Paisley was stunned by Desi's declaration.

Paula said, "That is a tremendous gesture, Desi, to give your gold medal to someone else."

"I never would have earned it if not for Paisley." Desi beamed. "I have plenty of time to rack up a couple more."

A passing fan handed Desi a US flag, and she held it high. "Team USA forever!" she cried.

By now, tears ran down Paisley's cheeks.

"Why are you crying, Mommy?" asked Megan. "Are you sad?"

"You don't always cry because you're sad, sweetie. Sometimes, you cry because you're very, very happy. And Mommy is happy and proud now."

"I can't wait to see Desi's gold medal," Megan declared. "I'm going swimming now."

Her daughter ran from the room, and Paisley turned to Sawyer. Her husband framed her face with his large hands.

"That's incredibly thoughtful of Desi to give you so much credit. And her gold medal."

"I can't take it from her," she protested. "She's the one who earned it. Not me."

"Take it. At least, for now. She wants you to have it. And not having it herself motivates her to set a goal to claim another one." Sawyer smiled. "You can always give it back to her eventually."

"I could," she agreed as his thumbs wiped away her tears.

"I'm proud of you, Paisley. Proud of all your accomplishments. Proud of what a terrific mother you are. But most of all, I'm proud we're in this together. We've built a satisfying life and family so far."

She smiled at him. "And we'll keep on doing what we both love. We're good together, Sawyer. I love being your wife and the mom to our kids. I love what we have. I can't wait to see what the future holds for us."

"Some challenges. Some fun. And a whole lot of love," he told her.

Her husband kissed her, and contentment—as well as love—flowed through Paisley. Her heart belonged to Hawthorne and this incredible man. She didn't know what their future might hold, only that they would face it together.

And live the best years of their lives in love.

Coming Home

The Lyrics of Love

Finding Home

HOLLYWOOD NAME GAME

Hollywood Heartbreaker

Hollywood Flirt

Hollywood Player

Hollywood Double

Hollywood Enigma

LAWMEN OF THE WEST

Runaway Hearts

Blind Faith

Love and the Lawman

Ballad Beauty

SAGEBRUSH BRIDES

A Game of Chance

Written in the Cards

Outlaw Muse

KNIGHTS OF REDEMPTION

A Bit of Heaven on Earth

A Knight for Kallen

SUDDENLY A DUKE

Portrait of the Duke

Music for the Duke

Polishing the Duke

Designs on the Duke

Fashioning the Duke

Love Blooms with the Duke

Training the Duke

Investigating the Duke

SECOND SONS OF LONDON

Educated by the Earl

Debating with the Duke

Empowered by the Earl

Made for the Marquess

Dubious about the Duke

Valued by the Viscount

Meant for the Marquess

DUKES DONE WRONG

Discouraging the Duke

Deflecting the Duke

Disrupting the Duke

Delighting the Duke

Destiny with a Duke

DUKES OF DISTINCTION

Duke of Renown

Duke of Charm

Duke of Disrepute

Duke of Arrogance

Duke of Honor

SOLDIERS AND SOULMATES

To Heal an Earl

To Tame a Rogue

To Trust a Duke

To Save a Love

To Win a Widow

THE ST. CLAIRS

Devoted to the Duke

Midnight with the Marquess

Embracing the Earl

Defending the Duke

Suddenly a St. Clair

STANDALONE ROMANTIC THRILLERS

Leave Yesterday Behind

Illusions of Death

About the Author

USA Today and Amazon Top 100 bestselling author Alexa Aston lives with her husband in a Dallas suburb, where she eats her fair share of dark chocolate and plots out stories while she walks every morning. She enjoys travel, sports, and binge-watching—and never misses an episode of *Survivor*.

Alexa brings her characters to life in steamy historicals, contemporary romances, and romantic suspense novels that resonate with passion, intensity, and heart.

KEEP UP WITH ALEXA
Visit her website
Newsletter Sign-Up

MORE WAYS TO CONNECT WITH ALEXA